The Secret of Grey Walls

"Of course we don't know what's in store for us all," Jenny said, "but I just don't fear any fate now we're all together and all Lone Piners."

"When you've all finished being sorry to each other," Mary broke in, "somebody had better come over here and see if they can see what I see."

Dickie was at her side before she had finished speaking.

"No need for anyone to worry any more," he said. "We're saved. Mary's saved us. This adventure is over."

But Dickie was wrong. The adventure wasn't over and had hardly begun.

Also available in the Lone Pine series

Mystery at Witchend

Malcolm Saville's
LONE PINE CLUB

The Secret of Grey Walls

Hippo

For my wife

Scholastic Children's Books
7–9 Pratt Street, London NW1 0AE, UK
a division of Scholastic Publications Ltd,
London ~ New York ~ Toronto ~ Sydney ~ Auckland

First published by George Newnes Ltd, 1947
This edition published by Scholastic Publications Ltd, 1995

Copyright © Malcolm Saville, 1947

ISBN 0 590 55919 2

Typeset by TW Typesetting, Midsomer Norton, Avon
Printed by Cox & Wyman Ltd, Reading, Berks.

10 9 8 7 6 5 4 3 2 1

Contents

	Foreword	1
	The Lone Pine Club	4
1	Peter's Dream	9
2	Penny Makes a Friend	36
3	The Caravan	59
4	Peter's Ride	86
5	Mr Cantor	103
6	Bury Fields	131
7	That Van Again	154
8	Into Action	173
9	Offa's Dyke	196
10	The Boys' Adventure	221
11	Tom on His Own	241
12	The Girls to the Rescue	253
13	Explanations	280

Map of the
Grey Walls Country
drawn by David Morton

Railway → To Hereford

Here the Lone Piners
met Jon and Penny

CRAVEN ARMS
STATION

River Clun   CLUN

CASTLE
H.Q.3

Here the
Lone Piners
met the Caravan

REY WALLS
OFFA'S DYKE
Bury Fields
Secret Sheep Pens
The Spinney
Here Penny met Mr. Clancy
X
River Clun
Peter and Sally came this way

Foreword

Clungunford and Clunbury, Clunton and Clun,
Are the quietest places under the Sun.

If you can find a map large enough to show the towns
and villages in the counties of Shropshire, Hereford
and Radnor, and then study it carefully, you may find
for yourself the four villages mentioned in the old
rhyme. Clun, the last-named, is the scene of this story.

Look for it this way. First find Shrewsbury on your
map and then follow the black railway line south in the
direction of Ludlow and Hereford until you come to a
strangely-named junction called Craven Arms. Look
now for a road leaving this little town and running west
– this is the road along which all the Lone Piners except
Peter travelled on that cold December day on which
their adventure started – and follow it until you find, as
they did, that Clun might well be the quietest place
under the sun.

Clun is the largest of the four places named after the
little river which rises over the Welsh border and slips
down the valley between the wooded hills by the Craven
Arms road.

There seems no particular reason why Clun should exist today, but it does, and you can go there for yourself. You can stand on the narrow stone bridge where Penny and the others stood while Alan Denton dashed past them on his bicycle on his way to find Clun's only policeman. You can climb the grassy hill up which the twins led the two new members of the Club and stand beside the ruins of the mighty castle which was built soon after the Norman Conquest. From here, high above the crowded roofs of Clun town, while the sweet wind sings in your ears, you can look west, over wild and rolling country into Wales, which is only a few miles distant. All this land was once a forest.

If you are not afraid of walking you can discover Offa's Dyke for yourself. It wants some finding, but for many miles it still runs as straight as a rule through the heather.

All this country is rich in history and tradition. Climb Bury Hill and look for the remains of the camps and forts the ancient Britons made; you may be lucky enough, as many others have, to pick up a flint arrowhead. Explore the road that swings up and down hill to the market town of Bishop's Castle and then, another day, try to find an old inn that reminds you of the one to which Mr Cantor took Dickie and Mary.

There is no other place in England quite like hidden, mysterious Clun, but although the castle, the bridge and the river are real enough, you will never find the house called Keep View, nor the farm Bury Fields, and neither, I am sorry to tell you, is there really a mysterious house called Grey Walls. I made all these up and they are as imaginary as the characters you will meet in these pages.

But I hope you will like the children and people you can never actually meet as much as the real Clun and its wild hills if you are ever lucky enough to go there.

M. S.

The Lone Pine Club

The Lone Pine Club was started by some boys and girls during the war at a lonely farmhouse called Witchend in the highlands of Shropshire. If you have not read the three earlier books about their adventures you may like to know something about the Club before you begin this story. It is only fair to tell you now that the members of the Lone Pine Club do not grow up! Readers who know them don't want them to get any older, and so they will go on having adventures at their present ages.

The rules of the Club, which were signed in the blood of the members, were very simple. The most important of these was "To be true to each other whatever happens," and the others were kindness to animals and a statement that the Club was for "exploring, and watching birds and trailing strangers." So far the members have trailed strangers far more than they have watched birds! Headquarters are at a secret camp under a lonely pine tree in the Witchend valley.

*   *   *

The Members

DAVID MORTON. He is sixteen and the captain of the Club. Steady, fearless, and always to be relied upon. While his father was in the R.A.F. he came with his mother to Witchend. He has one brother and one sister, who are twins.

RICHARD ("DICKIE") MORTON and MARY MORTON. These two are ten. Although they now go to separate boarding-schools they are inseparable in the holidays. They are alike in looks, speech, and even in thought, and often finish sentences for each other. Dickie is cheeky, but with a terrific sense of fun. Mary perhaps is the leader of the two, for although a dreamer, she is more level-headed. But their greatest qualities are their courage and tremendous loyalty to each other.

PETRONELLA ("PETER") STERLING. Peter is sixteen. She has no mother, brothers nor sisters, but lives in the holidays with her old father, who is in charge of a reservoir in the hills, in a tiny house called Hatchholt, near Witchend. She goes to boarding-school in Shrewsbury, but is only really happy when she is roaming her beloved hills and valleys on her pony Sally. Imagine Peter with two fair plaits, blue eyes and a clear brown skin. She looks her best in jodhpurs and a blue shirt. She knows the stars and loves everything in the open air. She swims faster than most boys of her age, and rides a hundred times better. Her life was changed when the Mortons came to Witchend, for then she learned for the first time how lonely she had been. David is her special friend.

TOM INGLES. Tom is a Londoner sent from the

bombing to help his uncle farm, half-a-mile from Witchend. He is small for fifteen-and-a-half but very wiry, and is now becoming reconciled to country life. At first he was suspicious of the Mortons and impatient with the twins, but although he would never admit it, he is intensely proud of his membership of the Club. He is quick, brave, and liked by everyone who knows him.

JENNY HARMAN. Jenny has not played much part in the Club's exploits. She is nearly fifteen, and Peter befriended her in the adventure of the Seven White Gates, when she needed a friend very badly. She has a stepmother who is unkind to her but she has plenty of pluck, and although David sometimes loses patience with her, Tom never does. She lives at the post-office of Barton Beach some distance from Witchend, so the other members do not see her very often.

Then there are two more people you must know about, and they are made members in this book. They are cousins.

JONATHAN WARRENDER. Tall, lanky, untidy and bespectacled, Jon is one of those boys who find exams easy! He is a little older than David, and like most really clever people has very little to say. He has no father, is still at boarding-school but in the holidays lives with his mother who owns the *Gay Dolphin* Hotel at Rye, where he met the Mortons and had an astonishing adventure with them.

PENELOPE ("PENNY") WARRENDER is Jon's cousin, and is one year younger. Her parents are abroad and she lives at the *Gay Dolphin* in the school holidays. Penny is grey-eyed and red-haired, and she has all the qualities that go with red hair! She is affectionate and loyal, impetuous and independent, and a rare fighter. In many ways she is old for her years, and for as long as she can remember the most important person in her short life has been her cousin Jon, whom she teases and infuriates, but would follow to the end of the world.

MACBETH is a black Scottie dog and a member of the Morton family. He loves them all, but especially Mary, who has nearly wrecked many an adventure because she will carry Mackie when his short legs tire.

The Lone Piners' secret signal to each other is a whistled imitation of the peewit's mournful call.

Chapter 1

Peter's Dream

Almost as high as the streams begin at the head of one of the little secret valleys which slip down from the windy heights of the Long Mynd in the county of Shropshire, there is a hidden reservoir. Its name, which is given also to the valley and to the sturdy little house which is built beside it, is Hatchholt.

The reservoir is one of several built in these hills and in the mountains of Wales to supply the thirsty midland cities, and as from time to time the clear water must be sent down the pipe-lines, a man lives in Hatchholt to work the sluices. It is a lonely life even in summer, for the house is more than two miles from the village of Onnybrook and it was only a few years ago that the water companies insisted that a telephone must connect their old and faithful servant, Jasper Sterling, with the outside world. But Mr Sterling is not afraid of solitude. Once or twice a week the postman pushes his bicycle up the rough track and brings newspapers as well as letters, and when he does arrive he is asked into the tiny kitchen for a cup of tea. Mr Sterling lives alone in term time, for his wife died when his only daughter Petronella was born sixteen years ago. Petronella – who is called Peter by everyone except her father – is at boarding-school in

Shrewsbury, and although she likes school she is never happier than when she is roaming the hills of home.

This story begins two nights after Christmas in Peter's little bedroom high under the roof of Hatchholt. It was a cold, bright night, with millions of stars blazing out of a velvet sky. Although the moon was not yet up the reservoir glistened like a sheet of black glass, for a film of ice was already forming on its still surface. Above and beyond the water, the heathery slopes of moorland rolled up towards the summit of the Mynd, and all the world was quiet.

Peter was dreaming – a strangely vivid dream, which was almost more real than reality. Before she was able to look around her in her dream she was aware that she was searching for someone or something very important. She had often dreamed that she was running for a train or hurrying desperately to meet someone who was waiting for her, but her feeling in this dream was even more urgent. There was something which had to be done and which she was sure nobody could do better than herself, but she struggled in vain to remember what it was.

Then, like the veil of gauze that is raised sometimes before the last scene of a pantomime, Peter began to see the dream country through which she was running. First, she realized that everything around her was cold and grey, but the light was so weird that she could not tell whether it was day or night. Then, she noticed that she was stumbling downhill through heather that scratched her legs, towards a little clump of pine trees in a hollow. She turned her head and, with a sudden shock, saw that she was not alone. A few yards to her left a girl of about her own age was running with her, and as, in her dream, Peter looked at her with curiosity, the girl turned towards her and gave her a friendly smile.

Peter was quite certain that she had never seen her companion before but, oddly enough, she felt that she also was searching and, in a way, felt that they were perhaps both seeking the same thing. Unlike many dreams Peter found that she had lost the power of speech; this was particularly annoying as the newcomer looked nice. So, without words, the two girls ran on down the slope while a bitter wind whistled round them and swayed the branches of the trees in the spinney below. The country was wild and desolate and Peter was sure that she had never seen it before, because although her own hillsides were thick with heather and bilberries, there was a loneliness about this strange landscape which was very different from the solitudes which she knew and loved.

At last they reached the trees and stood, still without words, while the strong wind at their backs moaned through the treetops. For a long minute Peter felt that they were both waiting for something to happen, for suddenly even the wind died away and the trees around them stood still like silent sentinels. Then the girl at her side broke the spell by stepping forward a few paces to where they could see, between the trees, a rough cart-track winding downhill. She clutched Peter's arm and pointed ahead, and suddenly Peter sensed that the ugly, grey-walled house squatting in the hollow below them was one of the things for which she had been searching.

What did she want in this strange house? What secret was it keeping from her and why did she feel so strongly even now that she must go down to the big double gates

11

set in the high stone walls to see what else she could discover?

Without a word to each other the two girls left the whispering trees behind them and went on down the cart-track together. And as they went it seemed to Peter that the light was changing, and before they had gone many yards the dream country was bathed in silver moonlight. Another few steps and the sky was flecked with scarlet, and when she turned to look over her shoulder Peter saw that all the moorland behind was on fire. Without either fear or surprise the two girls stood and watched the trees in the spinney flare up like giant torches and then, as the cruel wind swept the flames down towards them and the strange house, Peter woke.

It was still very cold. As usual her bedroom window was wide open, and the curtains were rustling gently in the wind. Her window, under the eaves, faced east and as she turned over and snuggled down in the warm bed, Peter saw that the sun was up and knew that it must be just after eight o'clock. She was slipping back into sleep again when she heard footsteps on the stairs, and her bedroom door was opened. She sat up in bed.

"Daddy darling! You've brought me a cup of tea. You're spoiling me."

Mr Sterling did not answer until he had placed a tray with a white cloth on the chest of drawers. Then he turned and smiled slowly at his daughter over the top of his spectacles.

"So you are awake, my dear ... I have started every day with a cup of tea for over forty years, and I've been thinking you're old enough now to be joining me."

"But I ought to be getting it for you, Daddy! I *would* do it every morning but I can't wake early enough ... I've tried but it just won't work ... But I do love tea, and you bringing it to me makes me feel very grown-up ... Throw me my dressing-gown off the door, darling, and close the window and let's be cosy."

Mr Sterling did as he was asked and then looked disapprovingly at the untidy pile of garments on the chair by the bed. Peter, for once, misunderstood this look – or perhaps she did not want to understand – and said,

"Just push them on the floor, Daddy, and sit down next to me. No! Give them to me and I'll put them on the bed. It'll keep them warmer."

"You must be more tidy, child," her father muttered as he handed her a tea-cup. "Your untidiness distresses me very much."

Peter looked down meekly into her saucer.

"Very well, Daddy. I'm sorry ... But I'm not often told that I'm untidy at school."

"Then there is something very seriously wrong with the school," her father replied promptly, "and I have long suspected that they did not pay enough attention to tidiness ... What are you going to do today?"

Peter put the cup into his hand and noted with horror that he winced when some tea slopped over into the saucer. Then she twisted round in bed and answered his question with another.

"Daddy. What did I do all the time before the Mortons came to Witchend? Do you remember that day I brought them back here after we'd pulled young Dickie out of the bog?"

"I mind it very well," Mr Sterling nodded. "I'm not likely to forget it, for they all spilled crumbs on the clean floor ... Untidy young rascals they were and still are."

"I must have been lonely in a way, although I never minded going out on my own really and of course I've nearly always had Sally."

"That pony is too fat ... You'll have to ride her more than you do in the holidays or else we'll sell her. She eats us out of the place in winter time."

Peter evaded this subject skilfully. It was raised frequently by Mr Sterling but nothing else ever happened.

"I'm going to Witchend again for the day. Mrs Morton asked me last night. You don't mind much do you, Daddy? I'd love them all to come here more often but it's such a lot of us for you, and besides they have got Agnes at Witchend to help and we've got nobody except us. You're not mad with me for going after breakfast are you? ... I don't quite know what we're going to do. Maybe David and I will go off somewhere, or p'raps we'll find Tom and see if Mr Ingles will let him off work for a bit and go and see how the camp is getting on – we haven't been up there yet these hols."

If Mr Sterling's eyes behind his spectacles glistened a little Peter did not see them, and if she had noticed she would not have known how much he missed her now that, in holiday time, she had found other friends. He knew well enough how lonely it was for her at Hatchholt, but he knew too how long each term was for him without her. So all that he did now was to clear his throat and place his cup and saucer back so precisely on the tray that there was room for Peter's cup when she was ready, and say,

"The Mortons are very kind to you, my dear, and if the weather holds you will have a good day. A few more frosts and we shall be able to invite them all to skate on the water here. Much better to have a party outside because then they can't all make a muddle indoors ... Breakfast in ten minutes."

When Peter came down the sun was high enough to shine in through the kitchen windows and set all the brass and copper and china plates gleaming. It was David Morton who had once said that the Hatchholt kitchen reminded him of a lighthouse because everything was so bright and clean, and Peter had never forgotten this. Her father was at the stove when she came in, but, as usual, the plates were on the table as soon as she had sat down.

After she had helped him wash up Peter ran out to find her pony Sally. At the top of the sloping garden was a fence of wire-netting to keep the rabbits out, and a little gate leading to a rough field. The moor had made many attempts to capture this field, and even now the top edge was brown with dead bracken and in the corners were the first clumps of the invading heather. But there was still enough pasture for Sally, who had been bred in the Welsh hills not many miles away, and who never saw the inside of a stable unless the snow was thick on the ground.

Peter put her fingers to her mouth and whistled shrill and clear, and Sally came trotting over to her and nuzzled for the potatoes or carrot which she knew her mistress was hiding in her pocket. Sally was not a show pony and not even very good looking, but she was faithful, intelligent, and almost tireless in the hill country, and Peter could do anything with her. Girl and pony had grown up together, and Peter could hardly remember a time when she was not riding Sally.

When the pony was saddled and tied to the gatepost Peter ran in for her gloves and two extra jerseys, for although the sun was well up the sky now, it was still bitterly cold. The underneath jersey was as blue as the shirt she always wore with her jodhpurs, but the top jersey with its rolled collar was scarlet. Mrs Morton had knitted this for Peter and given it to her for Christmas, "So that we can see you coming to visit us, darling," she had said as Peter undid the parcel with shaking fingers.

"When will you be back?" Mr Sterling asked plaintively as his daughter swung into the saddle.

"Not to dinner, Daddy ... Tea, probably ... Expect me when you see me, and don't worry. 'Bye!"

As she rode down the winding valley she knew so well she noticed how on one side the bracken glowed golden in the sunshine, while on the other the frost powdered the brittle fronds which still stood in cold shadow. Sally could have picked her way blindfold down the stony track, so Peter let her make her own pace while she flicked back her fair plaits and whistled to greet another lovely day. As they travelled down the valley the hills came in closer and steeper, and little streams came tumbling down the side valleys to join the brook which chattered over a stony bed close to the path. And sometimes on one side of the track and sometimes on the other, and sometimes hidden by the bracken, the four great iron pipes carrying the water from the reservoir ran straight down the valley the quickest way to the plains.

One more turn between the enfolding hills and Peter knew she would see the track running off to the right which led to the next valley called Dark Hollow and thence on to Witchend. As Sally stepped delicately over the brook which just here ran across the path, her ears went forward. Peter checked her own whistle, wondering what the pony had heard. Then she laughed and touched Sally's sides with her heels, as sweet and clear through the still air came the haunting cry of the peewit ... "Peeeewit! Peeeewit!"

The clink of the pony's shoes on the loose stones as she broke into a trot rather drowned Peter's reply, but she knew whom she would see as soon as they turned the corner.

David Morton was leaning against the gnarled trunk of a hawthorn tree whittling at a stick with a big knife. He looked up and grinned as Peter came into sight.

"Hullo, Peter!" he said. "You look like a fire station or a pillar-box! That jersey really is terrific. I don't think you ought to go about in it. Isn't Sally scared? Or do you have to wear something over it until you're on her back?"

"If it was pink with orange stripes on it I should still wear it if your mother gave it to me," Peter retorted. "Why did you come to meet me if you don't like it?"

David still grinned.

"I had no idea you'd be coming this way," he said. "I just wanted a walk ... Matter of fact I'd forgotten you were coming over today ... Or are you going somewhere else?"

17

Just in time Peter remembered that she did not often get the best of this sort of idiotic discussion with David, so she took no more notice.

"What are we going to do today?" she asked. "Could we get Tom and go up to the camp, do you think? How are the twins?"

"Awful," David replied, answering the last question first as he swung along by her side. "They're much worse since they were separated in term-time ... That's why I came out really – just to escape them."

"Time we had another adventure, David," Peter laughed. "However irritating the twins may be, they're jolly good when we have an adventure ... David! We must get Tom and try and fix something up, and we must get Jenny over from Barton Beach before the hols are over ... Do you realize we're nearly half-way through them?"

David nodded. "I know. The club ought to be doing something, and it would be silly to close it up just because it's winter-time. Trouble is, of course, that Tom is kept so busy and young Jenny can hardly get here and back home again in a day."

"I know Jenny is difficult," Peter broke in, "and you've never liked her much, David, but she *is* a member, and now that her father is home that old stepmother of hers has to behave herself ... I like Jenny. She's fun, and she's had a beastly time, and I believe she'd come over even for a day if we asked her."

"Jenny's all right, I know," David said, "but she either makes me laugh or makes me mad. She always seems to be scared of something round the corner."

"So would you be if you'd had such a rotten time…
Anyway, let's try and arrange a meeting of the club soon,
and if we can't make an adventure perhaps one will
happen to us … If not, ask Dickie and Mary to make one
for us. They will!"

"I tell you what would be fun, Peter. I wish we could
have Jon and Penny Warrender up here for a bit – you
know who I mean, don't you? Penny is very jolly and has
red hair and an awful temper. I know you'd like her."

"I'm sure I would," Peter said a trifle coldly, for she
had yet to forget how disappointed she had been to miss
the adventure of the diamond necklace in a smuggler's
secret passage at Rye.*

"Trouble is," David went on, quite unperturbed and
blissfully unaware of Peter's feelings, "that we've no
room for them at Witchend, and you can't put them up
at Hatchholt, and there's no place where they could stay
in Onnybrook. They're frightfully keen to join the Lone
Piners, and I know you'd like them, Peter."

"I'm sure I should," she said as briefly as before.

"And, of course, they are really keen to join. Even
Jon is keen, and he's so brainy over exams and things
that he scares me. We could have a grand time with them
up here, and I know they'd come if we asked them."

"I'm sure they would," Peter murmured, and then,
suddenly feeling sorry for her stupid jealousy, she said,
"Let's talk it over with the others and see if there's some
way of asking them here for a week. Your father and
mother know Mrs Warrender, don't they?"

They had crossed the Dark Hollow valley now and
were within sight of the chimney-pots of Witchend.

* See *The Gay Dolphin Adventure*.

Next to Hatchholt Peter would have chosen to live at Witchend, which, like her own home, had been built right against the sides of the hill, but in this case almost at the bottom of a valley instead of at the top. Opposite the old house with its thatched roof a dense larch wood clung to the hillside, and further up the valley they could see the head of the great pine tree which marked the secret camp which they had made their own.

The track along which they had come now joined the lane which faded out where a big white gate showed that the stretch of green turf before the house was private property. A rushing stream crossed the grass, swirled through a culvert under the wall, and ran down the side of the lane into which Sally now turned without pressure on her bit.

"Hullo, chaps," Peter called as she recognized the two figures on the top bar of the gate. "Hi, Mackie."

The Morton twins looked up at the sound of her voice, smiled politely and simultaneously, and then continued in earnest conversation. The black Scottie dog sitting below them got up languidly, stretched, yawned, wagged his tail as Peter called him a second time, and then sat down with his ears well forward and his head on one side. He looked as if he would have liked to welcome Peter in person, but a word from Mary seated above him kept him still.

Peter rode up to them and David said, "Get down and open the gate for Peter! Buck up!"

"Look who's here, Dickie!" Mary said with an innocent smile.

"It must be Peter," her twin replied. "How did she get

here, I wonder? ... We were just talking about he weren't we, twin? Oh, look, Mary ... David's been to meet her. *He'd* better open the gate, hadn't you, David?"

"We wondered why you had your breakfast early and hurried off," Mary broke in. "Acksherly we didn't mind because we had two extra sausages, but we do think you ought to tell us where you are going when you run off like that..." But as David strode towards them they jumped from the gate and fled from his wrath with Macbeth at their heels.

Peter slipped from the saddle as David opened the gate for her, looped Sally's reins over the hook in the gate-post and walked over to greet Mr and Mrs Morton.

"Well, Peter, we can certainly see you coming in that jersey," Mr Morton said. "It makes me feel hot just to look at you."

"Does it keep you warm and cheerful, darling?" his wife added, "because that's all that really matters -- except, of course, that you look very nice in it as well."

Peter leaned forward and kissed her, and this was such an unusual thing for her to do that Mr Morton and David, who had just sauntered up, showed their surprise. But Mrs Morton knew Peter very well now, and smiled her thanks before giving her hand a quick squeeze and saying, "What are you going to do today? You're staying to lunch, anyway, aren't you, Peter?"

"We thought of going down to Ingles and seeing if Tom could get the day off," David said. "It seems too good a day to stay at home, doesn't it? We're rather hoping something will turn up, Father."

Mr Morton nodded towards the gate.

"Here comes your adventure," he smiled, "for here's the postman. Every unopened letter is a mystery and may be an adventure, too ... Let's see what he's got for us this morning ... Good morning, George – how are the rheumatics?"

"Nicely, thank you," the old man replied as he leaned his bicycle against the open gate and walked across to him. "But I've not many for you this morning, though there's one from London ... Then there's two with penny stamps on them, but I reckon they're not worth looking at ... and there's one for old Agnes, too, although I'd better not let her be hearing me calling her old ... it's just that we've known each other hereabouts for a goodish while ... Thank you kindly, ma'am, but I'll not have a cup just now ... Good morning, Peter. Nothing in my bag for you, I'm afraid ... Good morning, all," and he turned and ambled back to his old cycle and pedalled away slowly without knowing that he had brought two letters which were to change the Christmas holidays for all the members of the Lone Pine Club.

"Agnes," Mrs Morton called, "here's a letter for you."

The mournful humming of a hymn from within the house stopped and Agnes, the Mortons' beloved house-keeper, came to the door.

"For me?" she said, and then, before Mrs Morton could answer, "So you're here again, Peter, but we're always pleased to see you, so I'll say no more..." She took the letter as gingerly as if it were red-hot and would burn her fingers.

"But it can't be for me? There'll be someone having a joke with me and sending me a letter. Maybe it's those two young limbs? They did it once before on Valentine's Day, I remember!"

"Why not open it and see?" Mr Morton smiled, and then caught sight of his wife's face as she read the letter which had come from London. Peter noticed also and strolled over to the stream, realizing that other people's letters were no business of hers.

David soon joined her.

"Something has happened, Peter," he said glumly; "I'm sure of it ... They're both looking jolly worried."

Then the twins appeared.

"I say," Dickie began, "what do you think? Something's up ... Agnes has got a letter in the kitchen and she looks as if she's crying."

"And Mummy and Daddy have got another one," Mary broke in, "and they just turned us out of the room when we strolled in, and they're talking like anything."

"Well, we shall soon know," David said, "because here comes Father, and he looks grim."

"Don't go away, Peter," Mr Morton called as he came over to them. "We count you one of the family, anyway ... And don't look so worried, David. Nothing very desperate has happened, but it looks as if your mother and I will have to go to London for a little while ... No, nobody has died and nobody is ill, but we've both got to go tomorrow or the next day and see the lawyers about signing some business papers, and there is no getting out of it. But you mustn't let this spoil your holidays. Agnes will look after you all, but you must promise – specially you twins – to make everything as easy as you can for her ... Promise, Dickie? Word of honour, Mary?"

The twins nodded, and then Dickie said, "I'spose you wouldn't care for us to come with you and help cheer up those lawyers?"

"If it's any help we'll come with pleasure," Mary added.

"No, thank you, Mary," her father said politely. "Nice of you to think of it, but I don't believe it would help."

"Are you sure something hasn't happened to Agnes, too?" Dickie asked. "She was crying like anything when we came through the kitchen."

"I think there's a crisis," Mary said tersely.

And Mary was right, for suddenly through the open door came the sound of loud lamentation, and then Mrs Morton's voice saying:

"Now, Agnes, please don't make such a fuss. I'm sure the news isn't as bad as it sounds, and, anyway, Mr Morton can take you over in the car today to see your sister, and then you can talk things over together and make your plans."

"But the little 'uns," Agnes cried. "How can I go away and leave them and you going off to Lunnon an' all just at this very time? I canna' go … and yet I must…"

Even Mr Morton was startled at this outburst, while Mary looked almost as if she was responsible for the crisis she had predicted.

"Maybe we'd better stay out here and let your mother deal with Agnes," he said at last. "But I've no idea what has happened to her … and I didn't even know that she had a sister."

So they all fidgeted about by the stream in the morning sunshine, and Peter couldn't help feeling that she was in the way, although she loved them all very much. It seemed such a beautiful morning for bad news to come, and on the way down the valley before she had met David she had looked forward to a glorious day.

Idly she called to Macbeth. The little dog, who seemed to understand that something distressing had happened, was standing sadly with drooping tail, staring at the running water. At Peter's call he looked up, moved his tail and with an apologetic glance at Mary, walked slowly over to Peter and licked her hand as she bent to stroke him. Mackie liked Peter, sensing, as did any animal with whom she came in contact, the sympathy which she had for all living things.

At last Mrs Morton came out and smiled at the glum faces waiting for her.

"Fetch some chairs out of the shed, David," she said, "and let's all sit here in the sunshine and have a council of war, like we used to do when Daddy was away at the war. The lovely part of our valley is that it gets all the sun there is, and even now it's almost as warm as summer – Agnes is bringing us some more coffee in a minute…"

"What's happened to Agnes, Mummy? That's what we want to know," Dickie said.

Mrs Morton sat down in the chair David had brought her, and went on talking … "I shall hate leaving Witchend even for a few days … Peter, come over here, darling!"

And not until they were all sitting round her in the porch and Agnes, now intoning "Rock of Ages, cleft for me," had retired to her kitchen after bringing out the coffee, did she tell them what they all wanted to know.

"I can see that your father has told you that we've both got to go to London for a few days. Of course, we shouldn't mind leaving you here with Agnes, but unfortunately she has had some worrying news, too. I didn't know before, but she has a sister who keeps a small guest-house at a place called Clun, which is somewhere down south of Ludlow by the Welsh border. Her letter this morning was from this sister who has to go into hospital at once for an operation, and she wants Agnes to go over and look after the house for her while she is away. Poor Agnes wants to help her sister and wants to help us, too, as she always does, particularly as I told her about our visit to London before she told me her news...

"Now, I don't quite know what we are going to do, but I've promised that Daddy shall take Agnes over to Clun today, and I'm afraid we shall have to split you all up and close Witchend until we get back ... unless, of course..." she paused and looked across at Peter – "unless Mr Sterling could be persuaded to part with Peter ... No! It's not fair to ask him. We mustn't do it."

"What were you going to ask him, Mrs Morton?" Peter asked.

"I was wondering whether you would come and live over here and help keep them all in order, but I don't think it's the best idea ... Perhaps Mrs Ingles could squeeze the twins in somewhere..."

"No, thank you, Mummy," Dickie said. "I don't think we'd care for that."

"We've got a better idea than that," Mary added. "At least I think we have ... You say it, twin."

"I was only going to ask how many live in this guest-house at that place with a funny name. I mean, how many are living there *now*," Dickie said.

Mary laughed. "Of course! We get all the ideas. We'll all go and live with Agnes and help to cheer her up," and before anyone could stop her she ran into the house.

Mr Morton looked across at his wife and shrugged his shoulders, but before he could speak his daughter re-appeared, dragging Agnes by the hand.

"How would I know, my pet?" the latter was saying. "But it's just like your darling kind heart to think of old Agnes and want to come and keep her company … But just let me look at the letter again…" and while she fumbled in the pocket of her overall David winked at Peter, and Dickie slipped round and stood on Agnes's other side and looked in the other pocket for her spectacles.

"Don't take any notice of Mary, Agnes," Mrs Morton said. "You ought to know by now that they both say the craziest things. Of course, you mustn't think of the children coming to Clun with you."

But Agnes was not even listening. Her glasses were crooked on her nose as she turned the pages of her letter. Her mouth moved as she read the fateful words again, until the lips of all those watching her twitched in silent sympathy.

"There now!" she said triumphantly, raising her head and smiling round at all the tense faces. "The child was right after all, for here it is in black and white in my sister's own handwriting, and I should know my own sister's writing by now, I should hope."

"Yes, Agnes," said Mr Morton patiently, "we're sure

you know your sister's writing, but what is it she says in black and white?"

Agnes looked at him as if this was an unfair question, and then pushed her spectacles more firmly on her nose.

"I was just about to tell you, sir" – she only called Mr Morton "sir" when she was upset or angry – "I was about to remark that my sister says that there is nobody else in the house now, but she won't be lying easy in hospital if the house be closed up … And I hope I make myself clear to ye, SIR."

Before Mr Morton could give a satisfactory answer Agnes turned to her mistress.

"But I'd be right glad and happy to have them all with me, for there's other help in the house she says, and this maybe will solve all your worries while you're away."

Mary, with shining eyes, swung round to face Peter.

"And you're to come, too, Peter … Of course you must … We won't go without her, will we, David? I'll come with you and ask Mr Sterling, but, of course, he'll be glad for you to go."

"It will be a real Lone Pine holiday," Dickie interrupted. "Let's ask Tom to come, too."

"And Jenny," Mary said.

"And the Warrenders from Rye," came from David quickly. "We could ask them now. Just the chance we wanted … Would there really be room for us, Agnes, do you think? You know we wouldn't be any trouble…"

"Nonsense, David," Mr Morton interrupted. "It's no use discussing it. We can't possibly saddle Agnes with the lot of you. I think your mother is right, and you'll have to split up. Bad luck in the holidays, but we'll all

28

have to make the best of it. Sorry, chaps!"

But Agnes had now made up her mind and nothing could shake her.

"It'll be a bit of company that I'll be needing over there in that great barn of a house, and who better than these I know and who know old Agnes ... and the other two that Mr David mentioned. Let them be asked as well, for I've no doubt there's room for all and it'll be a kindness to my sister for the house to be full after Christmas, and a great help to her with her operation and all..."

This last appeal was very cunning, and it was easy to see that Mr Morton was impressed. Meanwhile, Mary squeezed Agnes's hand and murmured, "You're wonderful, Agnes dear. We'll all come with you."

And after a lot more discussion between the grown-ups it was settled that if Agnes found when she got to Clun that there was room for them all, and that if she had enough help in the house, and that if her sister had no objection, then they could go. It was also agreed that Tom Ingles, Jenny Harman and the two Warrenders could be asked to join them.

Everyone seemed happier when the decision had been made, but Peter was worried about leaving her father for a week.

"You could telephone him every day," David reminded her.

"I know I could, but he hates the 'phone, and I'm afraid he might not answer. I always answer it when I'm at home."

"I'll write to your father, Peter, and you can take the

note when you go back this afternoon. Daddy and Agnes won't be home until dark, but why don't you all go and see Tom now and get your letters written ready for posting first thing in the morning? I shall have to write to Mrs Warrender, and, I suppose, to Jenny's father, too."

"I've got a better idea than that," David said. "As soon as Dad gets back and we know it's all right for us to go we'll go down to the post office in Onnybrook and telephone. I know they're closed, but Mrs Smithson knows us and will let us in. Jenny Harman's shop is on the 'phone, and I've got the number of the *Gay Dolphin* ... that will be a trunk call, but it's worth it, isn't it?"

Then Agnes appeared wearing her best hat – a wonderful creation from which coloured cherries dangled – and a coat with a brown fur collar. It was difficult to realize that she would be back in a few hours for she made her farewells as if she would never see any of them again. But at last they got her into the car and waved until it had turned the corner of the lane.

"Poor dear Agnes," Mrs Morton sighed. "What should we do without her? Perhaps, after all, this idea of you all going with her is a good one, because I can't think what she would do without us either. Now you go up to Ingles and I'll start some of this letter-writing while the house is quiet."

As soon as their mother had disappeared into the house the twins turned on David and Peter.

"Can't you even say thank you?" Dickie began. "Can't you see what a marvellous idea we made?"

" 'Course, we're sorry for Agnes and her sister," Mary

continued, "but I wouldn't be surprised if we don't have an adventure in that Clun place. Would you, twin?"

"We jolly well have to think of everything," Dickie went on, "and it makes us jolly tired. Partikerly when you two just don't say 'thanks' when we have the ideas … Oh, well! If you don't want to say anything you needn't."

"We'll go and tell Tom all about it," Mary said. "We like Tom. He's nice."

"He's got manners. He says 'thank you,' " and the two of them sauntered as one, with Macbeth between them, through the gate and along the lane towards Ingles' farm.

David laughed. "Let 'em go, Peter. We'll cut round by the corner of the wood. It's all working out well enough, isn't it?"

Peter nodded. "It sounds grand fun. Will you mind if I take Sally if we can go? I'd love to ride her over there, although I should have to start earlier than you. You know, David, it *was* a jolly good idea of the twins. They do get them sometimes. I hope Daddy won't mind me coming with you … Do you think the Warrenders will come?"

"Sure of it. Nothing will stop Penny if she makes up her mind to it. She's red-headed."

"So you said before," Peter said coldly. "I'm sick of hearing about it. Let's go and find Tom."

They followed the twins up the lane after all, and had not gone very far before they heard the throb of a tractor and the rattle of machinery.

"Bother! I'd forgotten for the minute," David said,

"but, of course, Mr Ingles is threshing today, so Tom will be busy. I believe they started yesterday and should be through tonight ... Let's go and see."

They found the twins sitting in their favourite position on the top bar of Mr Ingles' farmyard gate, watching the thresher and its gang at work. They saw Tom on the top of a stack, flinging sheaves of corn on to the moving band of the elevator which carried them up to the hungry mouth of the shaking, roaring monster. At the other end of the machine a stream of golden grain poured out into the waiting sacks, and Peter ran over and dabbled her fingers in its cool smoothness. Mr Ingles saw her and roared a welcome, and Tom raised a hand in salute and grinned. He dare not stop tossing down the sheaves to speak to them, however, for the threshing machine had a giant's appetite. At last they got the stack down to within a few feet of the ground, and the children at the gate saw the rats beginning to break cover and hurl themselves into a panic against the fence of wire-netting stretched round the rick. Two terriers, now having the time of their lives, yelped excitedly and began their work, and Macbeth, forgetting all his protestations of loyalty to the twins, dragged his head free of his collar, streaked across the farmyard, leaped the low fence and joined happily in the massacre.

"No use waiting here for Tom," Peter said after a little. "Let's go and see Mrs Ingles and ask her first."

This was an excellent idea, for within a very few minutes of their surprise visit to the kitchen Mrs Ingles had agreed to persuade her husband to let Tom go away for a week. When Mrs Ingles made up her mind that something was going to happen, it *did* happen, and so when Tom came in for his dinner his aunt had already had ten minutes with Mr Ingles, and the matter was settled so quickly that Tom could hardly believe it.

"Thanks a lot, Uncle," he said as he pushed a hot potato into his mouth. "It's a grand idea, and it's decent of you to spare me ... But threshing will be finished today, I reckon, so maybe you'll manage without me."

Mr Ingles slapped his knee and roared with delight. "D'you hear that, Mother? D'you mind what our Tom said? He reckons I'll just about manage without him for a week ... and that's the lad didn't know difference 'twixt a cow and a goat two years back ... Good luck to you, Tom, lad. You deserve a holiday if any of us do. Where are those twins and the other two?"

Tom's face was very red as he said, "Outside, Uncle, waiting to hear what you'd say."

Mr Ingles bellowed his delight again, and as he was of the opinion that he, and he alone, had decided to let Tom go, his wife hid her smiles and allowed him to be pleased with himself.

As soon as he had finished his meal Tom went out into the sunshine and found the others.

"All OK," he called as he closed the door. "I can come ... I say, though, who had this brainwave? I've never heard of the place before."

Dickie and Mary looked down modestly at their shoes until their silence was the most obvious answer to Tom's question.

"I'll walk back with you," Tom went on. "Threshing won't start again for ten minutes. Tell me all the news."

So they told him the full story of their idea for getting all the Lone Pine Club members together under one roof and introducing two new members as well.

"And there's Jenny, Tom," Peter said. "What about her? Do you think her father will let her come?"

"I'm not going if Jenny can't come," Tom said stoutly. "Let's telephone her tonight like you said. And if your mother sends a letter to Mr Harman, he'll let her go … Now I must cut back … Pick me up on your way down to Onnybrook tonight, will you, David, and I'll come, too. I know old Mother Smithson will let us telephone from inside the shop and not from the box … Cheerio!"

As soon as he was out of sight they heard the clear lament of the peewit's cry, which Peter answered.

Dickie, who was in front kicking a pebble down the roadway, turned and said, "Are you grateful to us now, you two selfish beasts?"

"Perhaps we will be tonight about six, when Father gets home and Agnes tell us that it's all right and that we can go."

"Gosh!" said Peter. "Nearly six hours still to go, and I shan't know 'cos I must get home before dark. How can you let me know, David?"

"Telephone you, too, you chump. After we've spoken to Rye and Barton Beach … Buck up, you two midgets. I want my dinner … Afterwards we might go up and have a look at the camp, and maybe light a fire."

"That's all very well," Peter said, "but I wish I knew what was happening at Clun – if they've got there yet. It all seems too good to be real … I mean that we can all go together to a fresh place."

"I like it," Dickie said as he opened the gate of Witchend. "It's a holiday in a holiday." He patted Sally as he passed. "Reckon you ought to give this old donkey a carrot, Peter," he said rudely as he ran ahead into the house.

Chapter 2

Penny Makes a Friend

Two hundred and ten miles away from the Long Mynd and Witchend, in the south-eastern corner of Sussex, the ancient town of Rye stands on a pyramid of rock facing the sea which deserted it hundreds of years ago.

Rye is a town of surprises. Its streets are winding and cobbled, and most of its houses look just as they did in the days when the smugglers from Romney Marsh climbed up the hill and trod the narrow passages and courtyards in the dark, with mysterious bundles on their backs.

Down by the muddy banks of the tidal river which slides round Rye's hill are the tall black wooden huts where the fishermen's nets hang to dry, and there are shipyards, too, where sturdy boats are still made by the descendants of the men of the Cinque Ports who made warships of Sussex oak felled when the British Navy was born.

There are many old inns in Rye, too – houses with creaking, twisting stairs panelled in oak that is now so black and shining that you can see your face in it. But of all the inns that many visitors come to see, none is more famous than the jolly *Gay Dolphin*, which stands at the end of Trader's Street, with most of its windows looking out over the green levels of the sheep-dotted marshes to the sea. Only the church in Rye stands higher than the *Dolphin*, which is built within six feet of the edge of the cliff above the river.

On the same evening that the Lone Piners met at Witchend the moon was silvering the huddled roofs of Rye town. There was no wind and the great wooden signboard of the *Dolphin* hung straight and still over the archway leading into the yard where the shadows were thick and black. On one side of the courtyard the guests of the hotel were enjoying the fire of logs in the great brick fireplace, and on the other Mrs Warrender, the owner of the hotel, sat in her tiny dining-room with her son Jonathan and her niece Penelope.

The room was dark but for the light of the four shaded candles on the table, and as Jon passed one of these to his mother for her cigarette, Penny pushed aside her coffee cup with a clatter.

"Nobody could say that I'm not a reasonable sort of person, but I don't jolly well see why I shouldn't speak to the guests downstairs if they want to speak to me..." she began breathlessly.

"Don't get excited," Jon interrupted in his methodical way. "Just be quiet until Mother has finished talking."

The candlelight glinted on his spectacles as he looked over at his cousin. The green band of ribbon over her red curls had slipped, her face was flushed with excitement and although her mouth was mutinous her eyes sparkled with fun before she looked down at her cup and said:

"Sorry, Auntie! ... It's Jon's fault. Why don't you tell

him to mind his own business? He's no right to boss me about just because an accident of birth has made him a bit older … I didn't mean to be rude."

Mrs Warrender, who had looked startled at the mention of her son's birth, smiled again at the apology.

"All right, darling, but I've told you before that you must not go into the hotel when we are full up as we are now and chatter to the guests."

"But it's very difficult for me, Auntie, because some of them seem to like little Penny … Jon doesn't understand because nobody is ever likely to want to talk to him. It's different with me. I s'pose it's because I've got personality…" and here, as Jon spluttered with rage, she turned in his direction and smiled demurely.

"You must understand, Mother," Jon said, "that our Penny is now building herself a social life. It's the fattish boy with pimples since Christmas Day…"

"He has *not* got pimples, you great…"

Mrs Warrender intervened again.

"You're both being stupid. I've told you before that I know this life is difficult for you in the holidays, but I've got to run the *Dolphin* myself, and it's the only home we've got, and neither of you must forget that this side of the yard is your home and not the other. It's different when we're not so busy, of course … Now, why don't you go off to the pictures?"

"Seen it," said Jon.

"No money, darling," from Penny. Then, as she flicked back her curls, "I feel like something happening to me – something really terrific. I don't suppose you know that feeling, Jon … Poor boy! You don't know what you're missing! Does he, Auntie?"

"I know what you're missing at this moment," her cousin retorted, "and I'd jolly well like to stop you missing it…"

Then, just as that morning the postman had brought news to Witchend, the telephone rang to bring news to the Warrenders.

"I'll go," Jon said, "but it's probably for you, Mother."

The telephone was in the dark little hall outside the dining-room, and as Jon left the door open the other two could hear every word he said. At first Penny, idly tickling the back of one leg with the toe of her shoe under the table, stared before her at the candle flame wavering in the draught. Then, as she heard Jon's astonished voice say, "Not David *Morton*? … Speak up whoever it is … Sounds like David Morton … It *is* you, is it, David, you old ass? … David Morton from Witchend? … Gosh, David! How are you? What's wrong?" Penny jumped from her chair and darted out into the hall.

"Give it to me, Jon," she hissed through clenched teeth. "Give it to me. Let me speak to David. I've got a right to speak to him, haven't I? You can't understand him, anyway, so let me talk…"

"SHUT UP, Penny!" Jon yelled, and then back into the receiver, "So sorry, David! It's Penny hopping about here … Go on … Tell me again … Gosh! How marvellous! … I don't see why we shouldn't … and your mother is writing, and so are you? … Grand! … Day after tomorrow? … Why not? … Sooner the better … SHUT UP, PENNY … How are the twins? … Good! …

39

All right, David … We'll send a wire tomorrow after Mother gets Mrs Morton's letter … See you soon … 'Bye."

When he put the receiver down and turned round, Penny flew at him. She stood on tiptoe, grabbed the lapels of his coat and shook him till her eyes filled with tears of humiliation.

"You beast, Jon! Why *are* you such a beast to me? Why didn't you let me speak to him? What is it? What does he want? Why did he ring up? Don't stand there saying nothing, Jon. *Answer me*, you great lout!"

Jon shook her off rather as a mastiff would dispose of an aggressive pekinese.

"How can I answer you when you never stop talking? Try and behave yourself."

Then he looked down at her, pretended not to notice the tears still in her eyes, put his hand on the back of her neck, and pushed her gently into the room before him.

"What's all that, Jon?" his mother asked. "It sounds exciting."

Jon pulled his chair round to Penny's side of the table and sat down next to her.

"It is. That was David Morton, and they want us – Penny and me – to go up in a day or two and join them and their friends at some place in Shropshire I've never heard of for a holiday … I couldn't understand it all, for he sounded a long way off, but Mrs Morton has written to you … Funny thing is they want Penny, too … Doesn't make sense to me."

Penny jumped up and hugged her aunt. "Say we can go, darling. Don't hesitate – don't say but and if – don't worry, 'cos we'll be all right … PLEASE let us go, whatever it's all about! … Jon won't tell me properly what it is, but you know, darling, that this very minute is what I've been waiting for all day, and nearly every day, these hols … I know this is going to be the terrific thing I wanted to happen…"

Mrs Warrender disentangled herself.

"What did he say, Jon? Just tell me again."

Two mornings later Jon and Penny began their exciting journey.

Penny was awake long before it was light – an hour before Fred Vasson, the porter at the *Dolphin*, tapped on her door. She jumped out of bed and shivered as she felt the cold from the open window. She looked out, and could just see the outline of the garden wall which had been rebuilt only last autumn after the gale which had showed them the way to the *Dolphin*'s treasure.* The hands of the little clock which Jon had given her last birthday showed twenty minutes past five, but they were catching the half-past six train, so had not really much time. When she crept down the creaking stairs into the lounge – for Penny's room was in the hotel part of the *Dolphin* – Fred was on his knees blowing the embers of the great wood fire into flame. He looked round at her and smiled slowly as she said, "D'you think you can manage without me, Fred? We'll be away for a week at least."

"Don't make a noise with the door, Miss Penny, and hurry across and get your breakfast. I'll have the car ready for you both at six-fifteen prompt."

Jon was already sitting down at the table when Penny

*See *The Gay Dolphin Adventure*

came in and kissed her aunt. She was too excited to eat much and was fidgeting about the room while Jon was still eating toast steadily.

"Sit down for goodness' sake," he said. "We can't start for another ten minutes, anyway, so we might just as well make good use of the time."

But at last Fred arrived to say he was ready. The two suitcases and two knapsacks and a big parcel of sandwiches were already in the car.

Mrs Warrender came out into the yard with them.

"You don't really mind us going, do you, Mother?" Jon said. "We haven't seen much of you these hols, but I think this will be fun."

"I've never had an 'away holiday' in the Christmas hols before," Penny added. "Take care of yourself, Auntie darling. We'll write when we can, but when we get with the Mortons we seem to be very busy.".

"Look after her, Jon," Mrs Warrender smiled. "She's an awful responsibility for you ... Try and get a taxi to Paddington from Charing Cross, and don't eat your sandwiches until you have to ... Goodbye to you both, and have a lovely time."

Vasson switched on the headlights and the car slid slowly out into Trader's Street. Jon and Penny looked back to see Mrs Warrender standing silhouetted in the orange light of the open doorway, and then turned to face their new adventure. The car bumped over the cobbles and the lights played strange tricks on the fronts of the closed and silent houses. A cat, with green eyes gleaming, ran back startled into a porch; the big tree at the corner of the churchyard threw fantastic shadows on the white walls of another house as the car turned, and almost before they could notice that the narrow High Street was deserted but for a lonely milkman, they were at the station.

Vasson carried their luggage on to the platform and waited while Jon got the tickets from the sleepy clerk in the booking office.

"You've but a few minutes to wait, Mister Jonathan," he said in his slow Sussex speech. "Crossing gates be opening. I'll be saying good luck to you now, for I've my work at the *Dolphin* to be through by breakfast."

"Goodbye, Fred," Penny said. "We'll be back soon ... and thanks for bringing us down."

A bell clanged in the signal-box, the red light changed to green, an old porter came out on the platform blowing on his hands and looked at them in surprise. Far away, from the direction of Winchelsea and Hastings, came the sound of the train. Jon took his eyes from the hissing gas-lamp over his head and laughed down at Penny.

"Thrilled, aren't you, kid?"

"Don't be so pompous, Jon. You know you're as excited as I am, only you just pretend it's grown-up not to show it. Here it comes ... You bring the luggage and I'll find a carriage."

The train was nearly empty, so she had no difficulty in finding an empty compartment. For a while they were both quiet. A railway journey in the dark of an early winter morning is always an odd experience, and now, as they crossed the flat country of Romney Marsh, the sky began to lighten a little in the east, and one by one the windows of the few cottages and farms which the train passed glowed yellow. The train stopped at every little station. Milk churns were banged about on the platforms, and bundles of newspapers thrown out. Slowly the wintry landscape came to life. As they left the Marsh behind them the bare branches of the trees could be seen against the pale sky. For a time the stars seemed to burn brighter and then to fade, and soon afterwards they reached Ashford.

Others got into the carriage here, so Jon moved over and sat beside his cousin.

"I wonder what this place Clun is like," he said. "I like going to fresh places, don't you, Penny?"

He took David Morton's letter from his pocket, and although they had both read it several times already, they turned the pages again as the train roared along through the wintry dawn towards London.

"... Rather a rag for us all to go together to a new place," they read, "and although Clun is not really very far from here it's odd that we've never been ... It's no use expecting Agnes to explain, of course. Did we tell you about Agnes when we were at the *Dolphin* in the summer? She's our housekeeper and has lived in Shropshire all her life. She's a funny old soul, but we're all very fond of her. Of course, the aged parents have put us on our honour not to make things difficult for her and to help all we can, but as far as we can discover she'll only have to look after her sister's house for her while she is in hospital. It's called – the house, I mean – Keep View, and she says that's because Clun has a very old castle now in ruins and practically only the keep now stands ... Dickie is very excited about this castle because he says there's sure to be some secret passages about somewhere and we're jolly good at those…

"I'm looking forward to you meeting the others – Peter, Tom and Jenny. We're all going on our bikes if it's not raining, except Peter, who insists on riding Sally. I don't know what she will do with Sally when she gets there, but she won't go without her, so that's that. Mackie has got to come, too, but Mary will bring him in a basket a gipsy made specially for him once … Anyway, have a good journey, although I'll bet you'll be sick of trains by the time you get to Craven Arms and we meet you there. If we're not there when you arrive, ask in the booking office for a message because I'll telephone … I hope you remembered to send your bikes on by passenger train, because they ought to be waiting for you at the station. We'll manage about your luggage some-how. I expect there's a bus or a carrier or something…"

Penny raised her red head.

"He thinks of everything, doesn't he, Jon? Gosh! This is a thrill. Do you think our bikes will be there? I wish we'd brought them with us now."

"I don't," Jon replied. "They'd have been an awful nuisance in London … It's light now, Penny, and we're getting on. Shan't be long now … I'm jolly hungry."

"So am I, but let's save our sandwiches for the other train in case we can't get into the restaurant car … You know, Jon, I like meals, but I don't think any are such fun as those you get on a train."

They sat back and watched the countryside change. The fields and hedges were far behind them now for they were roaring through the sprawling suburbs.

Station after station with crowded platforms flashed by, and soon even the suburbs were passed and they were riding high over the squalid roofs of south London. The other people in the compartment reached for their coats and luggage. The train stopped for a signal, an electric train rattled past them, and then they slowly crossed the muddy Thames and slid into Charing Cross.

"Do you remember starting off from here for Rye the first time?" Penny asked as they got out on to the platform.

Jon nodded. "Shall I ever forget? You chose the carriage and Miss Ballinger got in."

"Wonder what's happened to her," Penny went on. "I sometimes feel we'll see her again some time. She won't like us much, will she, Jon? If we do meet I think I'll be scared stiff of her … I say, Jon, there's an awful lot of people about, isn't there? What do we do now?"

Jon looked down at her in his quizzical way and then took her suitcase as well as his own.

"You give up the tickets, Newpenny, and leave the luggage to me, and then we'll get a taxi … You're not big enough for busy London. People just don't notice you…" And here, strangely enough, Penny found it impossible to answer, for the crowd surging through the barrier forced her to fight to keep her place.

Outside they stood in a queue for a taxi. The morning was dull, grey and damp, and it seemed as they waited that everybody in London was surging round them and rushing out into the busy Strand. The air was thick with petrol fumes and noises.

Penny wrinkled her nose in disgust.

"I hate it," she said. "Once I thought I liked London when we had to live near it, but now I hate it. It's not as real as Rye or country places. Everyone here rushes about … Oh, Jon! Look! What a marvellous dog. Look! I'm sure she hates London as much as we do."

They were now in the front of the queue, and as a taxi drew up Jon looked over his shoulder and saw a slim collie dog standing close to a man in a raincoat and a brown cap. The dog's eyes were fixed on her master, but her tail was down and, as Penny had remarked, she looked as if she hated her surroundings.

"Where to?" the taxi-driver grumbled. "Can't stay here all day."

"Paddington, please," Jon said as he opened the door and flung in the haversacks. As Penny got in the man with the dog stepped out of the queue and smiled at them.

"I wonder if you'd mind me sharing with you?" he said slowly. "I heard you tell him Paddington, and I've got to get there, too … And besides," he added, "I reckon I don't know London, and what I do know I hates and my dog don't like it either."

Penny beamed at him.

"Of *course*," she said. "We'd love you to come, wouldn't we, Jon? … I noticed your dog just now and thought she looked very sad, and I was just that minute saying to my cousin here that I don't like London either, so, you see … Ow! That was your elbow, Jon! You are clumsy."

But Jon looked grim as he helped the man in with his suitcase. For a minute he almost hoped that he *had* hurt Penny, just because she was so irritating in the way she would talk to anybody. As she bent to stroke the dog it was evident she had no idea that she had been reminded about this, for she went on talking just the same.

"Do tell me her name. I think she's marvellous. Has she had any puppies? If she does and I give you my name and address, will you please keep one for me? Please do. I'll pay, of course. I mean, I'd pay anything to have a dog like that for my very own. Have you any idea when she will … I mean when she will have some puppies, 'cos I probably ought to start saving up now…"

The stranger smiled slowly at her, and when he smiled he looked very nice. His face was brown, his hair under his ugly cap was fair and his eyes were grey. Jon noticed that his hands were brown and strong, and wondered for a moment whether he was a sailor on leave. When he spoke his accent was soft and unusual.

"I don't know about pups," he said. "But I've only had her a few days. She's a sheep-dog and a gift to me from my uncle down south."

After that he did not seem inclined to say any more, and although Penny made one or two attempts to make him talk again she had not succeeded by the time they reached Paddington. All she discovered was that the dog's name was "Lady." Almost before the taxi stopped the stranger thanked them, paid his share of the fare, and disappeared with his dog and his bag into the crowd in the booking hall.

"I think he was nice, but shy," Penny said as she got out.

"Nobody could accuse *you* of being shy," Jon retorted. "You make me blush for you."

"Then I should think that I'm the only thing that could do *that*," said Penny, walking off with her head in the air.

They got on to the platform before their train came in, and a friendly old porter told them where to stand for the Shrewsbury section. "And the diner'll be about 'ere," he added, looking Jon up and down, and then, having decided that Jon did not look as if he would disappoint him, he went on, "Just give me your bags and I'll get two corners ... Here she comes now, so look slippy ... Just follow me."

They did follow him very thankfully, and Jon gave him sixpence just as if he had been doing that sort of thing all his life. While the train was waiting and filling up they ate their sandwiches.

"They're getting rather a nuisance, anyway," Penny remarked, "and I want to enjoy my lunch presently, so I think we'd better get them out of the way."

At last they started on the second stage of their journey. The other people in the compartment were not very interesting, neither did they seem to be interested in the Warrenders and this depressed Penny, who, after a little, went to sleep. The journey was not even very exciting to Jon, who was a train enthusiast – or train maniac, as Penny sometimes called this particular interest of his.

They stopped at Banbury and Leamington Spa, and in just over two hours from London slid smoothly into Snow Hill, Birmingham, and here they were called in to lunch. They were put at a table for four and Jon was studying the menu – which in reality was simple enough, for the meal looked as if there was not much alternative to soup and sausages – when Penny, at his side, nudged him violently and said, "Hullo! Fancy seeing you again! ... And you've brought Lady, too. What fun!"

Jon looked up and recognized their companion of the taxi as he slipped into the seat opposite. He looked much nicer without his cap and raincoat, but seemed to be very worried.

"Don't notice Lady," he whispered. "Don't take any notice of her. I'm going to hide her under the table because they didn't want me to bring her in."

"Didn't want you to bring her in?" Penny breathed with wide eyes. "The brutes! You couldn't possibly leave her, could you? I mean I couldn't ever be parted from a dog like her."

For the first time the man seemed to regard them with some interest.

"Of course I couldn't leave her, and I've got to eat ... But don't either of you mention her again, and maybe we'll get away with it. Depends on who comes into this other seat..."

When a fat man with horn-rimmed glasses squeezed into the empty place Penny slid her hand under the table and patted the collie's head. She felt her move under the caress and then a warm, damp tongue licked her hand in appreciation. The soup came then, and the fat man settled down to it noisily, while Lady, under the table, stayed still.

Penny nudged Jon.

"Say something," she hissed. "I can't do all the talking all the time, and I think he's nice."

Jon looked up gloomily. The stranger certainly did look nice, but somehow very out of place in a restaurant car. His brown tweed suit and rather garish tie made him look as if he was from the country, but he didn't seem very cheerful or as if he was travelling for pleasure.

After another long pause Jon said, "Funny we didn't see you on the platform at Paddington. Are you going far?"

"Home, thank goodness," the man smiled. "I don't like the south really, and I like London less. Where are you going?"

"We've got to change at Shrewsbury," Penny said eagerly. "And then we're going to a station that doesn't sound real to me because it's called Craven Arms, and from there we're going to a mysterious place called Clun … C-L-U-N it's spelled. We've never been before. Have you heard of it?"

The fat man never even looked up from his plate – indeed, it had been obvious from the moment of his arrival that he had come to eat and did not intend to be distracted. But their new acquaintance dropped his knife with a clatter.

"Of course I've heard of it. I live near there. What on earth are you going to Clun in winter for? Nobody comes to Clun except some odd people in the summer who dig about for flint arrowheads on the hills."

Penny's eyes widened still further.

"There you are, Jon! I always knew this holiday was going to be thrilling, and now, almost before we've started, this has happened. Now this gentleman … I say, do tell us your name, please. This is going to be fun. I'm Penny Warrender, and this is my cousin Jon."

"And my name is Alan Denton, and I'm a sheep farmer – at least I'm just starting to be one in earnest … I haven't been out of the Navy very long, and while I was away my dad died, and I'm trying now to make it all work for Mother."

The fat man pushed his plate away from him and started to work with a toothpick. Now that he had finished all that had been put before him, he apparently realized that he was sharing the table with three others, and seemed inclined to enter the conversation. Penny didn't like the look of him at all and was desperately afraid that Lady might take a dislike to his fat knees also and make a scene. Alan Denton looked anxious, too, for it was vital that the stranger should leave the table first. So as the waiter came swaying down the narrow gangway with a tray balanced on one hand, he turned again to Penny and said, "I hope you two will have some coffee? Have it with me, will you, and then perhaps you can tell me why you are coming to Clun and I'll tell you something about the place in exchange?"

While saying this he winked slowly and then looked meaningly at the fat man, who was now lighting a large cigar. It was a cigar with a very strong smell, and Penny felt Lady tremble as the fumes troubled her sensitive nose. The coffee was poured next, and suddenly the fat man spoke. He had an absurdly small voice.

"I think there's something strange under this table," he piped. "I shall call the steward … Have you anything under the table, child?" to Penny, who for once was stricken with fear into silence.

Jon spoke up. "We've only got our haversacks under

there, sir. Sorry if they're in the way, but we didn't like to leave them in the compartment. We're going as soon as we've finished our coffee."

Before the stranger could answer, Penny recovered.

"I'm most *frightfully* sorry," she said with wide eyes. "I'm absolutely ashamed of myself, but I'm afraid that cigar makes me feel sick. Cigars always make me feel ill, and now I just couldn't move, *whatever* happened ... I'm *so* sorry ... I know it's rude of me, but I would never have sat here if I'd known there was going to be a cigar..." and here, to her everlasting shame, she put her hands to her face and lowered her head as if in pain.

Jon had the sense to look alarmed, while Alan Denton merely looked astonished. But the fat man, after a quick glance at Penny's now shaking shoulders, beckoned the steward, paid his bill, heaved himself out of his seat and waddled away.

Jon nudged his cousin.

"All right. You can recover now. He's gone."

"Don't you really like cigars?" Denton asked gravely, and then smiled as Penny burst out laughing. "That was a smart way of getting rid of him, anyhow. Let's pay our bills and go ... Maybe there's room in my carriage now, and perhaps you two would like to come in with me?"

As soon as the steward had turned his back they slipped out into the corridor, where Lady shook herself and then wagged her tail as Penny stroked her ears. There was much more room in Denton's carriage, so the Warrenders, who were only in the next coach, brought their luggage along and settled down opposite to him.

"Hope you don't mind a pipe?" he grinned at Penny.

"Now tell me why you're coming to Clun, of all places. I'm curious – and so is Lady."

Jon polished his glasses violently, and after glaring so fiercely at Penny that for once she remained silent, he told their new friend quite briefly that they were joining some old friends from another part of Shropshire and going to stay together at Keep View.

"Do you know that place?" he went on. "It's a sort of boarding house, isn't it?"

Denton nodded.

"Yes, 'tis ... Nice old soul runs it, but I can't just recall her name ... quite a lot of people come to Clun in summer they say, but I reckoned she'd be more or less closed up in winter time ... But I still can't understand why you're all coming to the place now ... What made you choose Clun?"

Somehow Jon did not feel inclined to tell him what little he did know of the reasons for their visit, so he countered this by asking,

"But you tell us something about the place. That's what we want to know. Have you always lived there?"

"Bury Fields our place is called, but 'tis three miles or more from Clun. Dentons have always been there I'm told. We never leave. We've been rearing sheep on those hills since William the Conqueror's time maybe. We don't go to Clun so often really. The Castle – Bishop's Castle is its real name – and Knighton are bigger towns for shopping and the like. There's a fine market at The Castle and Craven Arms is pretty well-known to all sheep farmers round Shropshire and Hereford way for they have big sheep sales there in August and September."

"But what's Clun *like*?" Penny demanded. "I've tried and tried to imagine it but I can't … Just give us an idea."

Denton scratched his head and then pointed out of the window as the train slowed down.

"I'll try in a minute … This is Wellington and you're in Shropshire now. See that smooth-looking mountain? That's the Wrekin and every Shropshire man knows that … Now you want to know what Clun is like … Funny, but it's difficult to explain something you take for granted, but I should know I s'pose for I've seen it and been told about it often enough.

"First of all, then, Clun is just a little town that seems to ha' been forgotten although 'tis said that it stands on one of the old coaching roads from Wales into England … You know it's got no railway and 'tis never likely to have."

"But the castle?" Penny interrupted. "Tell us about that? How old is it? Can you go in it? Has it got secret passages?"

"Steady! Not so fast! 'Tis funny, but I don't mind ever being told a lot about the castle and though I've seen it all my life I reckon I must take it for granted. Maybe I was told at school, but I believe 'twas built in Stephen's reign … It's just bits o' the keep that you can see standing on the hill now … But you'll soon see that for yourselves so don't bother me about that … Then we've got a river called Clun and a fine old bridge over it though 'tis much too narrow now."

He took his pipe from his mouth and looked out of the window for a long minute.

"But you can't explain it," he said at last. "Reckon you've got to feel it. 'Tis not the town but the hills and the country round about where I live that make the place something to remember ... They say some o' the first men in England lived in the hills around Clun, and you can pick up the flint arrowheads they made today ... And there's a circle of mighty great stones at Pen-y-wern – and these I've seen many a time – and an even bigger stone stands in another field nearby, and I mind there's a story which says a line stretched from the big stone to centre of the circle shows where the sun rises on December 21st! ... Do you know what that means?" he added with a sly glance at Penny.

Jon answered. "Sun worshippers I should think. Same as the Druids at Stonehenge ... But go on ... Tell us some more."

"I don't know that there's much more to tell ... There are hills all round Clun, and this is the country I know for 'tis mine and where our sheep are bred ... Once it was all forest ... From the tops o' our hills you can see other hills – the Long Mynd over Stretton way, the Stiperstones and over to the south the Black Mountains in Wales."

He paused again, and after a little Penny said, "Tell us about your farm ... And may we come and see you?"

Alan smiled, and the faraway look that had been in his eyes when he talked about the hills round his home disappeared.

"Of course you can ... Come when you like and welcome if you can find us! There's only Mother and me now though we're hoping to get some more help." He turned to Jon. "Are you interested in sheep? D'you know anything about 'em?"

Jon shook his head.

" 'Fraid not. But we'd like to see yours."

"Every penny we've got is in our sheep … We reckon Dad built up finest flock for miles around and now 'tis my job to keep it so … Come and see us and bring your friends with you, but maybe then I'll not have the time to be polite!"

"What did you say your farm was called?" Penny asked.

"Bury Fields."

"Why? It's a peculiar name."

"I suppose 'tis … Dad told me once it must be because we're right near one of those burying places where you can dig up bones and ashes and the like if you've time."

"Thank you very much for making it all so exciting," Penny smiled. "I'd – we all would – I'd like to come and see you and your mother and your sheep, and your lovely Lady of course."

"Maybe we'll meet again then," Denton said as he reached for his luggage. "We're running into Shrewsbury now and I'll have to say Cheerio for I've to do something in the town and can't catch your connection … And many thanks for the lift in the taxi and for helping me to hide Lady."

Penny stooped and rubbed her curls against the dog's head.

"Where did you get her? I do so want one like her."

"My uncle who farms on the South Downs down Sussex way gave her to me … Tell you what, Ha'penny, or whatever your name is – when I see him again I'll ask him to keep a pup for you unless Lady has 'em first."

"*Write* to him please," Penny pleaded. "Don't wait till you see him. That might be years!"

Alan laughed as he put on his cap.

"One day I'll learn to be a sheep farmer maybe," he said, "but I'll never learn how to be a letter writer!"

The train swung round a wide curve and glided alongside the long platform one minute before time.

Alan opened the door.

"Just look after Lady for me till I'm out with my baggage ... Right! Thank you ... So long, kids, and I hope we'll meet again!"

"So do I," Penny said, and then, under her breath, "I think he's absolutely smashing."

Jon looked at her coldly.

"Come on," he said. "Let's get on with it. We've got forty minutes if that clock is right, so we'll eat a bun."

But Penny was still gazing after Alan and Lady and did not seem to hear him.

Chapter 3

The Caravan

Mist hung low in the Witchend valley long after the darkness of the winter night had fled. It was very quiet. The stillness of the hills was broken only by the murmur of the little brook which ran so cheerfully down through the heather until it broadened into a pool before the front door of the house, dashed on again through a narrower channel under the stone wall, and then slid down the side of the lane that led to Ingles Farm.

Jemima, Mary's duck, suddenly removed her beak from the mud at the bottom of the pond, raised her head and quacked rather gloomily as the front door opened and Dickie and Mary came out. The twins were wearing green lumber jackets, brown corduroy shorts and balaclava helmets. As the latter completely covered Mary's curls the two looked more than ever alike. Macbeth, the Scottie, with a green ribbon tied to his collar, followed them a little way and then went back and sat in the porch. He knew that something was going to happen soon, and although suspicious, did not want to be left behind. With his head on one side he watched the twins until they disappeared round the corner of the house in the direction of the shed where the bicycles were kept. Then David appeared, patted the little dog absentmindedly, and said,

"Yes. You're coming, old boy. But you won't like the journey much." He raised his voice. "Where are you, kids? Buck up with the bikes else we shall be late ... Sun's coming out too."

The twins reappeared with their bicycles.

"Are your tyres hard?" David asked sternly. "Have you got your pumps? Have you forgotten your puncture sets as usual?"

Dickie looked aggrieved.

"Why do you speak to us like that, David? You're always picking on us. I'll bet that we'll be the ones that make no trouble at all."

"I remember the time that you got a puncture, David," Mary added, "and anyway I think you're the one who ought to blow up our tyres ... You're so big and strong ... An' now please don't interrupt any more because I've got to get Mackie's basket ready ... The little darling doesn't know yet that he's coming with us."

"Oh, yes, he does," David said as he went over to the shed for his own bicycle, "I've told him! Poor little blighter! It would be much kinder to leave him at home. Why don't you?"

"Don't notice him, twin!" Dickie comforted. "He's a cad ... Let's fix the basket."

Macbeth's basket had been made specially for him by some kind-hearted gipsies called Reuben and Miranda, who once brought the Lone Piners at Witchend a special message from Peter, who had been sent to a mysterious farmhouse away by the Stiperstones*. The little dog had

*See *Seven White Gates*

learned to ride in the basket without jumping out, but as he always laid his ears back and looked acutely miserable when he was travelling in it, David never missed an opportunity of teasing Mary about her "cruelty".

The basket was duly fixed to the carrier, and as they tightened the straps the sun came up over the tops of the pine trees above the house and swirled some of the mist away. David, still whistling cheerfully, came back with his cycle and grinned at them.

He was ignored.

Then their father and mother came out, and Mrs Morton said,

"Are you really sure you're going to be all right, twins? Are you certain it's not too far for you?"

"It's very strange," their father remarked as he took his pipe from his mouth, "that whenever we want you to walk or cycle anywhere for us you always say it's too far, or you're too tired, and can't we go in the car! You could all have come in the car yesterday when I took Agnes and your luggage over to Clun, but now you want to cycle! I think you're all crazy!" Then he laughed, and with each hand pulled up the twins' balaclavas into a peak and added, "... But I like you for it ... Take care of 'em, David, and go their pace and you'll be all right ... We'll ring up Keep View from London tonight to see if you've arrived safely, but I know we can trust you."

"You can, Dad, I promise," David said. "Get that little brute fixed in the back, Mary, and get your haversacks on your backs ... I bet Tom is waiting for us and as we've got to meet Jenny we shall mess up the whole programme if we're late."

"Come along, my little darling," Mary crooned as she lifted the quivering Macbeth into the basket. "Be Mummy's brave little boy and show David that you're not afraid of *anything*."

"Give my love to Agnes," Mrs Morton said as she kissed the twins. "Have lots of fun and we'll come back as soon as we can … Oh, and David, old man … My special love to Penny and Jon, and say we'd like them up here at Witchend in the Easter holidays if we can only fit them in. We'll talk it over and see if we can arrange something … You've got the sandwiches and the apples and the thermos … Goodbye, and good luck."

Mr Morton strolled over and opened the white gate for them.

"I'll bet Peter on Sally beats you all," he smiled. "Give her my love. If I know her at all she started her ride in the dark. Have a good time, and David – if the weather breaks today use your sense and don't cycle through snow or rain. Get to a station and then hire a car at Craven Arms for the last part of the trip."

They called goodbye, and when Mary turned to wave, her bicycle wobbled dangerously and poor Macbeth was nearly flung to the ground. Down the lane which they knew and loved so well they pedalled with the twins leading. As the sun gained power the mists fled and the brook, at the side of the road, sparkled in sympathy. Some crimson berries still blazed in the bare hedgerows and, up in the wood on their right, a bird called.

"Whistle the call, David," Dickie shouted over his shoulder. "I bet Tom will answer."

"They'll hear you in Onnybrook if you shout like

that," David replied. "Stop a sec and be quiet and we'll see if we can make him hear."

Soft, yet piercingly clear, David whistled the peewit's lament. Once, twice – and yet again the lonely little cry echoed down the lane and then, softer yet, came the reply and they knew that Tom had heard them.

He was waiting by the farmyard gate and David couldn't help remembering how thin and white he had looked when he had first come to his uncle's farm in the year when they themselves had come to Witchend. He was smaller and slighter still than David but his skin was brown, his hands hard, and his eyes now always seemed to be laughing. You hardly ever heard Tom pining for "the pictures" now, although he was still a Londoner at heart, and his happiest days were those when he was taken to Shrewsbury or further still to Birmingham.

"You're late," he said. "I've been up hours. You'd better just nip in and see Uncle and Auntie else they'll be upset. I b'lieve Uncle is hanging about specially to see you … I say, David! What d'you think? I had a letter from Jenny this morning. She's so excited she hasn't put any full stops so far as I can see – I'm not much good at letters but she ought to be ashamed of herself."

"Does she understand where we're going to meet? That's the point, Tom. Do you think she's going to manage on her own?"

"If she can't I'll go and meet her and catch you up later," Tom scowled. "Why shouldn't she understand, I'd like to know? Anyway she's the only one of us who's got to cycle on her own so we shall just jolly well have to wait for her."

"Peter's gone on her own, hasn't she?" David started indignantly, "and she's going the whole way by herself with nobody to meet her."

"Well, she likes it anyway," Tom rejoined. "It was her own suggestion. And you ought to jolly well remember that Jenny is nearly always on her own and doesn't have such a good time as we do."

Then he laughed good-humouredly and began to fidget in his pockets.

"Like to see her letter, David? … You kids cut in and see if you can find Uncle – he's waiting for you."

While the twins crossed the farmyard calling in duet, "Uncle Ingles! Uncle Alfred! Where are *you*? Where *are* you?" David and Tom leaned against the gate while the former tried to read Jenny's letter, which was as breathless and dramatic as its writer.

"Dear Tom I am writing this with my new fountain pen Dad gave me for Christmas but we cannot find the ink to fill it with so I must dip it in the shop. Everything is wonderful and most frightfully thrilling Tom I can't tell how much this means to me Dad says I can come with you all and good luck to us but I can't believe it yet until I see you Tom at the place you name in your letter…"

"Why doesn't she say Crown Farm instead of the place you name?" David asked as he turned the page. "And where does she take a breath?"

"You know she's like that, David. It's all those books she reads. She talks like it too, but she's a jolly good sort and nobody's going to say a word against Jenny," Tom said, rather red in the face, but before David could say he was sorry Mr and Mrs Ingles came out into the farmyard between the twins.

"GOOD LUCK TO YE," Mr Ingles roared in his usual cheerful bellow. "YOUNG TOM CAN STAY TILL YOU ALL COME BACK."

"Where's my darling Mackie?" Mary wailed suddenly. "What have you done with him, David? Where have you put him?"

But Macbeth had heard the voice of his mistress, and although he already most heartily despised and detested his basket he squeezed through a gap in the hedge where he had been exploring a rabbit-hole, approached Mary, and stood up to lick her bare knees.

So the cavalcade started again, and now David and Tom led the way.

Partly because they had planned to meet Jenny as soon as they could and partly because David felt that it would be more fun and wiser too to avoid the main road, he had chosen a rather roundabout route through lanes and over wild country. They had plenty of time before meeting the Warrenders at Craven Arms and he had been sure that the twins would keep going if they did not have to hurry and if they could have some good rests.

Once or twice David had to stop to consult his map. It was as well that he had allowed lots of time for, after two experiments, Mary absolutely refused to ride her bicycle down any hills.

Even Dickie thought she was crazy.

"You're just crackers," he said. "You've suddenly gone

it. Down hills is the best part of all biking 'cos it's like flying ... You always used to like going downhill, Mary. What's wrong?"

"You great stupid," Mary stormed at him. "Can't you see that it's Mackie? Every time I go downhill I go fast. Every time I go fast I bump. Every time I bump my poor darling is TORTURED AND TERRIFIED ... You can all jolly well go on your own way. I don't care. I'll catch you up if I want to – and not unless!" she gulped.

"You're just not going for a bike ride at all," Dickie muttered. "All you're doing is to take your bicycle for a walk and give it some fresh air. You walk it up hills and now you walk it down hills too, so it just doesn't make sense to me."

"Dickie!" Mary gasped. "I just can't believe it's you talkin'! ... I'll wake up any minute now. You must be ill to go against me like that ... Dickie! This is the most awful thing that's ever happened to me."

This discussion took place at the top of a long hill, and even David and Tom were silenced by Mary's wide-eyed horror of her twin's desertion.

Dickie began to fidget with his bicycle bell.

"Oh, well," he muttered after a horrible pause, "you don't want to get in a state over a bit of a joke, do you? 'Course I understand about Mackie ... What other people round here forget, Mary, is that we've all sworn in blood as members of the Lone Pine Club that we'll always be kind to animals ... We have, haven't we?"

"Well, Dickie, *we* didn't forget, but some people did, and I think it's jolly clever of you to remember that," Mary said in a more normal manner.

"An' there's another thing, twin … You know that joke I made just now about taking bikes for a walk?"

Mary nodded dismally.

"Well, if you and me *want* to take our bikes for a walk on this trip, I don't see why we shouldn't! I mean it's *our* holiday just as much as the others, however much they try and boss us about, isn't it, twin?"

Mary smiled cheerfully, for this was her real beloved Dickie again.

"O'course it is, Dickie … David was told not to go faster than we could manage, wasn't he?"

"That's all right, then," Dickie concluded triumphantly. "So now we'll jolly well *both* push our bikes down this hill and Mackie can walk … Come on, twin! I reckon David and Tom have had enough rest now!" And with this startling statement they set off down the road with Macbeth trotting sedately between them.

"Let them get well ahead," David said with his hand on Tom's sleeve. "It's no use fussing … Let them get on and then we shan't have to talk to them."

"That doesn't matter," Tom muttered. "I don't mind not talking to them when they're in this mood. Trouble is they never stop talking *to* us or *at* us … Anyway, I'm not walking down hills for anybody. I'll go on to Crown Farm, and if Jenny's not there yet I'll go along some of the way and meet her … Wait for us, David, if we're not there. So long!" and he jumped on his bike and whizzed down the hill.

With a wry smile David noticed that the twins did not even look up when Tom passed them.

At the foot of the hill Mackie was lifted into his basket

and the three Mortons cycled on together. Tom had been out of sight for some minutes.

The sun was well up the sky now, and as their road climbed steadily every break in the hedges showed the country spread out before them. Far away to the west they could see the tumbled mountains of Wales with their heads in the clouds. Before them rose the mass of the two Clees beyond Ludlow, and at their backs were their own hills and the more rugged Stiperstones from where Jenny was even now riding to meet them. David stopped at one gate on the left of the road and showed them the great vale spread out between Wenlock Edge and the hills they were now exploring. Far, far away a puff of white smoke marked the progress of a toy-like train on its way from Shrewsbury to Hereford.

"Do you think Jon and Penny are in that?" Dickie asked.

"Not that one – but that's the way they'll come. It'll be grand to have them up here, won't it, kids?"

Mary nodded happily.

"We'll make them members of the Club, won't we, David? They'll have to be sworn in just like Tom and Jenny were."

"And then I reckon we've got enough members," Dickie added. "We can't go on for ever makin' new ones … Yes! I'll like to see Jon and Penny again."

For another mile their lane wound steadily uphill, and then the hedges stopped and they found themselves coming to open moorland. David pointed ahead.

"See those buildings? That should be Crown Farm and a cross-roads, and that's where Jenny is supposed to meet us. Can you see her, Dickie? You're the chap with sharp eyes in this family."

Dickie strained ahead and then stood on the pedals.

"Yes!" he shouted triumphantly. "I can see her, I think. She's got a green blob of a hat on and she's standing by the signpost, and Tom's with her ... Up the Lone Piners!"

"Hold tight, Mackie darling," Mary implored as she accelerated. "We're going to bump a bit, so hold on with all four paws."

Jenny had recognized them now and they saw her snatch off her bright green beret and wave it frantically in welcome.

"She's done jolly well," David said as he waved back. "Wonder if Tom had to go far to meet her ... We'll pitch our first camp here and have some grub. Wonder how Peter is getting on?"

"She'll be all right," Mary said. "I'spect she's having all sorts of adventures by herself ... I think she's the only one of us all that doesn't mind being by herself a lot, don't you?"

David had no time to agree that this was a very wise remark, for now they had reached the cross-roads and Jenny was dancing about in the road to welcome them.

"D'you know, David, that I *really* was here first? I was here before Tom even, and he told me that he's hurried on specially. It was your map that did it, David. D'you know that I understood it nearly all and I didn't lose my way once ... And another thing, David. Dad says I can stay just as long as you'll all have me, and I'm so excited I just don't know what to do next ... Oh, hullo, you twins! Sorry not to say it before, but I *did* see you ...

Hullo, Mackie! Isn't he a pet, Mary? ... David, it was just absolutely marvellous of you to ask me ... I'm *utterly* bowed down with the weight of this haversack, but it's terrific down hills because I go so fast..." and here she paused for breath and David took the opportunity.

"We're all thrilled you could come, Jenny. If your father had said 'No,' we'd have come and carried you off."

"You *wouldn't*, David? Not *really*? Gosh! I wish he had said 'No.' ... Do you know I've always wanted to be carried off, but I don't s'pose it will ever happen to me?"

David couldn't help laughing at her as she stood there looking up at him so seriously. Her hair was not nearly so red and shiny as Penny's, and her eyes were darker, but he knew from their first adventure together that she was brave and true and loyal, and tremendous fun. He'd forgotten how jolly she was, and he was suddenly very pleased that she had, after all, been able to come with them.

"Tom says Peter is riding Sally," Jenny went on. "That's just like her, isn't it? I'm longing to see her ... And Tom says we're going to Craven Arms to meet those other friends of yours, too. That's fun! D'you think they'll like me, David?"

"It'll be their loss if they don't!" Tom said shortly. "I've not seen them before either, Jenny ... Maybe we won't like them, and that will be just too bad for them."

David looked rather startled. Jenny would never be short of a champion when Tom was about!

"We've got a lot of adventures to tell you, Jenny," Dickie was saying, "but I expect we'll have plenty of time at that Clun place … I'm jolly hungry now, and I bags we do something about it … And I tell you another thing! It's getting cold."

He was right about the change in the weather, for the wind seemed to be strengthening and to be coming from the north-east. The sun had disappeared, too, and quite suddenly the day did not seem as nice.

Mary shivered and picked up Macbeth.

"I'm cold. Let's make a fire right here by this signpost and get warm before we pursue our weary way … I've got an idea something is going to happen to us here."

"P'raps the farmer in this place is going to come out of that gate in a minute and say 'Hullo, Lone Piners! I'm jolly glad to see you, 'cos I've got a couple of big turkeys just out of the oven, and I want some help in eating 'em!' … P'raps that's what's going to happen?" Dickie said.

"I don't think it is, you greedy little blighter," Tom said, "but maybe Mary's right. Do you see what I see, Jenny? Do you, David? Coming up the road towards us, you chumps! Look! Is there another caravan like that round these parts, and is there another gipsy rides in the driving-seat like Reuben?"

"Gosh, Tom! You're right. I'm sure you are!" David shouted.

Up the road towards them came a gaily-painted caravan. Red and yellow were the sides, and yellow and red the wheels. The roof was green and so were the shafts, and there were white lace curtains in the windows. Smoke came from the little chimney and smoke from the short black pipe between the teeth of a jolly, handsome, brown-faced gipsy man in an old green hat who sat back with the

71

reins loose between his fingers. David and the twins ran out into the road and Mackie followed, barking excitedly.

"Reuben!" David yelled. "Reuben! Don't you know us? How are you all? Is Miranda there, and Fenella?"

"It's us, Mr Reuben," Mary shouted. "From Witchend. Do remember us, please, 'cos we've never forgotten you!"

The gipsy smiled with a flash of white teeth and pushed the old hat to the back of his head. His gold earrings gleamed and his eyes twinkled with delight as he checked the horse.

"Remember? How could we forget? Miranda! Fenella! Come you and greet the children from Witchend and the lad over yonder who farms with his uncle nearby, and a little miss here whose name I have forgotten, but whose fortune you can tell!"

And round from the back of the van came an olive-skinned woman with a bright handkerchief round her hair and ear-rings even bigger than her husband's! Then, very shyly, came the gipsy child called Fenella, who scowled at them all and yet was longing to talk to them.

Miranda greeted them in Romany and then turned and spoke to her husband in the same language.

"That's not fair!" Mary said. "What are you saying to him? … And have you noticed Mackie? He's come all the way in the basket you made him."

The gypsy turned to the twins with a brilliant smile.

"I was saying, little ones, that only this morning I said to Reuben here that we should meet old friends today."

Reuben jumped down and flung the reins across the horse's back.

"But before you tell us where you are going, tell us where is our friend Petronella, who saved Fenella's life and is the friend of the Romany for ever?"

"Peter's all right," David announced. "We're all going to Clun for a holiday, but she wanted to ride her pony on her own. She'll be there when we arrive tonight. Where are you going, Reuben? If you are going Onnybrook way, it's no use going up to Witchend because the house is empty ... If you look in at Ingles on the way up the lane you won't find Tom because he's here, and we all know you don't like the Stiperstones where Jenny comes from."

When David had mentioned Clun he noticed that the two gipsies glanced at each other rather meaningly, but before his question could be answered Dickie broke in:

"We were just going to have something to eat. Will you make a real gipsy fire and sit round it with us? We've only got sandwiches, but you're welcome to some of those if you like."

Reuben looked down at the boy, smiled and then, over his shoulder, said something to Fenella, who went into the caravan for a bundle of dry sticks.

Then the gipsies showed the Lone Piners how to make a fire in the open with only one match.

A tripod was set over the flames and a great pot of soup was heated over it and shared when it was hot enough, with the sandwiches. They were all glad of the fire, for the weather was getting steadily colder.

Mary began to explain why they were going to Clun, but Reuben interrupted to ask whether they had been there before.

David shook his head. "No; it's all new to us. I

suppose you've been there lots of times? Tell us what it's like."

Reuben shrugged. "The town? Like any other of its size, except perhaps that it is quieter. We go through it sometimes on the way to Wales from these parts, but there is no business there for us."

"You see," Miranda broke in, "you go to Clun and we come away."

"Have you just this moment left? I mean this morning?"

"We start in the night. But not from the town. On the other side of the town is the old forest land with sheep farms and many other old and mysterious things as well … That's the country we know and often go to … Now we do not like it as much, and maybe we never go back."

When pressed to explain his reasons for never going back to country that suited them Reuben admitted that sheep stealing was going on all over the Clun countryside, and that sooner or later – however innocent they really were – he was sure the gipsies would be accused.

"And so we go before the trouble starts," he finished. "Reuben and Miranda have a good name everywhere, but when sheep disappear from farms we have known for years we think 'tis best for us to move."

David held his hands to the leaping flames and looked up at the grey sky before he said:

"Do you really think so, Reuben? Of course, it's nothing to do with me, but aren't you afraid that people might think you really have got something to do with it if you go away? … I mean everyone who knows you – and you said all the farmers round about knew you –

realizes that you couldn't have anything to do with it…"

Reuben, who was leaning against the wheel of the caravan with his hands behind his head, blew a thin stream of smoke in the direction of the twins, who were now happily engaged with a large hunk of cake. Then he looked across at David and smiled slowly.

"What you say seems to make sense, but it is not so. Always it is the gipsies who are blamed for everything bad, and we do not like any of our friends to say, 'It is strange, but Reuben and Miranda with their van were not far away when the sheep disappeared. Maybe they had gipsy friends who know something about it if they did not do it themselves.'"

"I don't believe it," Tom said stoutly. "Nobody would say that, and we all hope you'll come back while we're at Clun. Don't we, Jenny?"

Jenny nodded and then turned to Miranda and said breathlessly:

"I say! I know it's awful cheek, but I s'pose you wouldn't tell my fortune, would you? I've never had it done, and I'd never really *dare*, but now you're here and if you wouldn't mind!…"

Miranda laughed, took her hand and pulled her down beside her. Then she turned the grubby little palm upwards, while Jenny, on her knees, with the crackling fire warming her back, stared at the gipsy with wide eyes.

"Is it *awful*?" she whispered. "Am I going to have an awful fate?"

Miranda closed her fingers over Jenny's and said, "Lots of good luck will come to you, my pretty dear, although you've not had much of it in the past. I think you've to learn never to be afraid, and I do not think you will find that difficult now. Good luck to you!"

David stood up and stretched.

"What's happening to the weather? Is it going to snow? I think we ought to be getting on, for we're to be at Craven Arms just after three."

"No snow yet," the gipsy said. " 'Tis too cold for that. Too cold for you to sit about here, I reckon, so you'd all best be getting on your way."

"Thank you *very* much for the soup," Dickie said politely. "We'd like to meet you every day, and we do hope you'll come and meet us in Clun."

"And Mackie thanks you again for his lovely basket, and for the bit of rabbit you gave him for dinner. He doesn't get much of that now. Please come back to Clun while we're there, or come again to Witchend in the holidays," Mary added.

"Thank you for the fortune," said a radiant Jenny.

"Don't worry about other people," Tom said. "We'll all say we know you if anyone says anything rotten."

Then Fenella came down the steps of the caravan with a bunch of white heather and Miranda gave them each a sprig.

But to David she gave two.

"One for you," she smiled, "and the other for Petronella, which you shall give to her for us. Tell her from Reuben and Miranda that we never forget her, and tell her never to forget the whistle that the Romany made for her and to use it when she needs their help."

Then Macbeth was lifted into his basket and with many goodbyes the Lone Piners started off again. The wind was very strong and David noticed that the twins were not proceeding with quite the same enthusiasm as they had showed in the morning. They were not talking as much either, but Jenny was making up for their silence. She was a most erratic cyclist, and her machine looked erratic, too, David noticed, and hoped most sincerely that it wouldn't fall to pieces until they got to Craven Arms. She was riding in front with Tom, but every now and then turned to talk over her shoulder to David. Every time she turned her green beret seemed to slip a little further to the back of her head. Every time this happened she clutched at it, and every time she did this her bicycle swerved across the road.

"Just concentrate on Tom," David yelled the fourth time that this happened. "Just remember all the things you want to tell me and don't talk to me until we get to the station!"

"It's just one thing I want to know, David," she shouted, and swerved again. "What did Miranda mean about the Romany whistle?"

David risked everything by closing the gap between them a little.

"Listen, Jenny. I won't ride three abreast for anybody. Not even for you. If you want to speak to me come back here or get Tom to go ahead."

"All right, David," she called. "I'll ask you again presently."

By now they seemed to have reached the highest point of their ride. At a cross-roads one arm of a signpost said "Clun" and the other "Craven Arms", and here Mary and Dickie stopped and Mackie, with the whites of his eyes showing and trembling in every limb, was given a run.

"It's awful torture for him," Mary admitted. "Look, twin! He's so stiff he's walking like an old man."

"Old dog, you mean," Dickie said. "I'm jolly cold. It would be all right if the sun would come out. I hate this place without the sun."

David brought out his map.

"We go left down the hill to Craven Arms. What are you going to do, Mary? Walk with your bike and Mackie, or ride?"

"I'm going to get this torture over, thank you all the same, David. We're going to ride down this hill, but promise me that if Mackie jumps out or falls out you'll rescue him. Promise faithful?"

David nodded. "I do. Now buck up and let's see if we can find a fire at the station and get warm before Jon and Penny arrive ... You two kids go first and mind the main road at the bottom."

As the road dropped downhill the moorland country was left behind. Then came the brown ploughed fields and some farms and cottages, and in a very short time they reached the outskirts of Craven Arms and rode into the station yard, twenty minutes before the train from Shrewsbury was due.

"Gosh!" said Dickie as he leaned his bicycle against a fence. "Gosh! I think I'm crippled for ever ... Stand still, Mary, and tell me if you feel what I feel. Although I'm standing still now it seems as if my legs are still going round and round on the pedals ... It's all very peculiar."

Mary stood still and shut her eyes for a moment.

"I don't get it the same," she said at last. "I just feel my legs are going to drop off!"

Even David felt stiff, and Tom said straight out that he wanted to sit down near a fire. Jenny alone seemed as fresh as when they had met her, and David couldn't help wondering whether this was because she was always talking so hard that she didn't really know that she was cycling!

They walked to the platform and the twins smiled sweetly at a nice young porter who was staring at them in amazement.

"None of that now," David muttered. "Just keep yourselves to yourselves, as Agnes says. I'm going to ask if the Warrenders' bikes have come, and you needn't all come into the parcels office with me either. See if there's a fire in the waiting-room."

The bicycles had arrived, and there was a fire in the waiting-room. It was a poor fire for a cold day, so Dickie and Mary lay on the floor and blew it into life with terrific puffs. It was unfortunate that at first they did not realize that it was wiser to blow alternately and not simultaneously, for when they got up again their faces were black.

At David's command they retired into a corner, licked Mary's handkerchief – Dickie had lost his, as usual – and tried to make their faces look normal again.

"You'd better not blow your nose on that dirty rag," Tom said as he saw the corner of the handkerchief, but before either of them could answer the signal bell clanged and they went on to the platform.

"Hope the Warrenders haven't missed it," David

muttered. "What shall we do if they have? I don't think those kids ought to cycle any further, anyway."

"I expect there's a bus they could catch," Jenny replied, "and they could go on that, anyway, if the man would take their bikes on the top. I'll go with them if you like … David, tell me about Peter's Romany whistle now."

"I don't know much about the whistle really, except that Reuben and Miranda and Fenella gave it to her and told her that if ever she was in trouble and blew the whistle, then any Romany in earshot would come to her help … I heard her try it once, but she wasn't in trouble at all then, and she blew it because she thought she recognized Reuben's caravan coming towards us."

"Did it work?" Jenny asked, gripping his arm.

"It did," David answered with a grim smile. "It *was* Reuben's caravan, and he was mad with her for joking with the whistle."

"Why did they give her the whistle?" Jenny persisted.

"Don't you know, Jenny? I thought you did. If I tell you, you must promise that you'll never tell Peter that I told you. Promise? Peter did the bravest thing I have ever known. She stopped the caravan you saw today when the horse was bolting down a hill towards her. The horse had been frightened at the top of the hill, and only Fenella was on the driving-seat. Peter will never say exactly how she did stop the horse, but I can guess. Anyway, she saved Fenella's life and the gipsies will never forget it … Here comes the train … You twins stand by the exit in case I miss them and hold tight to Mackie. He hates trains and stations."

"We know that very well, thank you, David," Mary said. "Come to mother, darling, and look out for Jon and Penny."

The long train slid slowly to a standstill, but before it had stopped, David saw Jon's head, with Penny's red one just behind it, looking anxiously out of an open window.

"Hi!" he yelled. "Here we are, chaps!" and rushed up the platform.

Jon, with his slow smile, was first out and then turned to help Penny, who, in her haste and excitement, flung her haversack out on to the platform and pushed her suitcase out after it. Then she jumped out herself, tripped over the luggage and fell against David.

"Oh, David!" she said as she clutched his arm, "it's just marvellous to be here at last. I'm sick of trains after today, but now we're really here nothing else matters. How are you, David? And the twins? Where are they? And how's Mackie? ... Tell me something, David. Do you think I look any older? I want to look older. I ought to now I'm growing up a bit, but I don't feel I am. Funny, isn't it? Oh! Sorry, Jon. What's that? Would I take my feet off your haversack? Of course I will. How stupid of me ... There are thc twins. Hullo, Dickie! Hullo, Mary!" and she rushed down the platform and flung her arms round them both while Mackie, clasped to Mary's bosom, wriggled and yelped in excitement.

Tom and Jenny, who were keeping in the background, were pulled forward by David next, and there was hand-shaking and grins all round, and they each said they had heard about the others, and they felt they were friends almost before they had left the platform.

The short winter day was dying now, but the weather was brighter, and it looked as if there might be a glorious sunset.

"Your bikes have arrived," David said, "but those who are going to cycle ought to start now because we should try and get there before dark. Who wants to go by bus?"

There was a long silence, until Mary said meekly, "I think Mackie does, and I don't think he's old enough to go by himself, so I'd better go, too."

"An' if Mary goes by bus I s'pose I've got to go as well, although, o'course, I'd much rather go on my bike," Dickie said.

"Of course you would, Dickie," David agreed hastily. "Everyone knows that! Jenny, do you mind going with them if they'll take your bike and luggage on the roof of the bus?"

Jenny agreed, although it was clear that she would rather have cycled; but those who got to know Jenny soon realized that this was the sort of thing which she was often doing for other people.

The bus was a real, friendly country bus with a little railing round its roof which had obviously been specially made to hold awkward or unwieldy luggage. The driver of the bus, who was also the conductor, climbed on to the roof while Jon and David heaved up three bicycles and all the luggage they had except the haversacks.

"Why not them 'aversacks?" the driver-conductor enquired with some concern.

"Well, we can carry those on our backs," David said, "and it doesn't seem fair to make your bus carry them as well."

"Come on with you!" the man said. "Up 'ere with the lot of 'em ... If you're biking to Clun you'll not want anything extra on your backs tonight. You've come some way by the look of you."

The bus was filling up now and David was rather glad he was not going in it, as there was every sign that the twins were looking forward to entertaining an enthusiastic audience on the journey. "Just behave yourselves," he begged as they clambered in, "and when you get there anyone will tell you how to find Keep View. Tell Agnes we're on our way and that we shall be cold and hungry. Maybe Peter will be there, too ... Thanks for going with them, Jenny ... We'll be as quick as we can."

The driver and all the passengers seemed to be very interested, and David had no doubt that the twins and Jenny would be well looked after. As the bus turned out of the station yard he said, "It's lucky we've all got lamps on our bikes because I think the cyclists should have a cup of tea before they start."

They found a little café and all felt much better after tea and toast.

"I bet Dickie would never have gone in the bus if he'd known we were going to do this," Jon said.

"Now I'm ready for anything," Penny added as she licked the crumbs from her lips in a most unladylike manner. "Let's go ... Oh! but we haven't told you about our adventure, David. I wonder when the next train from Shrewsbury comes in and whether Alan will be on it?"

"Alan?" David queried. "Who's Alan?"

"Friend of Penny's," Jon said. "You know what she's like, don't you? She's been getting into trouble at home because she will talk to strange men in the *Dolphin*. Tom doesn't know her yet, of course, and he's got a lot to learn."

So as they cycled out into the dusk David and Tom were told about Alan Denton and his sheep-dog, and the newcomers were told about the meeting with the gipsies.

There was not so much fun in the journey now, although the wind was not as strong, and they seemed to be riding right into an angry, flaming sunset. In the first village they passed, just by a bridge over the little river was a great tree with the remnants of many tattered flags hanging from its bare branches.

"I want to know why someone has done that," Penny said. "But I s'pose we can't stop now to ask?"

She was quickly told by the three boys that she was right, and they hurried on, counting the milestones as they rode. It was a lonely road and Jon remembered how Alan had told them that Clun itself seemed to be at the end of everything. The river was never far away, and on each side of the valley great hillsides shrouded in trees stretched up towards the darkening sky.

"I like Shropshire," Penny said. "I've never been in country like this before. It gets weirder and weirder, doesn't it? Funny to think that only on the morning of this very day Jon and I were crossing Romney Marsh, where there's hardly a tree to be seen … This is a jolly lonely road, too. Nothing much seems to happen on it."

"We must be nearly there," David said after another mile. "I think I can see some lights ahead … I'm tired, aren't you, Tom? Hope Agnes has got in the biggest supper I've ever seen."

"I expect the twins have eaten it," Tom said gloomily. "My legs tingle, and I never knew before that the saddle of this bike could be so hard ... Here we are, anyway – this must be Clun ... If it isn't I'm not going any further. Let's walk the last bit."

They got off their bicycles rather thankfully, for even Jon and Penny were tired after a long day's travel, and trudged into Clun. There was nothing very unusual about the village street but before they could ask the way to Keep View, Penny, who was in front of the little procession, stopped and pointed ahead.

Although it was nearly dark now the setting sun, at that very moment, flung out a final, fiery challenge to the dying day. Suddenly the western sky glowed red and orange and silhouetted against this strip of colour the travellers saw, for the first time, the ruins of the Castle of Clun dominated by its mighty keep.

Then, as, almost spellbound, they watched this dramatic welcome, they saw five tiny black cut-out figures move across the scene like marionettes on the stage of a toy theatre.

"I know who they are," Tom said quietly as the figures slowly climbed the edge of the hillside on which the ruins stood. "Dickie and Mary in front ... Then Peter with Sally ... and Jenny at the back. I bet Mackie's there, too, but he's too small for us to see. Wonder what they're up to already?"

Chapter 4

Peter's Ride

Mr Morton was right when he predicted that Peter would be up and away before it was light on the morning of the Lone Piners' journey to Clun. Getting up early and riding off alone on Sally was no unusual experience for Peter, for it was something she often did in the spring and summer. She was indeed so used to the solitude of Hatchholt that, although she liked visitors, she loved the loneliness and peace of the hills almost as much.

But on this particular morning, although as she dressed she was thrilled at the thought of the adventure before her, she did feel rather unhappy at the idea of leaving her father again. She heard his foot on the stair while she was still plaiting her hair, and by the time she got down the kitchen fire was burning cheerfully and the porridge cooking.

"Good morning, Petronella!" he said as she kissed him. "This is a ridiculous time to be starting your journey, and I am not sure that it is not a ridiculous journey when you could have gone by train or cycled with the others … But you are a headstrong child, I fear, and not as tidy and methodical as I should wish you to be." He paused here to cut some slices from the loaf.

"Let me make the toast, darling," Peter said, hoping that a change of occupation might change the subject. "It'll look like a zebra when we cook it in front of the bars."

"Very well. But put a paper on the floor to catch the crumbs ... Have you packed everything satisfactorily in your haversack, or must I check it for you?"

"I've got everything in, Daddy, I'm sure ... David fetched my suitcase, you know, and Mr Morton took that in the car for me when he took Agnes yesterday."

"That was very considerate of him ... Be careful! You are burning the toast."

But when they both sat down to their porridge Mr Sterling's mood changed, and he said no more to his daughter about tidiness and punctuality, but told her once again how glad he was that she had made such good friends as the Mortons and how he wished her to see as much of them as she could.

"In two more years, Petronella, I shall have finished my work here, and then doubtless we shall have to leave Hatchholt to make room for my successor. How will you like that?"

"Daddy!" Peter put down her toast. "Daddy! You don't mean we'll have to leave this house? Why, where else would we go?"

Mr Sterling twinkled at her over the top of his glasses. "You don't think you're always going to live with your old father, do you, my dear? That's why I'm sending you off to Clun now ... We have to get used to doing without each other."

Peter was very thoughtful as she lit a hurricane lamp

and went out to saddle Sally. Only the faintest lightening of the sky showed in the east. Above her the rolling grandeur of the hills blocked out the stars, and the air was clear and cold as it stung her cheeks. Sally came at her whistle and nuzzled at the pocket of her jacket as she saddled her quickly and competently.

Mr Sterling was waiting for her by the little gate of the cottage. Peter's haversack was at his feet and he had something shapeless over his arm.

"Are you warm enough, child?" he asked as he took the lantern from her and the orange light of the flame glinted from his spectacles.

"I've got my new jersey and a pullover under that, and my jacket and my fur gloves and my jodhpurs are like toast," but even as she spoke she shivered slightly, for up here in the hills it was much colder than in the shelter of the valleys.

Her father nodded.

"You are growing up, Petronella, and already as big as your old father. Put this on, my child, for you'll be glad enough of it later today and over on those hills round Clun. Put it on under your jacket," and he handed her the leather jacket lined with sheep's wool that he often wore in cold weather.

Peter protested, but he refused to be cajoled or bullied, and in the end he got his way.

"Now be off if you're going," he said gruffly as Peter hugged him. "Your flask and sandwiches are at the top of the haversack. Ride slowly and take care. Which way are you going? Down to Onnybrook or over the mountain?"

"Over the top," Peter said as she swung into the

saddle. "I'll telephone you if I'm in trouble, darling, or if I meet a highwayman or something. I could easily go with the others if I wanted to, but I have an idea I'd like to do all this on my own and get there first to welcome them! Goodbye, darling, and thank you for being such a beautiful father!" The pony's shoe struck a spark from a flint on the track as Peter turned to see the old man silhouetted for a moment against the warm light of the open door. Mr Sterling raised his hand as if to wave it, and Peter felt a sudden rush of tears to her eyes as she waved her own and called almost frantically, "Goodbye!"

She turned Sally by the reservoir and along the track that ran up the valley which led to the top of the mountain. As she rode through the dark she remembered how, from the hillside just above her, she and David Morton had hidden in a secret place and watched the woman who called herself Mrs Thurston spying for the enemy with whom they had been at war.* She remembered, too, that it was that same day that she and David swam a race in the reservoir, and that he had allowed her to beat him. She remembered this with flaming cheeks because she knew only too well why he had done it.

She had no need to guide Sally, for the pony knew every inch of these hills and picked her way delicately up the rough track by the side of the rushing stream. The valley narrowed as they rode on, but within half an hour of leaving home Sally turned up a path that could only have been made by rabbits and left behind the bog that was the source of the stream that fed Hatchholt's reservoir. Then she stopped and tossed her head, as if to say:

*See *Mystery at Witchend*

"There you are, Peter. I've brought you safely up again. We're at the top now."

The Long Mynd mountain up which they had climbed is a broad tableland of wild and lonely rolling moors. Peter knew it well in all its moods. She knew it in November when autumn mists clung like a soft white garment round the smooth hillsides; and in February, too, when a pale, clear sky gave promise of spring. In summer she had often climbed up there and lain for hours in the heather, while a myriad bees and insects sang round her head and the sun shone pinkly through her closed eyelids. And every September, for as many years as she could remember, she had come up the valley to pick bilberries where she now sat on Sally, until her fingers, and her mouth, too, were stained purple.

She knew, too, that it was possible to spend a day on these hills without seeing another human being, and that many a stranger trying to explore the Mynd for the first time had been frightened by the eerie solitudes, and turned back thankfully down one of the winding valleys to civilization again.

"Right, Sally," Peter whispered as she touched the pony's neck. "Let's be on our way."

The Mynd stretches from north-east to south-west across this part of Shropshire, and she proposed to ride along the top until she reached the southern end of the hill. Sally picked her way through the bilberries and heather until they reached a broad and grassy track. Peter had been told many stories about this path. It was called the Portway, and was a roadway of the ancient Britons which ran for six miles along the western edge of the Mynd. From this track she had often looked out over the plain to the rugged ridge of the Stiperstones in whose shadow lived her uncle at his farm, Seven Gates, and beyond that to the mountains of Wales.

She urged Sally into a canter now as the rising sun brightened the sky over to her left, and as the wind stung her cheeks she tried to imagine what she would do if she met a party of her skin-clad forbears as they travelled high above the dangers of the dense forests, which, in those far-off days, would have covered the plains below.

After a little she passed an evil and eerie-looking pool called Wildmoor, and then she forgot everything except the thrill of this gallop in the dawn. Below, in the valleys, the mist lay thick and white, but up here the sun, as it came up over the ridge of Wenlock Edge far away to the east, shone brightly in a clear sky and Sally's little hooves thudded on the yielding turf and every now and then she tossed her head and snorted with the joy of the morning.

David had told Peter of their route and that they planned to meet Jenny at Crown Farm just in case she wished to join them and finish the journey together, but when she left the Mynd behind she chose to make her own way. Sometimes she sang and whistled as she rode and always she waved and called "Good morning" to the men starting work in the fields and farms. Once she stopped for fifteen minutes to talk to an old brown man who was turning a tangled, overgrown hedge into a miracle of even tops and sides. While Sally contentedly cropped a little grass by the roadside Peter helped the hedger to gather up the clippings and stayed with him while he set them alight. The flames roared and crackled up into the still air and left a circle of grey ash flecked with red as Peter rode on again. At another farm a kindly woman smiled at her and asked her in for a cup of tea, judging correctly, as she did not know her face, that she had already ridden far.

But as she went on her way Peter found, as did the other Lone Piners, now not many miles distant, that the sun was not going to shine all day and that the weather was getting steadily colder. She was most grateful for her father's jacket, which kept her snug and warm.

It was while she was enjoying her sandwiches and flask of scalding coffee in the shelter of a big rick just inside a gate that she heard a heavy lorry coming along the road. She noticed this in particular, firstly because the road was narrow – indeed, little more than a lane – and this was the first motor vehicle she had met so far, and secondly because, although she did not know much about cars or their engines, she was quite sure that this one was making a most peculiar noise. First it seemed to bang very loudly and then to splutter. Then came a series of loud reports, and finally, after a horrible grinding, there was no sound but that of men's voices from the other side of the rick.

What happened next was so unpleasant that Peter was not sure what was the best thing to do. She was certain that the men in the lorry were annoyed and that they were quarrelling in a very nasty way. She heard the scrape of heavy boots on the roadway and the growl of ugly voices as one man snarled at the other as he strained at the starting-handle. Then, "Come and do it yourself, then," she heard quite plainly, but was rather glad that the answer to this invitation was not loud enough for her to catch. She had just decided to walk off quietly along the inside of the hedge and not come back until the men had gone, when one of the voices was raised in surprise, and she knew that she was discovered.

"Just look at that, George!" the voice rasped. "Am I a' seeing right, or is that a pony with a saddle on? Just there by corner of rick! Maybe we're in luck and can get a tow."

After that everything happened very quickly.

Before she could move she heard one of the men making ridiculous clucking noises, and then the clink of Sally's bridle as the pony moved away from whoever was trying to catch her. At the idea of some rough stranger laying hands on her beloved pony Peter's courage came back and she put her fingers in her mouth and whistled. Sally had never failed to answer this summons, and almost before Peter's hand was back in her pocket the pony trotted round the corner of the rick, followed by a man who looked as nasty as his voice had sounded. He was wearing dirty corduroy trousers with leggings, an old lumber jacket, and a check cap pulled over one eye. He stopped and glared furiously at Peter, who stared back at him with much more bravery than she felt. The man turned his head and out of the corner of his mouth said:

"Just come over 'ere, Alfie, and see 'oo's 'ere."

Alfie was not quite such an unpleasant-looking specimen as his companion. He was wearing a soft brown hat and a grubby overcoat, and the stub of a cigarette dangled from his lip. He stared insolently at Peter and said quietly:

"What are you doing here, miss?"

There was something about both these men that was very frightening, and yet Peter had the sense to realize that she must never show that she was afraid of them. So she drew herself up – and she wasn't really very tall – and faced them courageously enough as she said:

"I was having my lunch in the shelter of the rick before you came along and tried to catch my pony ... You wouldn't be able to catch her, anyway ... She only comes to me."

The two men glanced at each other and then the first – the one with the cap – grimaced in a way that was meant to be a smile and said, "That's orlright, missy ... Jus' surprised us, that's all. This is a lonely place this is on a cold winter's day, and we were surprised like to find you here ... Weren't we, Alfie? Surprised like, we were, to find a young lady with her pony round these parts."

Alfie's cigarette stub moved up and down as he said: "Better be getting on your way, miss, hadn't you? You don't want to take no notice of us. Just forget all about us! See?"

Peter was rather puzzled at this odd turn in the conversation, but she was sure that the best thing she could do was to get on her way as quickly as she could. So before she answered them she called Sally softly by name. The pony, who had been standing some yards off with her ears back and a nasty glint in her eye, trotted forward obediently, and before either of the men could move a step Peter was in the saddle. She felt safer there, for she knew now that they could never catch her. She wondered, too, why Alfie had suggested that she should forget all about them? It was true that she had never met two people that she disliked more, but she was not silly enough to think that they knew that! She edged Sally a little towards the open gate, suddenly curious to see the van that had broken down on this lonely road. As she did so the man with the cap – and Peter noticed now that he had a horrible squint in one eye – stepped towards her and snapped:

"Keep off the road, miss. Just ride along inside the field this side of the hedge."

"But why?" Peter asked innocently. "Why should I? You've broken down, haven't you? Would you like me to stop at the first garage or the first policeman and ask them to come and help you?"

Alfie took charge.

"No, miss. We wouldn't like you to do that. We shall manage and be away in ten minutes ... Don't you worry about us. Just forget us from now on."

Then a very strange thing happened. The wind, which was blowing from the road towards them in the field, suddenly strengthened and with it brought an un-expected scent, and a strangely muffled but familiar sound. Peter could hardly believe her nose or her ears, but she suddenly decided to see for herself why these men wanted to keep her off the road. She bent, patted the horse's neck and urged her forward as the man with the squint grabbed at the bridle and missed.

As she turned round the rick to make for the open gate she realized with a shock that a huge van was blocking her way out into the road. Like a flash she pulled Sally's head round and the good little pony pivoted and turned like a ballet dancer. Back into the field she cantered, past the two angry men who stood shaking their fists at her, and past the rick searching for another gate or a lower part of the hedge. Peter found the gap first and set Sally at it, praying that there would be a grass verge on the other side. The pony sailed through the hedge like a bird and landed safely in soft earth.

"You've never failed me, darling," Peter whispered as she patted her again. "Thank you." Then she looked back down the road.

The van was certainly a large one, and although she was now some distance away she was as sure as she could be that it was a furniture van. It was painted a dull red, and she thought she could just read the word "Wolver-hampton" on the back. As she strained her eyes the two men came out into the road and stood watching her.

Peter shuddered slightly, turned the pony's head and rode on her way with a puzzled frown on her forehead. It was certainly very odd that a furniture van from Wolverhampton should come along this narrow and lonely road, and stranger still that the driver and his mate should want to keep a schoolgirl away from it.

"Jiminy!" Peter said aloud suddenly. "I've just remembered that smell. Now I know what it was. It was *sheep* – and that noise was sheep baaing. That van was full of sheep, but what beasts those men were to keep the van closed up like that. P'raps that's why they didn't want me to go near, just in case I reported such cruelty to someone. I guess that's why they were so wild with me; but I still can't see why they couldn't have opened the back of the van ... I'm glad I've left them behind, anyway. I hated them both."

And so she rode on while the weather worsened, the sun disappeared, and a bitterly cold wind swept across the wide valley to the hillside along which she was now riding. She knew that the other Lone Piners would reach Clun from the direction of Craven Arms, but she had planned her ride so that she would discover the little secret town – as she called Clun in her own mind – from the other side. She had a map with her, of course, because in strange country her greatest difficulty was to avoid metalled roads. For Sally's sake at least it was important for her to find the bridle paths or lanes with a grass verge. There was only one big town on her way and that was called Bishop's Castle. She had been there once, but had determined to miss it today.

She lost her way twice. The first time two men working in a field put her right, but the second occasion was more troublesome, for the track she had been following lost itself in a glade in a little wood and she had to ride back a mile to find a farmhouse at the junction of two lanes.

Sally never seemed to tire, but Peter was very cold and stiff when she left the hill-tops behind her at last and reached a signpost which said "Clun 3 miles". The lane now was very steep, so she got off to stretch her legs and give the pony a rest. The woods here came right down to the road, and it was very dark under the trees. Almost for the first time today Peter wondered what her friends were doing and whether they had yet reached Craven Arms. And this thought made her wonder what Jon and Penny were like – and particularly Penny. She realized that it had really been her own idea that these two should join the Lone Pine Club, and she had made the suggestion without even meeting them. Now that they were really coming Peter wondered whether the original members wouldn't have had much more fun on their own. After all, the Club was big enough now that Tom and Jenny had joined. It had been such fun in the early days, and at Seven Gates, too, when they had met Jenny, and now these two strangers were coming and nothing would ever be quite the same again.

The road was level once more and the woods were behind them as Sally stopped obediently and Peter lifted herself into the saddle. The sky was red at her back, so she knew that she was riding east and that Clun could not be far away. Soon she caught the gleam of water and realized that this must be the River Clun itself on its way from the hills of Clun Forest to join the river Teme and then the mighty Severn. For another mile she rode on by the side of the stream, next through a little wood, and then she looked up to see a smooth, steep hill in front of her crowned with the ruins of a castle.

"We're here! We've done it, Sally!" Peter said as she bent forward to pat the pony's neck. "I hope we're first."

As she got nearer she realized that the town must be on the other side of the hill, for she could see no houses – only this great green mound round which the river slid, acting as a moat. She turned Sally to the left, for the slope of the hill was longer and gentler on that side, and joined the road again.

The sun had nearly gone but the broken stones of the ruins were tinged with the red light of his setting as she rode through an open gate on to the soft turf at the foot of the hill.

Then, hardly knowing whether to laugh or to cry with surprise, she put her fingers in her mouth and whistled a long, shrill "Pee-wit! *Pee-wit*!" As the echoes died away three human figures and a little black dog a quarter of the way up the hill turned their heads and looked back, but it was Mary who led the race down to her and flung her arms round her as she dismounted.

"Peter!" she shouted. "We've only just got here. Isn't this *marvellous*? Have you ever seen such a wonderful, weird, ghostly place in your life? Just as soon as we could escape from Agnes we came here."

"Hullo, Peter," Dickie said as he trotted up. "We're jolly pleased to see you, but now we've got to climb up this hill again, and I'm so tired and hungry I'm just one big, hollow ache."

"Oh, Peter," Jenny began when she was still ten yards away, "have you had any *marvellous* adventures? We have! We met the gipsies and I had my fortune told, and it's a good one, and oh, Peter, I'm having the most wonderful, amazing time."

Peter laughed. "Where are the others?"

"Coming on their bikes. We wanted to cycle, o' course, but that bully David wouldn't let us ... And, Peter, Agnes has got the most terrific tea-supper ready for us. We've been in to see her, and it's going to be grand – but we just had to come out and explore this place before the others came."

"Look! Look!" Jenny squealed suddenly. "There they are ... I can see Tom ... They're waving ... Now they're shouting ... Be quiet, Dickie, for just one second and we'll listen."

"Come down now," came faintly up to them. "Let's explore tomorrow ... Come back and show us where the house is."

"Of course we must go back," Jenny said. "It wasn't really fair to go exploring on our own first ... Come on! Let's go ... Shout to them, Dickie ... I don't know why it is, but my throat is quite sore."

Dickie put his hands to his mouth and yelled so that the echoes rang round the ruined walls of the castle above them and sent some big, black birds wheeling up into the twilight.

"All right. Wait for us! We're coming!"

As they turned to go down the hill again Peter bent down to pat Macbeth. Suddenly she felt ashamed of herself for thinking just now that she didn't want the Warrenders. But she felt unaccountably shy, too, and she and Sally were the last of the little procession that hurried down the opposite side of the hill to where she could now see lights in the windows of houses and David, Tom, a taller boy who must be Jon, and a slighter figure who must be Penny waiting for them.

Suddenly she felt tired. She had been up early and had ridden a long way without much to eat. All the afternoon it had been very cold, and then there had been the adventure with the two men and the lorry on the lonely road. She was stiff and sore and felt very grubby, and just at this minute didn't want to meet anyone new.

Then the others were all round her, talking and laughing. She stumbled a little with weariness, and realized that David was next to her and was saying:

"This is Peter, who I always wanted you to meet. She's the brains of this club of ours, as you'll soon find out. She's ridden Sally here a much longer way round than we came on bikes, and *I'm* so tired I can hardly stand … Dad said to me this morning that she would get here before we did, and I bet he was right. Nobody ever seems to beat Peter at anything that she makes up her mind about."

This was a very long speech for David, and Peter felt her cheeks burn as Jon shook hands with her and said, "It's too dark to see you properly, Peter, but it's grand for us to be here and to meet you all, and we can't thank you all enough for asking us."

And on her other side Penny slid an arm through hers, and for once had little to say beyond, "We think we've known you a long time, Peter. Ever since David and the twins came to Rye in the summer."

"If I don't eat soon I shall just faint," Tom said. "Let's find this house we're going to live in and all be polite to each other there … It's cold, too … Come on, Jenny. You know where it is. Come in front with me and let's get going."

They turned into a narrow lane which ran steeply downhill, turned left again, and found themselves in the main street.

"It's not far, thank goodness," Mary said. "It's just past that lamp-post. There are steps up to the front door, but when you get inside it's lovely, and there's a whacking big fire and lots to eat … Look! There's Agnes at the door now waitin' for us."

As they hurried under the lamp-post Peter and Penny looked at each other in the light and then laughed as they caught themselves doing it.

"Silly of me," Penny said, "'Cos I guessed what you looked like … Or I suppose it was what David told us about you."

Peter was now so weary that she had no answer to this. But she knew that she was going to like these Warrenders, and especially the girl with the red curls and laughing grey eyes at her side.

Then Sally stumbled, and she blundered against David, who had stopped on the pavement outside Keep View as Agnes came hurrying down the steps to greet them.

David turned. "Dickie knows where Sally's stable is – Agnes showed him. Give her to me, Peter, and Dickie and I will see to her. You come along presently and see that we haven't done everything wrong … Come on, Peter. Don't be silly. Sally knows me, and you're tired and cold … I'll put my bike away when we get back or Tom will take it in for me … Penny! Just grab hold of Peter and take her in."

And, somewhat to her own surprise, Peter found herself doing what she was told – and by David, too! As she stepped over the threshold of Keep View with Agnes' welcoming voice rambling on behind her, the light and warmth in the hall, and the smell of something hot and tasty to eat made every minute of the long day's adventure worth while.

Chapter 5

Mr Cantor

Peter and Penny shared a room at Keep View. Although each was anxious to get to know the other better they had no chance to do so on their first evening, for they were so tired that even during supper they had the greatest difficulty in keeping their eyes open. Just as soon as they could after the meal was over they went upstairs, smiled sleepily at each other once or twice as they undressed and cleaned their teeth, and then tumbled into bed.

Peter woke first, when it was still dark. She woke with that odd feeling that so often comes in a strange bed in a strange house – a feeling of not knowing where you are and that the bed is facing the wrong way, and that the window and door have changed places! Then, as she turned over and stretched, she remembered everything.

"This is going to be fun," she thought, and bravely moved her arms from the warm bedclothes and put her hands behind her head. The air from the open window blew cool on her bare arms, and the glimpse of a distant star reminded her of yesterday morning and of how the stars had swung up the sky as she had gone out into the dark to saddle Sally. She wondered about her father, and was grateful for the way David had said that he would telephone him for her last night. What a good friend David was! Never any fuss, but always seeming to be just in the right place at the right time!

A gentle snore, which was more like a purr, came from the bed on her left and disturbed these thoughts. Penny! She had almost forgotten her!

Peter groped among the clothes she had thrown on the chair last night until she found her torch. First she looked at her watch and saw that it was just after seven, and then she swung the beam round until it picked out Penny's tumbled red head on her pillow.

Peter looked at her carefully. She did not make friends easily, and although she was quite prepared to like the Warrenders for David's sake she was not necessarily prepared to accept them yet for their own. She remembered again how she had felt last evening when she had looked down from Clun Castle at the Warrenders waiting below to meet her.

Then, as she watched, one of Penny's curls fell across her forehead and tickled her cheek. She flicked it away with one hand but it fell back, and then, with her mouth slightly open, she tried to blow it away. She looked so funny that Peter laughed, leaned over and shook her shoulder.

Penny's grey eyes opened and she sat up in bed.

"What's happened? Where am I? Something bit me or hit me."

Peter laughed again.

"It's me, Penny. We're all at Keep View and I was feeling lonely so I woke you up. It's after seven. Shall we get up and explore?"

Penny slipped down into bed again.

"No fear," she said. "Let's put the light on and talk. I'm generally the first up in our house for Jon is *awful* in the mornings, so let's stay in bed for a change ... Let all the others get up and make a noise and fight for the bathroom while we stay here and be comfortable."

While they were talking about their schools and getting to know each other better there was a knock on the door and Agnes came in with two cups of tea.

"And let me tell you two great girls," she began, "that this is not going to happen every morning ... I'll be spoiling those two just for this once, I said to myself as I made my own tea downstairs, for I'm sure they were that weary last night I kept on yawning every time I looked at them."

Penny sat up again.

"Oh, Agnes," she said. "Everything about you is wonderful. You were wonderful last night, although I don't remember much about it, and you're just perfect this morning. I'm going to love you very much."

"Get along with you, my dear," Agnes said as she bustled round the room. "And for heaven's sake put something round yourself or close the windows or I'll be having you in bed all the time you're here ... And now I'll be waking those twins and those boys, and I'd better be warning you now that you'll not be all using the bathroom at the same time, and the water is to stay in the bath and not on the floor ... I'll be telling those lazy boys that you two will be in there first ... Breakfast at half-past eight on the dot and I'll thank you not to be late..." and she bustled out.

"Isn't she sweet, Penny? She's always like that, but she is really the grandest person and we've got to help her all we can ... Come on – let's get down first and explore."

Keep View was a very ordinary and rather ugly house. It was not old, but there are tens of thousands of boarding houses like it all over the country, particularly at the seaside. The stairs were steep and led straight down into the hall, which smelt of furniture polish and linoleum. There was some coloured glass in the front door, and the dining-room on the left, and what Agnes called "the lounge" on the right.

When the two girls came down and went into the dining-room a cheerful fire was already blazing in the grate and a table set for eight was in the window. Outside the morning looked cold, grey and uninviting.

Jenny was next down.

"Oooh!" she said as she saw the fire and ran to it. "Isn't this fun? I had Mary in with me and she's still asleep. Every time I tried to wake her she just said: 'Go away you beasts' ... Besides, Mackie is on her bed and he growled at me ... What shall we do this morning, do you think? ... Oh! I know what we must do, don't you, Peter? We'll have to have a secret meeting first, won't we? I do wish the others would come ... It's too bad of those boys to waste all this time. I know Dad said I could stay all the time until you all came back, but we do want to make the most of every minute, don't we? ... I mean it is a pity not to be all together all the time ... I mean it's a pity having to go to sleep often, but I do have some wizard dreams sometimes so I s'pose it's worth it ... Oh! Here they are ... Hullo, Tom, where are the others?"

Tom yawned.

"This is a rum place isn't it? Not a bit like I expected. I thought maybe it would be old and a bit what Mary calls ghosty."

Next Jon and David clattered down the stairs, and as the half hour struck Agnes appeared, opened the hatch in the wall and called, "Porridge for all. Come and help yourselves and then sit down and enjoy it while 'tis hot ... Hot porridge on a morning like this is as good as an overcoat my old father used to tell me..."

Then the twins, looking surprisingly bright and clean, slipped round the door and joined the end of the porridge queue.

"You see how it is, twin?" Dickie was heard to murmur. "Another second and they would have taken our porridge ... Nothing kept for us o' course."

"Just because we're the smallest, 'cept Mackie, we're kept out of the bathroom," Mary said, and then bowed almost graciously to Jon. "Good morning, big Jon! Was it you I heard snoring in a disgustin' manner in the middle of the night? ... Mackie and me were disturbed..."

Jon knew the twins well enough to ignore this and Mary was not surprised when he took the sugar from Dickie and got on with his porridge.

When the meal was over and they had helped Agnes to clear away, David beckoned Peter and led her across the hall into the lounge.

"I say, Peter," he began, "I wanted to ask you without the others whether you agree that we should make Jon and Penny Lone Piners? If we're going to do it I think we should do it this morning?"

"Why don't you ask the others as well?" Peter said, with her back to David so that he couldn't see her face.

"The Lone Pine is as much your club as mine," David replied. "Really it was your idea and we won't have them in yet unless you want them ... You know, Peter, I'm wondering if Jon won't think us awful asses over the Club business ... Of course he's a grand chap, but he's always passing exams and things and he might think we're behaving like kids over all this signing in blood ... Do you see what I mean?"

Peter whirled round and faced him with burning cheeks.

"Yes," she said, "I see what you mean, David! You're ashamed of the Club and afraid Jon will laugh at you ... Very well. You two had better go off together and be grown-up somewhere else. The twins and Tom and Jenny and me will make Penny a member..."

"All right! All right!" David interrupted. "You're wrong. I only wanted to ask you before I went after the others ... I didn't tell you before but I went up to the Lone Pine day before yesterday and dug up the tin with the rules. I've got 'em in my haversack ... Let's ask them, Peter? I'm sure Jon will be all right. I only wondered for a sec what he'd say."

"Ask him, then," Peter said shortly, "and see what he says. You know him and I don't. I've hardly spoken to him yet."

David crossed to the window.

"Got out of bed the wrong side, didn't you?" he said, but before she could answer they heard Jon's voice calling from the hall.

"Where are you, David? We want you and Peter."

David opened the door and Jon came in.

"Hope I'm not butting in," he said as he polished his spectacles, "but I wanted to catch you two and specially Peter."

"Whatever for?" Peter said. "If you want to talk to David I can go I 'spose."

Jon's eyebrows went up.

"No," he said quietly. "I wanted to ask you both if you'd let Penny and me be members of this secret club of yours. Of course, Peter, you may not think you know us well enough yet but we thought it would be a grand way to start this holiday if we could get it over this morning."

Peter caught David's eye and laughed rather shame-facedly.

"I think we were both wrong, David," she said as she turned to Jon. "Of course we'd love to have you and Penny. It's why we asked you up here anyway ... Do you two mind waiting here for a bit and we'll send you a messenger when we're ready for you."

Jon stood aside as Peter swept out into the hall, and perhaps it was just as well that she did not see the way in which David closed his left eye as he followed her out.

Ten minutes later the Lone Piners passed down Clun's main street towards Castle Hill. The twins, side by side, and in step, led the way with Mackie at their heels. Peter walked between the two boys while Jenny danced round the party until David complained that she was making him giddy. They climbed the hill, trying to guess where the drawbridge would have been when the castle was manned, until they were actually in the shadow of the mighty walls of the keep. From here they could look down over the roofs of the little town in one direction, over the river which curled round three sides of the hill in another, and, when they turned right round, they saw the rolling hills and woods which were all that now remained of Clun Forest and, in the far distance, the gaunt line of the Black Mountains, and the other tumbled hilltops over the Welsh border.

"This place is HQ Three," Dickie said. "One, is our own Lone Pine at home. HQ Two is the barn at Seven Gates, and right in this old castle is HQ Three … Who's going to fetch up those two and blindfold 'em and lead them here, David? Don't let's waste time."

Before he could answer, David sensed that someone was trying to attract his attention and turned to see Jenny gazing at him soulfully with her hands clasped in supplication before her.

"Let me do Penny, David?" she pleaded. "Only let me do her, David. I'll never ask you anything again if you'll only let me go and blindfold her and bring her here … *I'll curdle her blood on the way, David* … But let me do it, *please* … This is the sort of thing I've *lived* for, David."

"All right," David laughed. "You go first, Jenny, and then the twins can bring Jon."

And in this way the Warrenders were made members of the Lone Pine Club. The messenger sent back first to Keep View was Dickie, who strutted, a little breathless, into the hall and called,

"I got a message for you, Jon and Penny!"

When they appeared, Dickie took a deep breath and said what he had been told to say as quickly as possible.

"If you want to be proper sworn members of our secret club now is your last chance to say 'Yes' or 'No' or forever hold your peace – do you say 'Yes' or 'No'...?"

Here he paused and eyed Jon very sternly just in case the bigger boy had the temerity to smile. But Jon's face as he looked down at Dickie was deadly serious and he nodded slowly as he said:

"The answer is 'Yes' for me, Richard."

Dickie blinked at the "Richard" and turned to Penny, who hurriedly composed her face and stood with her hands folded modestly before her.

"Yes for me too, please," she said demurely.

"OK – I mean, very well," Dickie replied coldly. "Now we know where we are. You're the first victim, Penny, and you've jolly well got to be blindfolded and come with me."

"Is it far, Dickie?" Penny pleaded. "I mean I get giddy when I'm blindfolded and I just can't stand it."

"You gotta stand it," Dickie said remorselessly. "That's the idea. And it's about a hundred miles."

"Oh, dear!" Penny wailed. "Look after me, won't you, Dickie? Let's go now and get it over. Have I got to walk down the street blindfolded? What will everybody think?"

"Doesn't matter what they think. You gotta do it. Come on!" and he grabbed a scarf from the hallstand and tied the knots at the back of Penny's head himself.

"You just wait here," he said darkly to Jon. "We'll come back for you."

Dickie grabbed his victim's arm and led her firmly down the steps into the street. Penny remembered turning to the right and then crossing the road several times, but after that she was hopelessly lost. Once or twice she heard the voices of strangers apparently being sorry for her, and once Dickie said indignantly:

"Just you go away and leave us alone. I can manage her very well by myself, thank you … and you mustn't talk to her 'cos she's been VERY, VERY ILL, and it's bad for her to talk to strangers."

At last Penny felt grass under her shoes and realized that Dickie no longer held her arm. In a panic she stretched out her hands to find him.

"Where are you, Dickie? Don't be silly, come back here," and she raised her hands to the scarf round her eyes.

Immediately a horrid, croaking voice behind her said:

"Do not dare to touch that. If you give way now you will have failed the Club and can never be a member … I shall lead you further in a minute, but for the last time I ask you whether you are prepared to suffer tortures and anything else just to be a member of this Club?"

Penny nodded feebly. She was trying in vain to recognize this voice, but as she was now really giddy all that she wanted was to get rid of the scarf and see again!

Then a hot hand grasped her own and began to lead her uphill. As they climbed Penny felt the wind in her curls and almost giggled at the thought of Jon having to undergo an experience like this.

"You are smiling," said the croaking voice at her side, and her fingers were squeezed so hard that she almost cried out with the pain and surprise. "There is nothing to smile about now, for you must satisfy the Captain and

112

Vice-Captain that you can be a worthy member ... Can you shed your own blood for the sake of the Club?"

This sounded rather alarming, but Penny gulped and said she thought she could, and then they stopped and she heard the whisper of other voices round her and suddenly she found herself blinking into Peter's laughing face and saw that she and David were leaning against an old grey wall. When she looked up she saw the wintry sky above the ruins of the great keep of the castle.

"Who brought me up here after Dickie?" she asked. "Who was it with that beastly voice?"

Jenny, in the background, turned triumphantly to David.

"There you are, David! What did I tell you? I knew I could do it ... You didn't guess, did you, Penny? I bet I scared you!"

"I'll remember that, Jenny," Penny laughed. "One day I'll get my own back. Now what do I have to do?"

David produced an old tin and from it took a dirty piece of folded paper.

"These are the rules of the Lone Pine Club," he said. "We made them up the day we started the club and they're kept buried under the original lone pine tree at Witchend. Just read them, Penny, and then sign your name in your own blood under all the others ... Peter's got a needle so that you can prick your arm or your finger."

"Your finger'll be best," Jenny said. "Then you can press it hard and it SPURTS out!"

Penny took the grubby scrap of paper, which she knew had been hidden for over two years, and read the rules as well as she could. Three, four and five seemed the most important.

"The Club and Camp are so private that every member swears in blood to keep them secret."

"Every member promises to be kind to animals."

"The Club is for exploring and watching birds and animals, and tracking strangers."

"It's the last of all which is the important one," Peter said quietly. "The one on the other side. That's the only one that matters. It's the oath."

Penny turned the paper and read,

"Every member of the Lone Pine Club signed below swears to keep the rules and to be true to each other whatever happens always."

Then she glanced up and met Peter's blue eyes. The two girls looked at each other for a long minute without speaking. Then – "You're right, Peter," Penny said quietly. "Give me the needle. I'd like to sign this."

By the time she had done this they heard the sound of voices below them and ran across to see Dickie and Mary leading Jon up the hill. Try as they would the twins had found it impossible to disguise their identity; although Dickie, as soon as Jon had been blindfolded, had tried talking out of the side of his mouth, this had not been a success. Their victim had been very polite about it all and asked nicely if he might put his spectacles in his pocket, but the twins did not encourage general conversation as they led him along the street and up the hill to the ruined keep.

Neither David nor Peter need have worried about Jon's interest, for even if he was acting he did it extremely well.

When, like Penny, he had pricked his finger and signed the oath in his own blood, David took the paper back and said:

"If this is HQ Three then I suppose we ought to bury the documents here. What do you think, chaps?"

They all agreed that as this particular corner of the ruins was going to be the Club's meeting place when necessary the papers should be buried there.

"S'matter of fact," Dickie said, "I don't think anything ought to happen to those papers except them being buried."

Jon looked at the small boy in surprise.

"Don't they teach you English at school? That was the most disgusting sentence I've ever heard."

"Oho, big Jon!" Mary broke in, "then you haven't much to worry yourself about, have you? Don't you worry 'bout Dickie's sentences not being English 'cos the most intelligent people understand us! You just wait until you know us better, Jon, and then you'll begin to understand what we say."

To avoid further discussion David hurriedly produced his big knife, cut and lifted a slice of turf where they were standing and buried the sardine tin. When the turf was replaced they all looked at each other and grinned.

"This Club is nothing to laugh at, Jon and Penny," Mary said seriously. "And you've got something jolly important to learn too … Acksherly we ought to have a new rule that nobody can really be a member until they know how to do the Peewit's whistle."

As they walked down the hill towards the town Tom gave the new members some lessons in whistling the call, and found Penny a much better pupil than Jon.

"You just don't try, Jon," his cousin said. "You may think you're clever at some things but you're no good at whistling … Just suppose you were lost in a fog and wanted the other Lone Piners and found you couldn't whistle the call. Just suppose you were. What would you do?"

"I'd shout, you silly ass … You haven't got much sense this morning, have you?"

Penny turned her back on him and went ahead with Peter and David. At the foot of the hill they walked along the river bank until they came to the little stone bridge which carried the road from Clun into Wales.

"That's odd," Jon said, "but the arches aren't equal. Let's watch the river from up there and maybe we'll see some fish."

The bridge was very narrow and between each of the arches was a triangular recess where foot passengers could stand aside for traffic. For a few moments they stopped to watch the water from one of these recesses while Dickie ran from one side to the other to watch the progress of scraps of toffee paper which he was throwing in the swiftly-flowing river. Nobody was arguing with him, and although it was nearly lunch-time the little town seemed fast asleep. Suddenly, as Dickie made one of his dashes across the bridge, the silence was broken by the furious ringing of a bicycle bell. David grabbed his brother, and they all looked up as a bare-headed man rushed down the hill towards them.

Penny, who had only glanced up idly, suddenly stiffened and grabbed Jon's sleeve.

"It's Alan! HI, ALAN! Stop! It's us. Don't you remember us? HI! COME BACK."

But even as she shouted the cyclist whirled over the bridge, and although he undoubtedly heard Penny call his name and may have recognized her, he made no attempt to stop but merely called back something over his shoulder.

Penny was furious.

"Well!" she stormed. "Of all the mean, rude things. He knew us, didn't he, Jon? I'm sure he did ... I'll never speak to him again ... Where do you think he was going?"

"Do you know him then?" David asked. "Who is he? I thought he called out something about 'Police.'"

"I thought so too," Jon said. "He's the chap we met on the train – or Penny met really. He's got a sheep farm near here. Don't you remember we told you about meeting him last night?"

"Whoever he is he was in a hurry," Tom said. "He's the only person I've seen hurry since we've been here. I b'lieve everybody else is fast asleep."

"He said 'Police,' did he?" Penny said. "Are you sure that's what he said, David? Well, you ought to be sure. There's you and Jon standing right there almost next to him and with nothing to do at all except listen, and neither of you can be sure ... I think you're both dumb as well as deaf ... I'm going to the Police Station to see if he's there. Coming, Peter? I'd like to know why he was in such a hurry."

"P'raps someone has been murdered or kidnapped for an awful fate," Jenny added hopefully. "I'll come with you, Penny. I'd like to see if anything exciting has happened round here."

So when Alan Denton came out of the cottage in the High Street that had the words "County Police" over the door, he found what looked like a large crowd round his bicycle.

He soon picked out Penny's red head and said, "Oh, hullo! How are you? Sorry I couldn't stop on the bridge but I was in a hurry."

"We noticed that," Penny said coldly. "You nearly killed this poor little boy."

Dickie's eyes nearly popped out of his head, but Penny went on before he could think of anything to say to express his indignation. "We did think you were rather rude, Alan. I wanted you to meet all my friends."

Alan looked rather alarmed.

"Are these all really your friends? I thought there was a fire or something … Oh, hullo, Jon! I didn't see you before in the crowd. How are you? … Of course I'd like to meet you all but I'm afraid I can't wait long because something rather unpleasant has happened and I've got to get back to Bury Fields. Why don't you all walk some of the way with me? – I've got to walk up the hill anyway."

Jon introduced them all and David kicked Dickie's ankle none too gently as he edged forward with Mary close behind him. David knew very well that if not checked the twins would be only too willing to put on their famous "introduction act". Before Mary could open with "Good morning. I'm Mary Morton and this is my brother," etc., etc., Jon said:

"I hope there's nothing seriously wrong, Alan ... Just say so if there is and we'll clear off. We didn't mean to butt in, you know ... Or if there's anything we can do to help...?"

They had reached the bridge again now and were straggling across it when Alan Denton said, "I suppose there's no reason why I shouldn't tell you, but please don't talk about it to anyone else. Promise me that, all of you? Good! The truth is that sheep stealing has begun in the farms round here and last night I lost fifty or sixty of my best ewes and you can guess I'm feeling pretty sore ... Now I must get on, and I wish you all a good day, and the best holiday you have ever had ... Wish I'd got some time to show you round the woods and hills, but I will some day when we've found our sheep ... I reckon the gipsies have done this and if I had my way I'd move them on wherever they go, or better still maybe, I'd put them into prison ... There's two of 'em with a little girl often round these parts and I'd never be surprised if they didn't have something to do with it ... Those three are too sly, I'm sure."

"If you mean Reuben, Miranda and Fenella," David said indignantly, "then I can tell you you're quite wrong, for we met them on the road just about midday only yesterday, and they were coming *away* from all the farms and leaving this country."

Alan shrugged his shoulders.

"That may be what they told you! I don't see how you can know them anyway, but I don't trust any gipsies and I hope if you see any about you'll let Sandridge, the policeman here, know ... Now I must get along. Cheerio all! … Here! Just a minute … Why don't you all come over to Bury Fields tomorrow to see my mother? I'll have more time to show you round then. Will you come? Come early for tea, then you can get back before dark."

Peter stepped forward.

"Just before you go, Mr Denton, I think I ought to tell you something that happened to me yesterday." Alan got off his bicycle again and listened politely while Peter told him of her adventure with the furniture van from Wolverhampton.

"… and the two men were horrid," she finished, "and I'm quite sure that the van was full of sheep."

Alan put a finger on his chin as he always did when he was puzzled.

"Seems odd to me," he said at last, "But it just isn't possible to get somebody else's sheep into a furniture van in daylight, and it would be too noisy at night I should have thought … Still, thanks for mentioning it … See you all tomorrow … 'Bye."

Peter flushed with humiliation.

"He didn't believe me. I'm sure he didn't. He was nice about it, but I think he thought I was making it up."

"Maybe we didn't meet Reuben, either," Mary said. "P'raps it's all a dream. Anyway I want my dinner."

"Maybe it will be roast mutton," Dickie said with a grin. "Let's go and see."

It was very cold and dull after dinner, and Penny suggested that after they had helped Agnes to wash up they sit round the fire and tell each other stories.

"After all," she said as she reached for a wiping-up

120

cloth, "we don't *have* to be out all the time, do we? I like indoors in the winter and think it's a bit silly to keep on dashing about in the cold and wet ... And you just do your share, Jon, and David too ... You're neither of you too important to help wash up."

"I always drop things," Jon said plaintively. "You know I do, Newpenny ... I'm an expensive washer-up ... You'd better let David, Tom and me off ... There's too many in this kitchen anyhow ... Aren't we in your way, Agnes?"

Agnes straightened her back and brushed a wisp of greying hair from her forehead.

"You'll not be getting out of your share of the duties *that* way, Mister Jonathan, and you'll all please to stay here for I have something to tell you."

They crowded round her and Mackie yelped as somebody trod on him. When order was restored and Mary had been comforted, the housekeeper began again.

"'Tis very strange that just as soon as my poor sister is taken away the house fills up, but so it is and from tomorrow there'll be someone to wash the dishes I'm glad to say, so this is the very last time I'll be allowing any of you in my kitchen – and if it's Hooray I heard you say under your breath, young Richard Morton, I'll be teaching you to speak a little louder in the future ... and now what was it I was saying before that young limb flummoxed me with his rudery...?"

"You were saying the house is going to fill up now your sister has gone away, Agnes darling," Penny reminded her.

"So I was and thank you ... mind those glasses, Mister

David, for anyone might think you were in a circus … Where was I? Oh, yes! This very afternoon there's a new gentleman coming here to stay for a while."

"But he can't do that," Dickie said. "We don't want him, do we, twin?"

"I shouldn't think so," Mary said. "But we could look at him first."

"And that's just what I mean," Agnes said, turning round from the sink to face the Lone Pine Club grouped round her. "There's to be no nonsense. He spoke to me on that dratted telephone this very morning while you were out … Very nice and gentlemanly he sounded, but quiet and peace he must have because he's been sick and in hospital."

"Did you tell him we were all here, Agnes?" David asked.

"I did that, and he said he supposed he must just put up with that but he must have quiet, so maybe he'll order a fire in his bedroom and stay up there. He told me he's out walking a lot and collecting bits o' stone and the like from the hills around … But you must all promise Agnes that you'll behave yourselves with him so that he doesn't complain … I'm right sorry it's happened, but truth to tell he's going to pay us well and that will help my sister, for these operations seem to cost a lot of money … You'll all help Agnes now won't you?"

"I'll take him a cup of tea in the morning if he's nice," Penny volunteered.

"We'll cheer him up if he's downcast and weary," Mary said.

"Oh, no you won't," David interrupted, "That's just

122

out, was the only occasion on which they saw this suit which now seemed so out of place.

As Agnes closed the door behind her he looked rather as if he had been thrust into a cage of wild animals without chance of escape. In fact he looked so scared that all the Lone Piners stared at him rather rudely, until David remembered his manners and Peter, who was sitting on the hearth-rug leaning against his legs, suddenly found herself pushed forward as he jumped to his feet.

"Good afternoon, sir. Won't you come close to the fire? I'm afraid we're all rather piled round it, but there's plenty of room really."

Jon hauled himself off the sofa.

"Do you think you could stand the strain of being introduced to us all, sir? There's rather a lot of us to remember, but Agnes says you are going to be here for a few days and so are we, so perhaps we'd better try and get it over."

And after this long speech, during which Penny watched him in admiration, he took off his spectacles and polished them violently.

Mr Cantor started and stepped forward under the light.

"Bless my soul!" he said, in a strangely childlike voice. "Good gracious! What a variety of youngsters to be sure. Charming scene! Charming ... Thank you very much, my boy, and I will certainly do what I can to remember you all ... May I be presented to the young ladies first?"

Peter didn't care for this sort of thing very much and acknowledged the introduction rather coldly. Penny was frankly curious about any male, and so was particularly charming – so charming that she patted the vacant position on the sofa and invited Mr Cantor to sit by her. Jenny just didn't like him and made no effort to hide her feelings. Tom seemed to share the same opinion, and the twins were pretty confident of the effect they would have on this newcomer when their turn came. But on this occasion they were disappointed, because Mr Cantor looked at them both very carefully the first time and then, after being merely polite, seemed to lose all interest in them.

David noticed this and made a mental note to remind the twins not to try and get their own back. He had seen the results of non-cooperation with Dickie and Mary too often not to be nervous now.

After he had recovered his composure a little Mr Cantor began to enjoy himself, and when Agnes wheeled the tea-trolley into the room ten minutes later she was relieved to see how well he had settled down under circumstances which must have been very unusual for a middle-aged bachelor who had chosen Clun for a holiday in the middle of winter. And the more Agnes thought about Mr Cantor the more puzzled she became, but as her only business at present was to look after her sister's interests at Keep View and to make the Lone Piners as happy and comfortable as she could, she did not spend much time worrying about the new guest.

But Peter did. She couldn't make him out at all, and as she also disapproved of the way in which Penny seemed to be entertaining him, she was more than just curious. Several times during tea she thought she caught him looking at one or other of them rather keenly when he thought that he was not being watched, and she had the strange feeling, too, that he was pretending to be someone else. Peter knew that sometimes she had odd feelings about people and things. During her short life she had learned that these odd dreams and sometimes feelings of distrust or suspicion of others were not always reliable. She had learned, too, that she herself had a very rare understanding and sympathy for animals, who would often do anything for her. Here, almost as if her thoughts were read, Mr Cantor leaned forward and gave Macbeth a piece of cake. Peter knew very well, as did the twins, that Mackie took very strong dislikes to certain people and had proved his instinct right before now. On this occasion he took the offering gratefully and then sat against Mr Cantor's legs and looked up at him with his head on one side.

"What a fool I am!" Peter said to herself as she leaned forward again and threw another log on to the fire. Then she turned and said quite naturally:

"I wish you would tell us something about Clun, Mr Cantor. I'm sure you must know lots about it really, and we've only seen the castle so far. I suppose it's all very old round here, isn't it?"

Mr Cantor's spectacles gleamed red in the firelight as he turned to his questioner.

"Petronella, is it not? Ah, yes! Peter, to be sure! I shall remember that ... If you would all like to hear I can tell you something of this country. Do you all know that you are on haunted ground? Do you realize that here on the hills around this little town the oldest men in Britain lived and fought? Did you know that only a few miles away one of the mighty roads the Romans made still runs, straight as a rule, as it did when their legions marched this way? ... And have any of you heard of Offa's Dyke...?"

When Agnes came to clear the tea-things away Mr Cantor, with his pipe well alight, was sitting like a king enthroned, with the Lone Piners, his loyal subjects, grouped around him. Within ten minutes of Peter's question she had forgotten her suspicion, and even the twins and Jenny were quiet as he told them of the haunted country they hoped to explore.

First he told them that it was his job to be interested in history, old buildings and historical remains, and that he had come to Clun to explore some of the prehistoric burial places which had recently been discovered in the hills. He told them of flint arrowheads and human bones and great stones placed, and still found, in circles, and of how these were set up three thousand five hundred years ago.

"Tell us about that dyke," Dickie said. "We know something about dykes. Is it full of water?"

"Not this one, Richard. This is a very special dyke built twelve hundred years ago by wise King Offa. It is a wall of earth with a deep ditch on the western – that is the Welsh – side, running for one hundred and fifty miles north from Chepstow between the Severn and the Dee."

"Can you walk along it or in it now? And who was King Offa?" Mary asked.

"You can walk along it some of the way today. Not far

from here there is a long stretch for you to explore. Offa was a king of the Mercians, and Mercia was the kingdom which you would call the Midlands. He had the dyke built to mark the boundary between his kingdom and the marauding Welsh, and I expect that many battles were fought along its length."

Mary, who was sitting on the hearthrug with Mackie's head in her lap, suddenly knelt upright.

"Do you mean to tell us that we can *acksherly* go now – or tomorrow, 'cos it's dark now – and walk along that dyke that king made?"

"Of course you can. There's a stretch of it but a mile or two away."

"Gosh! Did you hear him, Dickie? We'll go and do that tomorrow … And are there any castles near?"

"All the border country is castle country, Mary," Mr Cantor said as he got up. "Now I must go and unpack. Thank you all for looking after me so well … I have a fire in my room so that I can work undisturbed, but we shall all meet at meals, I have no doubt … Good evening to you all."

Tom was the first to speak when they were alone.

"What a rum old fellow … Fancy us coming all this way just to have a holiday with him."

"I think you're very unfair," Penny replied. "I think he's nice, and he's not so very old."

"He hasn't got much hair, anyway," Dickie added, "and I bet he's about a hundred. How old do you think he is, Peter? You hardly spoke to him at all."

"Didn't I? I don't think he's a hundred, Dickie, and he was jolly interesting, wasn't he?"

Dickie nodded.

"I s'pose so. I listened some of the time, but it's all very well this talk about what happened once upon a time ... You know Mary and me don't care so much 'bout what happened a billion years ago. We want something to happen *now*!"

"That's true, twin," Mary said dreamily, looking into the fire. "We came yesterday and we haven't had a real adventure yet – unless you call Mr Cantor an adventure ... Oh, Dickie! I s'pose you noticed he was very rude to us when he first came in?"

Dickie nodded brightly. "I'm remembering that, twin!"

"Well," Mary went on, "p'raps we could make our adventure of him. It's time we had one."

"I like things to happen quickly, too," Penny said as she flicked back her curls.

Jon put down the book he had just picked up.

"They generally do with you about, Penny ... Coming out?"

Chapter 6

Bury Fields

Neither Jon nor David were good at getting up! On the following morning Agnes called them, banged on the door without response, and then walked into their room, switched on the light and flung up the window as far as it would go. After a few minutes Jon stirred, reached for his glasses and sat up.

"Here, David, did we turn the light out last night? … And did you open the window as wide as that?"

"Gerrout and go away," David growled as he turned over, but it was not long before the cold roused him and he realized where he was.

"Let's stay here for a bit till those kids have all got out of the bathroom. It's too cold out of bed, anyway, and if we go now we'd be keeping Mr Cantor out."

"That's a ridiculous argument," Jon answered. "And it's the sort of thing young Dickie would say. You're half asleep still and don't know what you're talking about … What do you think of our new friend?"

"Do you know," David answered as he turned over, "that I've been wondering what a cantor is, and I've suddenly remembered. At least I think I know. Isn't he a chap who sings in cathedrals? Come to think of it, he looks like that, doesn't he? Funny how some people's names fit them."

"Why don't you ask him?" Jon said. "I'll bet you haven't the nerve to ask him if he sings in a cathedral choir? ... You know, David, he struck me as being a very odd sort of chap."

"He knew all about Clun, anyway, and I thought he was decent enough."

"Peter didn't think so."

David sat up in bed, felt the draught from the open window and slid under the clothes again.

"How on earth do you know that, Jon?"

"I was watching her face while he was talking. You ask her."

And here their very interesting conversation was interrupted by Tom and Dickie, who came in to tell them what they thought of their laziness.

"Shut the window, Tom," David pleaded, "and then we'll get up. Is the bathroom free?"

"Shut the window yourself," Tom said tersely, "and I may as well tell you that the ice is about half an inch thick on the window and the bathroom has been empty for ten minutes."

"I think you two are the most disgustin' people I've ever met," Dickie said, "and I can't think how you can't see it yourselves. I'm going to fetch the girls to come in and see you," and with this parting shot he side-stepped the pillow which Jon flung at him and slammed the door.

Mr Cantor had his breakfast with them in the dining-room and sat at a little table near the fire. He beamed at them all when he came in and was still very bright and clean and shining. This morning he was dressed in a rather remarkable greenish tweed suit. The coat of the suit looked quite nice, but when Dickie and Tom noticed his very thin legs sticking out from a pair of baggy plus-fours and caught each other's eye, they both had to stifle their laughter. Dickie then choked over his porridge, Jenny began to giggle at the sight of his struggles, and Penny said far too loudly, "I do think you might share the joke."

The situation was saved by the innocent subject of the disturbance.

"And what are you all going to do today? The weather looks and feels extremely seasonable, and as I have a slight cold I believe I may stay in for the present ... But surely some of you will be out exploring?"

"I expect we shall, sir," David answered. "We don't know what we shall do this morning, but directly after dinner we're going off to find a farm near here called Bury Fields."

"Indeed? And may I ask why you are going and whether you know where it is?"

David opened his mouth to answer, but changed his mind as Peter kicked his ankle sharply under the table and spoke instead.

"Just some friends of ours, Mr Cantor. And we shall know how to find it, thank you."

Mr Cantor put down his knife, looked at her over the top of his glasses, but said nothing else. After he had finished his breakfast and left the room Penny said, "I think you were jolly rude to him, Peter."

"Maybe," Peter replied tersely, "but I didn't like the way he said 'And may I ask why?' I expect he's a very nice man really, but what we do is nothing to do with him."

After some discussion they arranged to do nothing special together in the morning, but to start off as early as possible for Bury Fields after dinner. David found the farm marked on the large-scale map he had brought and then settled down to write to his mother and father in London. The twins took Macbeth for a walk round the town. Peter went to attend to Sally and give her a little exercise, and Tom, Jon, Jenny and Penny wandered off to the castle ruins.

The sun was bright but the weather bitterly cold when they set off together after an early dinner over the bridge and up a winding lane that climbed steeply for a mile. When at the top they paused for breath and turned round they could see Clun and its castle on the hill and the silver gleam of the river like a toy town below them. On all sides the wild hills, looking darkly purple in the afternoon light, rolled and rumbled into the distance.

Mary put into words what they were all thinking.

"It's a very little town, and it looks lonely by itself down there, too."

"Which way now, David?" Dickie asked, "and I hope you'll remember the way back, 'cos this is all very wild."

David consulted his map, and after another hundred yards they came to the field gate he was seeking. It took them longer than they expected to find Bury Fields, for the track that led to it was not sign-posted and seemed to wander without a purpose first through fields and then over the actual moorland on which they noticed some sheep. The farm buildings were all of grey stone and the roofs were green with age and the action of the weather. The house looked as if it had grown out of the soil and was a real part of this particular country. But it looked a friendly little house, and as they walked down towards it a short figure came out of the front door, waved to them and then stepped out across the farmyard and up the track to meet them.

"You'll be the young friends Alan told me about?" she said when they were near enough to hear. "Come along in and welcome. It's a cold day to be walking these hills, and I'd rather be round the fire."

"So would we," Dickie said cheekily. "It's our brute of a big brother who drags us out like this. That's him! That one there! The glasses one is our friend Jon ... And this is Mary, my sister. We're twins ..."

"So I see," Mrs Denton said as she led them round the side of the house to a door which led directly into one of the most fascinating rooms they had ever seen. "My son told me about you ... Now you're all to make yourselves at home and be comfortable. Take off your gloves and scarves and put them on the top of the chest over there, and Alan will be along in a minute or two and we'll have tea ... You can see it's ready and waiting for you on the table and the kettle is on the boil."

Nobody could have helped feeling at home with Mrs Denton. She was small and plump and rosy, and certainly not as old as Agnes. Her speech was soft and slow and her smile rare, for her face was often sad. When Peter, who had gone over to the fire to help her, saw her hands, she noticed how they were worn with work.

The kitchen in which they found themselves was enormous. The floor was of stone, but covered with rugs and mats. The ceiling was crossed with great black

135

beams from which hung enticing bunches of herbs and bundles of onions. The fireplace must have been ten feet wide and four feet deep, with seats each side of the great oven in which a big fire was roaring. Against one wall was a long, narrow table with a bench each side, and on the table was the most magnificent tea that Dickie had ever seen.

Firelight and lamplight gleamed on brass and copper decorating the walls, and the only picture they could see was a framed photograph of a great ram with a black face. Then they heard Alan's step outside, and Mrs Denton's sad face lighted up as he came into the room with Lady, the sheepdog, at his heels. He bent to kiss his mother, who looked tinier than ever beside him, and then turned to the Lone Piners.

"Glad you found us," he smiled. "I can't possibly shake hands with you all, so if Mother's ready let's sit down and eat, and then I'll tell you my news."

"What sort of news, son?" Mrs Denton called from the fireplace as she poured the water into the great brown teapot.

"I'll tell you all in a minute, just as soon as we can get started. Everybody got something? Good! You'll looked after Mother up that end, won't you, Jon? I have to force her to eat most of the time."

"Any news of the missing sheep?" David said. "That's what we've been wanting to ask ever since we got here."

Alan took an enormous bite of scone and jam before answering.

"None, I'm afraid. Seems as if they got clean away." He turned to Mrs Denton and went on: "I've told these kids a bit about our trouble. No need to worry about them knowing, I'm sure, so I might as well tell the rest … The more people that know about what's going on in this part of the Forest the better, I reckon …"

He sounded so serious that everyone, including the twins, stopped eating and stared at him. Mrs Denton fidgeted with her teaspoon and said quickly: "What is it, Alan? What's your news?"

"I've been around this afternoon," Alan went on slowly. "I've been over to see Clancy at Three Oaks and Dixon at Little Hollow, and both of them are losing poultry now as well as sheep. Clancy says this business has got beyond a joke and that as the police can seemingly do nothing we've got to organize ourselves and keep watch at night. Dixon says that when he does sleep he'll have his gun at his side, and we're planning to take it in turns to keep guard at nights … Trouble is, o' course, there's not enough of us to cover all the country round, though I reckon we could all guard our own places somehow."

Tom and David spoke at once.

"Why don't you ask us? I'll come."

"Will you let us in? We'll help to keep guard."

"I'll lend you Mackie if you'll let me come, too," Mary said.

Alan looked down the table and smiled at his mother.

"I told you they were the right sort, didn't I?" Then, to the Lone Piners, "It's grand of you to offer to help, and there's a chance in a day or two that we might be grateful for some sentries or guards, but there's nothing you can do now except to keep a good look-out for anyone suspicious either in Clun or on the hills around here."

"Mary and me went for a walk in Clun this morning," Dickie said, "and we thought practically everybody looked suspicious at us. Maybe that's because we're new to them."

"It's at night the sheep stealing is done, obviously, and that's what makes it difficult for us to be in the right place at the right time," Alan went on. "But we'll get 'em in the end, and I hope they'll be in the way of my gun when we catch them!"

Dickie put down the piece of cake that was half way to his mouth.

"I think all this is just wonderful," he said. "Why don't you carry a pair of whacking big six-shooters low down like they do in the cowboys? You've got to be jolly quick on the draw, but I s'pose you know that."

"What could we do to help?" Penny asked plaintively. "Here's Peter and Jenny and me just as much use as any of the boys so long as you give us something subtle and cunning to do."

"I'd like to be disguised," Jenny began, but "What about that furniture van I saw?" Peter interrupted. "It was full of sheep I know, but when I told you yesterday you didn't seem very interested."

"I'm sorry, Peter," Alan said. "Maybe you're right about that after all, but nobody could bring a van up to a flock of sheep in daylight without somebody hearing it or seeing it."

Jon spoke for the first time in this conversation.

"Are you sure of that? It looks as if that's just what

they have done. More likely daylight than night I should think, because surely they couldn't see how to drive them into a van after dark. Besides, wouldn't sheep make a lot of noise at night if they were suddenly confronted with a furniture van?"

Alan nodded.

"Maybe that's so, Jon, but whoever is on this job is a very clever enemy … Anyway that's enough of that now … I'll promise I'll ask you to help if the others agree and if we need you very badly … Meanwhile, just keep your ears and eyes open and I wouldn't trouble to tell that policeman in Clun after all. Tell me!"

Everyone was quieter than usual for the rest of tea, for the older ones, at any rate, could see how upset Mrs Denton was and how serious was this matter of stealing the farmers' livelihood. As soon as the meal was over the girls helped Mrs Denton clear the table and wash up. Alan took the boys round the farm, but after fifteen minutes or so said, "I don't much like the look o' the weather. The wind has gone and it smells foggy to me. I think you'd better be on your way but I hope you'll come again whenever you can. Mother's lonely – misses Dad o' course – and life's not very easy for her. Fresh people cheer her up. And I'd like you to come round with me and Lady one day and see the flock and learn a bit about sheep maybe."

They went back to the house and told the girls to hurry, but it was another fifteen minutes before they all waved "Goodbye" to the Dentons and walked up the track down which they had come two hours ago. They had been longer at Bury Fields than they realized and it was already dusk as they looked back at the golden glow of the farm-house windows below them.

"I like them all very much," Mary said, "but I don't like where they live ... I mean it's a nice house inside and I s'pose it's all right outside, but it's too lonely."

Tom heard her and turned round.

"You're not lonely at Witchend, are you, Mary, and this house is no lonelier than Hatchholt, is it?"

"We're miles from anywhere up there of course," Peter replied, "but I know what Mary means. This country is different somehow, and you can't help feeling lonely in it. I wouldn't like to live here. I can't help thinking about all the *old* things that happened round here. Do you know what I mean, Penny?"

"Yes, I do. It makes me feel creepy. Ancient Britons and more ancient than them may have walked along here where we are now ... And do you remember that nice little Mr Cantor told us about them all being buried under those mounds and barrows ... I say, Peter! I suppose those boys know where they're going, 'cos I don't believe we came this way."

"Neither do I. Hi! David! Wait for us."

The boys and Jenny and Mary, who were about fifty yards ahead, heard her call and waited for them to come up.

"I suppose you know where we are ..." Penny began breathlessly, and then stopped at the look on Jon's face. There was a long pause while they all looked at each other and Mary picked up Mackie and said, "The little darling's coat is all wet ... David! It's getting foggy and it's jolly cold too."

"I'm sorry, chaps, but I'm afraid I've been an awful fool," David said slowly. "I'm not sure that I know where we are and I've been idiot enough to leave the map at the Dentons' – it must be on that sofa thing we sat on before tea."

There was another long silence until Penny laughed a little nervously and said, "I s'pose it's not funny really, but it's fun."

Then Peter spoke up. "Don't look so fed up, David. It's not really your fault and any of us might have lost the map. I think it's jolly decent of you always to take on the job of guide, anyway. There's nothing to worry about really. We're all together."

"Oh, isn't there something to worry about?" Dickie snorted. "That's all you know, Peter. First of all it will soon be supper time, and next you've never been lost in a fog and Mary and me have. And let me tell you it's jolly beastly. Shall we tell you how we were lost in the fog that day on the Mynd?"

"No!" the others all shouted.

"Very well then, I will," Dickie continued, not in the least put out, but when David turned and said seriously, "Don't be an ass, Dickie," he just grinned ruefully and kept quiet.

The light had nearly gone now and although the fog was not thick it looked as if it might soon be very unpleasant. For a minute or two they wondered whether it would be worth while trying to find their way back to Bury Fields, but Jon and Tom were against that.

"We can't be far away from a road," the latter argued, "and this track must lead somewhere. If we go back it will mean Alan will have to turn out and guide us and he's got enough worries. We're supposed to be helping him, and a fine lot we shall look if we all troop back there and say we've lost ourselves."

"Let's go on and chance it," Jon said. "This must go somewhere. Tracks lead to roads and I think nearly all the roads round here must lead to Clun in the end. Don't you worry, twins. We'll be all right."

"*We're* not worried, thank you, Jon – we've had an adventure like this before. We'll go first with Mackie if you like and maybe he'll act like one of those Bernard dogs."

So they went on in the gathering gloom for another ten minutes without passing any tree or stone or hedge that they could remember.

Suddenly Tom, who was in front with a very subdued Jenny, turned round and shouted, "The track goes downhill now and I can see some trees in front. I think maybe we're getting somewhere."

But all that they found was a small cluster of pine trees in a hollow. Their track led them into it and then joined another rough road.

"Now we must be nearer something," Jon said, "for this road has been used lately and looks quite important for this sort of country. Trouble is, which way shall we go – to the right downhill, or up to the left?"

"If only I hadn't been such a fool about the map," David groaned. "I'm sure these trees and this other road would be marked and then it would have been easy."

"Don't keep on so," Penny said. "You've said all that before, David, and nobody wants to hear it again."

"Of course we don't know what's in store for us all," Jenny said, "but I just don't fear any fate now we're all together and all Lone Piners."

"When you've all finished being sorry to each other," Mary broke in, "somebody had better come over here and see if they can see what I see."

Dickie was at her side before she had finished speaking.

"No need for anyone to worry any more," he said. "We're saved. Mary's saved us. This adventure is over."

But Dickie was wrong. The adventure wasn't over and had hardly begun.

They all crowded round Mary and looked where she was pointing. While they had been standing at the junction of the two tracks she had turned to the right and taken a few steps down the hill. Now, in the deepening twilight they could just see below them an ugly, squat house which appeared to be surrounded by high stone walls.

"I don't believe it," Penny said. "It can't just be there. I mean why didn't we see it as we came along that other path? We ought to have done. This is a mirage."

"I'm not sure what a mirage is," Tom said, "but it looks like a prison. P'raps we've walked to Dartmoor and didn't know it. My feet feel as if we had."

Mary tucked Mackie under one arm and then felt for Peter's hand. "I hate it," she said and shuddered.

Jon, who was the tallest, made one of his rare remarks.

"Looks to me as if there's a pair of big wooden gates in the wall at the bottom of the hill here. Tom's right. It does look like a prison, and it looks empty too."

"Let's go and ask where we are and for a drink of water," was Dickie's bright suggestion.

"I can't think of anything I'd hate more than a drink of water," Tom replied. "But we'd better go and see if anyone lives there and can help us."

After some argument Jon, David and Tom went down to explore.

"And don't any of you move from here," were David's parting words. "It's nearly dark, but it's silly for us all to go down there looking like a circus. We'll soon be back. Look after them, Peter," and they disappeared into the shadows.

As soon as they were clear of the trees they noticed something else very odd about this strange house.

"Look to the right of those big doors," Tom said. "It seems as if there's a big bank stretching along in front of the walls."

"You're right, Tom," David replied. "It might almost be the wall of a moat."

"I bet it is," Jon said promptly. "I bet that's Offa's Dyke that old Cantor told us about ... Look! It runs in a straight line as far as you can see on that side of the house and I dare say that it goes up the hill the other side if we could only see properly ... You know, chaps, this *is* an odd sort of place. Those walls must be at least eight feet high and it looks to me as if they've got broken glass on the top ... Wonder if they want to stop people from getting in or prevent them from getting out ... And I still can't understand why we didn't see it before we got to that little wood."

"Here we are, anyway," David said. "And what do we

do now? Tap on the door politely, or stand out here and sing? I shouldn't think anyone has lived here for years."

"I believe they have," Jon said looking at the ground. "This track has been used recently, anyway … Surely there's a bell somewhere?"

They found a rusty iron bell-pull on the brick pillar at the right hand side of the wooden gates. Tom reached up and pulled it heartily, but although they listened intently for an answering peal no sound broke the silence.

"I'm sure that bell has been used," Tom said. "It pulls easily enough and it didn't squeak. You try it, David. Seems to me it was oiled."

So David tried, but with no more success, and while they stood there uneasily in the dark wondering what was the best thing to do there came down to them through the mist the sound of the peewit's whistle.

"That's Peter or Dickie," David said at once. "They're the best whistlers – I wonder what's wrong?"

"Maybe they're warning us," Tom said. "P'raps someone is coming. What shall we do? I'll call them back."

Tom was the best whistler of them all and his answering signal was so real that David almost looked up, expecting to see the shy little bird with the crested head wheeling and tumbling over the heather. Then he felt Jon's hand gripping his arm and heard him say under his breath:

"Turn round carelessly in a sec. I think there's someone watching us through a little window in the doors … Don't let them see that you've noticed."

David felt his mouth go dry with excitement as he said normally, "Call them again, Tom." Then, as the peewit's lament wailed through the gloom he turned casually with his hands in his pockets and looked as closely as he could at the surface of the great doors. He kicked a pebble idly and moved a step or two nearer, pretending – and not finding this very difficult – to be fidgeting about because they didn't know what to do. Then he thought he noticed a slight movement on the surface of the nearest door. Jon was right, then; they *were* being watched.

David felt that he could now make some amends for leaving the map behind. By a stroke of good fortune his electric torch was in his jacket pocket, although he had forgotten it until now. He had it out in a flash and calling suddenly, "Watch the doors," he pressed the button and swung the beam up until it picked out a little door about three inches square in the centre of the big, right hand gateway. As Jon and Tom wheeled round at David's warning the trap closed with a click, but not before David had seen a human eye watching them. It had disappeared before he could have counted three, but even so it had given them a shock.

Not only was there something unpleasantly different about the eye, but the idea of someone watching them while refusing to answer the bell was maddening. David felt himself go hot with anger and was surprised to hear his own voice shouting, "Whoever you are please open the doors. We're lost – a big party of us – and we need help and to know where we are. Open the door!"

And Tom, who had also been just in time to catch the glimpse of the sinister eye, rushed forward and banged on the doors with his fists.

"Let us in!" he yelled. "Open the door. Answer us."

They waited for another minute and then called again, but there was no sound which even suggested life within these strange, grey walls. Then Jon said quietly, "That's very odd. I think we'd better go back to the others as we're not going to get any help here. Bit of luck you finding your torch, David. I couldn't see properly of course but I thought I saw that peephole open ... I can hear the peewit whistle again. Come on. Let's get back."

"I suppose there's a back entrance somewhere," Tom said. "Shall we follow the wall right round and see what we find?"

"No. Jon's right, Tom. I think maybe the others have got some news. Let's get back. I shall have to save my battery as much as I can and it will be quite dark in a minute or two. Come on."

Halfway up the rough track which led to the wood they heard running footsteps coming towards them.

"Whistle, Tom!" David said urgently. "Quick!" Again the call wailed and this time was answered – but not with a whistle.

"It's me! Penny!" a familiar voice called, and then she was with them and clinging to Jon's arm while she tried to recover her breath.

"What's wrong, Penny?" David said. "Take your time."

"We think we're being watched up there in the wood. The twins are sure of it and say someone is spying on us. It may sound silly to you but I felt it too, and I think Peter's quite sure ... Did you have any luck?"

"No, we didn't," Jon said shortly. "The gates are locked and barred and there's no other way in and we think the place is deserted."

Tom started to speak and then stopped.

"But we heard you shouting as if you'd all gone mad," Penny said.

"We thought we'd try making a noise but it was no good. We'll just have to keep walking and hope for the best. Don't scare the twins, Penny, will you?"

"Could I? Could you? Don't be silly, Jon … Well, if we're lost we're lost, and that's all there is to it. I'm not scared when we're all together, although Jenny is a bit jumpy. Come on! Let's get back."

The light had gone now but the fog was no worse and a yellow moon was poking her rim over the little spinney where the others were waiting. As the boys and Penny reached the trees they heard Jenny's voice, pitched just a little too high.

"I don't care what you say, Peter. I don't like this place and my teeth are chattering. Let's get away from these beastly, ghostly trees before the others come back. We can soon join up with them somewhere but I hate this *and I want to get out*!"

They could not hear Peter's reply in words, but David was thankful when he recognized her quiet, level voice. Peter would never get panicky or lose her head or scream. The twins were standing quietly together leaning against the same pine tree, and David had perhaps never admired them more than now when, without asking him any futile questions, Dickie said, "What are we going to do? Go on or stay?"

"We're going right back to Clun now," David answered. "The moon is coming up and I've got an idea that the right way is to follow this new track up the hill."

"I'm sure it's been used recently," Jon said again. "Sure of it. If we follow it up through the trees I'll bet it takes us eventually to a road … Come on – let's go!"

They set off, close together, up the rough track between the sighing trees. Dickie edged up to David and whispered, "Did Penny tell you that we're being tracked and watched?"

"She did, Dickie. Are you sure? Have you seen anybody?"

"Not exactly, but we know we're right. We heard somebody at the edge of the wood."

"It's no use looking like that, David," Mary broke in. "We know you don't believe us when you look like that. This time you're wrong again. Ask Peter."

"Yes, I do think there's someone skulking about round us," Peter said. "While you were down at the house I know I heard a twig snap and thought I saw a shadow moving through the trees … Let's try and prove it … Looks as if there's a little hill ahead. As soon as we're all over the top two of us had better flop down in the heather and watch the path to see if someone comes out of the wood and follows."

"Right, Peter. You and I will do that … You others go on slowly once you're over the top and just keep on talking."

Although it was very difficult to be certain, they both agreed that some sort of dark human figure came out of the trees, looked towards them for a long minute, and then started to follow them.

"Quick, David," Peter whispered. "Back to the others and warn them. We'll catch this chap somehow."

As soon as they caught them up David gave his orders.

"There *is* somebody. The twins were right ... Divide up and some go one side of the track and some the other. Don't get too near because we don't want him to see us. Let him walk between us and we'll trail him and see where he's going. If he does nothing else maybe he'll lead us to Clun, and I should think Alan would like to know about him. Quick now and quiet. Nobody to make a move after he's passed until I do."

They scattered obediently – David, Peter, Jenny and Dickie to the left of the path and the others, with Mackie, on the right. They lay full-length in the heather watching the top of the little hill over which the stranger must come. Jenny, as she lay beside David, was sure the enemy would hear her heart beating, and she almost screamed when a dim figure did appear against the skyline. But now they had a surprise, for instead of running towards them the figure stopped, looked round intently, and then disappeared again. The Lone Piners lay still waiting for David's signal. They saw him stand up and were just ready to follow him when he signalled them down again and flung himself flat on his face. Then they heard an odd rattle or jangle, and suddenly a figure on a bicycle appeared at the top of the hill and came bumping down the track between them.

It was too dark and they were all too far away for any of them to recognize the cyclist, and they could not even be sure that it was the same man who had come out of the wood. As soon as possible they scrambled through the heather to the track, but by then there was no sign of the mysterious cyclist, although they could hear the rattle of something loose on his machine as it bumped over the uneven track long after he had disappeared.

Nobody said much. If the cyclist was the man who had been watching them from the spinney and again from the top of the rise he had certainly made them all look rather foolish.

"P'raps he's got an invisible bike," Dickie said. "I mean invisible some of the time ... I'm jolly cold and I want my supper, but you all see now that Mary and me were right, don't you?"

The path led downhill and after ten more minutes they found themselves between hedges and David's torch proved that the track was now a rough lane.

"We'll be all right now," Tom said thankfully. "I've had enough of today."

He was right for, soon after, they came to a road and a signpost, the righthand finger of which said "Clun".

When, tired, cold and hungry, they clattered at last up the steps of Keep View it was to find an angry Agnes waiting for them. She was very cross indeed and threatened to send the twins to bed at once.

"But it's you bigger ones, and specially Mister David and Mister Jonathan, that ought to be ashamed of yourselves a'worrying of me into my grave, and me responsible for you all."

"Just let me have my supper, Agnes," Dickie pleaded, "and then be mad with us all after. You know how sorry we are, but it's like Jenny says and fate was against us."

"And we've done some most important secret work," Mary added, "and maybe the police or somebody like that will give us a medal presently, and so you must forgive us, Agnes."

"One day p'raps you'll be proud of us all for this day's work," Jenny added.

When at last they were sitting down to supper Peter asked where Mr Cantor was, and Agnes explained that he had had his meal upstairs in his room some time ago. As soon as she had closed the door behind her Dickie clapped his hand to his head and cried out as if in pain. Neither David nor Mary looked up from their soup, but the latter said:

"Don't worry, anyone. He's got an idea and I bet it's a big one. What is it, Dickie? I'm trying to think, but I'm not sure."

Dickie looked round the table triumphantly.

"I bet you'd all like to know who was riding that bike up there on the moor, wouldn't you? I bet I know who it was. Would you like to know…? Here, Mary. Just come exploring with me and we'll prove it and be back in a sec."

The others got on with their meal without much comment when the twins had gone, but David did say: "Dickie must be on to something if he's left his supper. You can never be quite sure with him."

Suddenly the door burst open to disclose the twins, open-mouthed and triumphant.

"What did we tell you…?" Mary began, but Dickie stopped her with a dramatic gesture and closed the door behind them. They both strutted to the fire and stood in front of it.

"What did we tell you?" Mary went on. "We've done

it again for the Lone Piners – you can't do without us. Now listen! That bike with the rattling bell that the spy escaped on is Mr Cantor's."

There was a long pause and then knives and forks clattered on to plates as the others stared at them in amazement.

Then, "Don't be ridiculous!" Penny said. "You two are trying to be funny again. How can you possibly know that? He's not the sort of man to have a bicycle."

"Go on, Dickie," Peter said quietly. "Tell us how you know."

Dickie spoke soberly now.

"I'll tell you. This morning after we'd been for a walk with Mackie we explored round the back here. There's a sort of garden which is rather messy and a shed with all sorts of things in it. There was a man's bike in there and it had a label on the handlebars addressed to Mr Cantor here. We had a look at the bike and I noticed that the bell was loose and rattled … The bike is there now but in a different place. The label has gone and there are lamps on it now, but the bell still rattles and we bet that man on that bike was Mr Cantor spying on us – or up to some dirty trick."

Chapter 7

That Van Again

As soon as supper was cleared away they gathered round the fire and began to discuss the day's adventures. Nothing that the elder ones could say could make Dickie change his mind about Mr Cantor.

"It's no use you trying to bully us, David and Jon," Mary said in defence of her twin, "and we don't care what you say but you're jolly well wrong and we're right. We 'zamined that bike in the shed this morning, and if you want to know we did just take it out on the garden path and sort of try it, and the bell jangled."

"And there's no need for you to say anything about us just trying the stupid old bike," Dickie added, " 'cos that's nobody's business but ours. We didn't hurt the thing but we did put it away quickly because the bell was loose and jangled."

"Yes, Dickie, we quite understand about the jangling bell and you needn't mention it again, but how do you know it was Mr Cantor riding it this evening?" David said.

"Acksherly," Mary took up the tale, "Acksherly we were just giving Mackie a little, teeny ride on the saddle and that was why we took it out of the shed."

Jon glared at her. "Never mind about darling Mackie.

Nobody is really interested in that dog except you … All right! All right! I'm sorry. We all love him very dearly, but tell us, Dickie, how you know it was Mr Cantor this evening."

"Well, you see," Dickie began a little doubtfully, "we know it was his bike, and after all nobody would want to come breaking into this house and garden and borrow his bicycle and go riding it in the fog and the dark all over those beastly hills where we got lost, would they? I mean it just doesn't make sense."

"Of course it doesn't make sense," Peter broke in. "I think you're right, Dickie. I've always been suspicious of Mr Cantor and now I'm sure I'm right. He looks too smug to me, and anyway it's a silly time of year to go crawling or cycling about the country to look for old bones and things."

Then the door opened and Agnes came in.

"And what was it made me wonder whether those two little ones had gone to bed? You're both tired out and it's getting late. Be off with you! Goodness gracious me, but you're both yawning while I look at you. Come along and no arguments."

The twins looked at her, then at each other, and decided that Agnes was right and that this was no time for further argument. At the door Dickie turned and hissed, "Why don't you go and jolly well look for yourselves? *You know where I mean!*"

"And another thing," Mary said, "don't any of you dare to plan anything without us. It's only because we're not as big as you that we're driven off to bed in this brutal way. And you're all yawning! Why don't you make *them* go to bed, Agnes? You just don't know how I wish I was older so that I didn't have to do things like this."

When the door had closed behind them David said, "I've got a brainwave. What Mary said is true about us being tired. I suggest that Jon and Tom and I go out and examine that bicycle and then we all go to bed—"

"I must say that's a futile sort of idea," Penny broke in. "Our adventure has just about started and all you can suggest is bed. Why, I think that's awful, David! I didn't think the Lone Pine Club was like that!"

"It isn't," David said coldly. "If you hadn't interrupted me I was going on to suggest that we all meet in Jon's and my room about midnight for a Council of War. And anyway, Penny, you're yawning now. What do you others think? Is it a good idea?"

"It's a good idea," Peter agreed, "but how do we wake up? And what about the twins? They'll be mad about it, but they ought to get a night's rest."

"That's all right," Jon replied. "I've got a little alarm clock. We'll come and wake you all."

"Well, don't bang on *my* door," Tom said. "Come in and shake my shoulder, but for the sake of peace and quietness don't wake Dickie."

"Same with me please!" Jenny pleaded. "I shall be dead asleep, I know, and generally Mary wakes before I do. So be specially quiet whoever wakes me ... Oh, David! This is the most wonderful thing that ever happened to me. All my life I've been wanting to have a midnight Council of War, and now it's come and I'm so afraid I'll never be awake enough to be my best."

"I'll wake you," Penny said grimly. "Don't you worry,

Jenny. You'll be wide enough awake by the time I've finished with you! I seem to remember being led blind-fold up a hill with someone croaking in my ear!"

"You girls go up now then," David said. "We're going to look at the bike and we'll see you all later. And for goodness sake be quiet at midnight, else we shall wake Agnes and Mr Cantor. I'm sorry about the twins, but they can't expect to be in everything…"

"Can't they?" Peter grinned. "Cheerio for the present."

Jon had put his alarm clock under his pillow so that its shrilling should wake nobody but themselves. It rang soon after twelve and although he was sleeping deeply he woke at once. This idea of a meeting seemed for a few minutes to be particularly stupid, for bed seemed the best of all places; but at last he reached over and shook David, who stirred and then sat up, instantly awake for once.

"Close the windows," he said, "and pull the curtains right across. I'll light the gas fire and go and wake the others. Lend me your torch, Jon?"

He tried Tom first and the door squeaked horribly so that Dickie sighed, stirred in his sleep and then turned over with a grunt. David crept over to Tom's bed, shook him and then whispered in his ears till he awoke and remembered.

"I think we're all crackers," he muttered as he swung his legs out of bed. "All right, David. I'll go along to your room, but I hope we're not too long."

Peter answered the second soft knock and within five minutes they were all, except the twins, round the gas fire in David's room. Penny and Peter had brought their own eiderdowns, so they all sat on the floor and kept each other as warm as they could.

"Do you think we ought to sign in blood again?" Jenny asked with chattering teeth, "I mean just to make it more real."

They all looked at her pityingly, so she just smiled brightly at them and leaned back against Peter's knees with a sigh of content. This was real life to Jenny who, until the Lone Piners came to the Stiperstones, had hardly any friends. She felt now, although she thought longingly once or twice of her warm bed, that she would follow any of them to the end of the world.

"I must tell you girls first," David began, "that we went down with a torch and had a look at the bike and that we think Dickie is right about Mr Cantor. It sounds amazing, I know, but there's no doubt that the bike had been used this evening. The tyres had got fresh mud on them, and there was a scrap of heather jammed between the handlebars and the jangling bell, and Jon found some fresh soil on one of the pedals which proves, we think, that the bike had been dropped or hidden in the heather. There doesn't seem much doubt to us that Mr Cantor is a very suspicious character and that we should watch him closely now that this sheep stealing has started. We've got to make plans for tomorrow, and for the next day, and decide whether we should go over tomorrow and tell Alan Denton all we suspect or whether we should hang around and try and watch Cantor. What do you think, chaps?"

Penny spoke first. "You may be quite right about the bicycle, David, but I think he's too nice to do a thing like stealing. I think we ought to take it in turns to watch him anyway if everybody else thinks he's acting suspiciously."

"Well, I don't like him," Peter said in her straight-forward and honest way, "and I never have, and I still can't see why he should want to come and stay at Clun at this time of the year. I'll believe him when he proves himself, and meanwhile I vote that we follow him when he goes out and see if he really does practise what he preaches, or whether he steals sheep ... I feel certain that he's up to something very mysterious and I shall watch him as much as I possibly can. Perhaps he'll be the beginning of another big adventure for us? ... What do you think about it all, Jon?"

Jon shrugged. "I'm beginning to think with you, Peter. He's a very odd chap and now that we've decided that he's to be watched I think we shall have a lot of fun from it. What about you, Jenny?"

"Oooh, Jon! What do you mean, what about me?"

"I mean – what do you think of Mr Cantor?"

"I don't quite think I ever think about him much, but I'm sure you're all right – specially Peter."

After some more talk David got up from the floor and went over and lay on his bed.

"I don't know about you chaps but I'm jolly tired. I wish you'd all go away and by breakfast time I hope I'll have thought of a way for us to watch him without him knowing ... or perhaps somebody else could get an idea? If anybody does have a brainwave, come up here and bang on the door in good time before breakfast ... Penny's yawning. Look at her! She'll be no good at guarding us or dogging Mr Cantor tomorrow unless she goes to bed now … Good night all.”

When Peter got back to her own room she felt strangely wide-awake. The few hours' sleep she had enjoyed before the meeting in the boys' room had freshened her and now her mind was so active that she would have liked to have gone on talking. But Penny was asleep in a few minutes and no company at all, so she tossed and turned on her pillow thinking again of all that had happened in the last twenty-four hours. Half-an-hour ago she had said that the discovery of Mr Cantor's suspicious behaviour might be the beginning of a new adventure, but considering all that had happened since she rode away from Hatchholt in the dawn two days ago, she realized that they were in the midst of one already. Now that she came to think of it again there was a strange atmosphere of unreality about Clun and this unusual, lonely countryside. In spite of certain intuitions which came to her sometimes, Peter was a very practical person, but as she lay uneasily in her bed in this bare little room at Keep View she could not quite banish the odd feeling that they were all living in a story.

She could not have put this into words if she had been asked to do so, but when she thought again of the eerie loneliness of the hills after they had left Bury Fields this afternoon she remembered that the word which had stuck in her mind as she had trudged along with Penny in the mist and as she had waited for the boys in that horrible, lonely, little spinney, was “haunted”. She did not feel particularly frightened, for she was not the sort of girl who was easily scared and was used to the solitudes of a wild countryside; but she was puzzled.

And while she lay there in the quiet dark with Penny breathing gently beside her the light of the moon crept through the window and patterned the foot of her bed with silver. The sash was open and, after a little, the cry of an owl broke the silence. She turned over again to find a cooler patch on the pillow and then sat up suddenly, for there was now a new sound in the night. Far, far away she heard the faint, pulsating throb of the engine of a car. As soon as she sat up the silence of the night surged back again so that she wondered if her ears or brain were playing tricks. Then it came again and now it was nearer and there was a whine in the pulse of the heavy engine which told her that the car was coming up a hill. Or was it a car? She listened intently, as the sound became muffled again and then burst into new life. Now she could hear the rumble of heavy wheels coming rapidly closer, and suddenly she was sure of what she would see if she went to the window.

She was out of bed in a trice, and pushed up the sash still further so that she could see up and down Clun's moonlit street. No living thing moved except a sly, black cat mincing along in the shadows opposite. The noise of the approaching engine was louder now and echoing back from the houses built close to Clun's little bridge. Peter leaned far out so that the bitter cold struck through her pyjamas and started her teeth chattering. Then a great lorry with only two small, dimmed headlights swung round into the main street. It was travelling dangerously fast – too fast for Peter to notice how many men were in the driving seat, but even as the red tail-light swung out of sight round the corner she had recognized the van as that she had met on the day she rode to Clun. But one thing was different. She was quite, quite certain that this time the lettering on the side of the van read "Thompsons of Manchester".

Peter had made up her mind even before her feet touched the floor again and she had closed the window. She ran over to the door and switched on the light and then moved to Penny's bed. She put her mouth close to her friend's ear and whispered as she shook her shoulder:

"Wake up, Penny. Don't make a noise, but wake up quickly. Please be quiet, Penny … Yes, it's me. It's Peter. It's urgent, Penny. Wake up … I'm sorry, Penny, but you *must*. This is something for the Lone Piners…"

At the last words Penny sat up and rubbed her eyes.

"Am I mad, Peter? I suppose I am, 'cos I'm quite sure that all this has happened before."

"What do you mean, Penny? … Are you really awake now? I've got something terrific to tell you."

"Yes, I'm awake, I s'pose. It seemed to me that I've been woken up like this once before tonight. What's happened? Is the house on fire, 'cos if it is it's jolly cold and quiet … Peter, what are you dressing for? You're putting on your jodhpurs … Oh dear! I s'pose we're both mad."

"Get up and get dressed," Peter whispered. "Put on the warmest things you've got. I've just seen that furniture van again and I bet it's full of sheep, and we must go and warn the Dentons … This is a job for the Club, Penny, and we're all pledged to stick together, you know. Get up. I'm going to wake the boys."

Penny did not even stop to argue, but had reached for her clothes before Peter had closed the door behind her.

Peter had trouble with the boys, but she went boldly into their room and switched on the light. If she had had time she would have smiled to herself because they looked such babies lying there with their tousled heads. She shook David first.

"Peter! What's wrong?"

She told him in a few words.

"Right," he said. "Wake Jenny. I'll see to Tom and Jon. Don't wake the twins. We'll be downstairs in the hall in five minutes."

He reached up and pulled one of the plaits which she had not undone after the council of war.

"Good old Peter!" he grinned.

And she was so pleased with this that she was thankful he could not see her burning cheeks as she went back to the door. Penny was dressed by the time she had wakened Jenny and got back to her own room.

"Down in the hall," she whispered. "We'll all be there except the twins. Not a sound."

One stair creaked badly, but within five minutes they were all down. Jenny looked as if she was walking in her sleep and Tom was obviously furious, but he grinned happily when David herded them all into the dining-room and began his whispered story.

"Peter has just seen that furniture van again. She says it was travelling fast, but she's certain it's the one she met the other day full of sheep. Peter says – but it's her idea, not mine, and she ought to be doing the talking…"

"*Go on, David!*" Peter implored.

"Peter says we ought to split up and try to warn the Dentons and any other farmers we can reach. I think it's a grand idea. We've all got bikes except Peter, and she's going on Sally to Bury Fields. Let's get out of here as quickly and quietly as we can, and we'll make further plans as we go up the hill. We can't cycle up that. Come on … Bike shed next."

They crept out like hunted criminals, down the front steps and round the side of the house to the shed where Dickie had first found the bicycle with the jangling bell.

"There's going to be some trouble over all this," Tom muttered as he wheeled out his bicycle.

"Who from?" Jon whispered.

"Those twins! Just think what they're going to say when they find out we've deserted them. I'm frightened to death of 'em. Always have been … Where's Peter?"

"Gone for Sally," David said. "We're going to meet on the bridge. Come on. Let's get out of here. I've an awful idea Mr Cantor may suddenly open his window and spot us."

Jenny's teeth were chattering again as they got on their bicycles and glided silently down the still moonlit street to the bridge. While they waited for Peter she stood close to Tom, and if for a moment she laid her cheek against the rough tweed of his coat-sleeve nobody noticed. She wasn't really scared and was grateful for being included in the party, but she had made up her mind that she wasn't going to leave Tom for anything or anybody. Tom seemed to understand, for as the clip-clop of Sally's hooves came nearer he looked down at her and said, "We'll stick together, Jen, shall we?"

At the top of the hill where the houses stopped they stood under the sign-post for a few minutes and made their plans.

"We'll all meet here in two hours' time if we can," David said. "I think that's the best scheme. Peter is going on her own to Denton's because she'll be quicker on Sally than we shall on bikes. I suppose the rest of us had better split up and explore as much as we can, keeping a good look-out for anybody suspicious or for that van."

"What do we do if we come to a farm and there's nobody about?" Jon asked. "Wake 'em all up and tell them Peter saw a furniture van in Clun?"

Before David could answer Tom said, "You can split as much as you like, but Jenny and me aren't splitting!"

"I think the best idea," Penny said, "is for those of us with bikes to go together much further down this lane till we come to the cross-roads we struck this afternoon where four roads meet. Some of us can stay on guard there and the rest can take it in turns to go off on bikes and keep a good look-out. Isn't that a better scheme than all meeting here, which is really too near the town? What do you think, everybody?"

Jon patted her on the back.

"Smart, bright little Newpenny!"

She put out her tongue at him as Peter said, "Of course. That's a brainwave. Agreed, David?"

"Rather! Let's go."

The moon was high in the sky and it was nearly as light as day. Every trace of the evening's mist had gone, but it was bitterly cold to their ears and finger-tips.

"Just think," Tom said ten minutes later as he let his

cycle fall on the frosty grass at the foot of the sign-post, "Just think that we might all be in bed. I was wondering just now, when I thought my ears had fallen off, how it was that Peter has persuaded us all to do this ... There she goes. Just like a cowboy on the pictures ... What do we do now, David?"

David blew on his fingers.

"I thought you two girls might stay here on guard while we three went on a bit further and then split up if we came to a likely path or saw a farmhouse."

"You're wrong," Penny said. "I don't want to be split, and I'll freeze to death if I stay here. I'm coming with whoever is on the attacking party."

"I'm going to be with Tom," Jenny said quite simply, and as Tom seemed to have no objection to the job of sentinel this was soon settled.

"There are four roads here and only three of us," Jon said. "If each one takes a road, which one shall we miss?"

"You're not as bright as usual, little boy," Penny laughed. "We won't bother about the one we've come along, of course," and for once Jon looked a little sheepish.

And it was Penny who had the next adventure. She rode off in the moonlight down the road that the others had chosen for her, whistling cheerfully. This was the first time in her life that she had ever been out at half-past two in the morning, and she was enjoying the experience. She was too excited to be tired and the cold air was like a tonic. Frost sparkled on the road surface in front of her, and every now and then she beat a gloved hand on her knee to keep it warm. After a little she came to a steep hill with some trees at the bottom and was free-wheeling blithely down this when a car came out of a hidden turning in the shadows and headed towards her. Penny was so astonished that she put on her brakes too hard and felt the back wheel begin to slide on the slippery road surface. The car seemed to rush up to meet her, and although she wrenched at the handlebars, her bicycle began to behave like a mad thing. She felt herself slipping, put out her left foot, touched the grass verge and fell in a heap with her bicycle on the top of her.

After a moment she sat up and noticed that the car had stopped opposite and that a man was getting out. Suddenly she felt defenceless and afraid and wished that she was not out alone on this absurd adventure. Then, rather cautiously, she looked at the man in front of her and saw that he was studying her, too. He was small, and wearing a soft felt hat with the brim turned down all the way round and a heavy tweed overcoat. He had a rather fierce-looking moustache, which seemed too big for his face, and he was carrying something long under his arm.

Suddenly Penny gasped and put a hand to her mouth. The "something" was undoubtedly a gun. He was the sheep thief and was going to shoot her! What could she do? What could she say? Her teeth chattered as the stranger and she examined each other in the moonlight, and then her courage and common sense came back with a rush and she scrambled to her feet and picked up the bicycle. Then she smiled at the stranger rather disarmingly – and Penny could smile very disarmingly when she liked – and said, "You did scare me coming rushing up the hill like that. I do hope the bike is all right, 'cos I've got a long way to go on it. Will you help me if it isn't? And if that's a gun it won't pop off or anything, will it?"

The moustache still regarded her fiercely.

"Who are you?" it barked suddenly. "Are you hurt? What are you doing out here at this time of night? Where are you going? Why aren't you in bed?"

Penny was playing for time. Should she make a dash for it? If she did it would have to be down the hill and away from the others, whose help she needed now. And would her bicycle stand it? It seemed all right. Her knee hurt and she thought she had grazed it badly. She gave a rather shaky laugh.

"That's not fair! I can't answer all those questions at once. And I don't like that gun thing."

"Where do you come from?" the little man barked again. "I don't know your face. Come here and let me look at you. What are you doing? Running away?"

Penny felt a lump rise in her throat. She was very lonely and defenceless. Then she remembered she was a Lone Piner, swallowed the lump and held her chin up high.

"Why should you know my face? Do you live here?"

"Live here? Of course I do. Lived here for fifty years ... Now speak up and tell me who you are."

"I will if you will ... No! Don't touch me! Keep away! I'm not afraid of you."

A noise came from under the moustache that might have been a laugh.

"All right, child, don't fear. I won't hurt you, but tell me what you're doing out here on a bicycle at this time in the morning, but be quick because I'm in a hurry.

Have you met anybody on your way? Seen anybody driving sheep along?"

"No, I haven't," Penny said soberly. "But do please tell me who you are."

The man opened the door of the car and tossed in the gun.

"Name of Clancy," he said. "Farmed here all my life."

Penny nearly sobbed with relief and her voice was very shaky as she said, "That's marvellous. I remember Alan Denton saying that name ... Mr Clancy, I've got some news for you. Let me get in with you, and if you go up the hill and about two miles further on you'll come to a signpost and the others will be there ... Oh! I should have asked you this first. Are all your sheep safe? If you have any, I mean. We've all come out to warn you..."

"Jump in beside me," Mr Clancy barked. "Leave your cycle and I'll get it for you some time. This all sounds crazy to me, but tell me what you know as we go ... I've lost fifty sheep this night."

Penny did her best to explain as they roared along the empty road, but she realized that her story was very confused.

"... It was Peter who saw the van go through Clun tonight, and she's gone off on her pony to warn Alan."

"Oh, he has, has he?"

"It isn't a he. Peter's a girl like me, only a bit older, but there's quite a lot of us staying at Keep View in Clun and trying to help you all if you'll let us."

Mr Clancy grunted.

"I've had no sleep for three nights and reckon I must have dropped off for an hour or two tonight," he muttered, almost to himself. "They could do the trick with a lorry or van somewhere near, o' course. Well, young lady, I don't know what to make of your story, but I was on my way to pick up young Denton, and here's the cross-roads, and by the looks of it there's some of your crazy friends too, so I reckon what you've told me is the truth."

Before Penny could answer he stopped the car as Tom and Jon stepped into the road in front of it.

Penny jumped out. "It's all right, Jon; it's me. And this is Mr Clancy the farmer, and he's had fifty sheep stolen tonight ... Where's David? Has anyone else been along?"

Jenny, who was leaning against the signpost, spoke up.

"No, Penny, nobody has come this way. You're the only one so far who has found anything ... and fancy getting a ride back. Where's your bike?"

Mr Clancy barked again before Penny could answer. "Seems like a school outing to me! Can't make any sense out of you youngsters wandering all over the country in the middle of the night. I'm going down here to find young Denton. You say he knows all about you?"

"He does," Jon said. "We're all friends of his and we're trying to help him, and you, too, sir, if you'll let us ... I think we've a clue over this sheep-stealing, but I agree that it is a good idea to try and find Mr Denton as well."

"I think he's coming now," Jenny said. "Or if it's not him it's Peter. I can hear horses ... Oh, and here's David coming, too, and he looks out of breath and fed up ... Hullo, David! We're still on guard, and look what we've found – a farmer in a motor-car!"

David got off his bicycle and let it fall distastefully on to the grass verge, but before he could say anything they all heard the thudding of hooves and turned to see a man on a fine slim horse come cantering up to the gate in the corner of the field. A hundred yards behind him came Peter, sitting easily and comfortably on little Sally, who, now that she had become used to working in the night air, was coming along at a splendid pace. Tom strolled across and opened the gate as Alan slipped off his hunter and turned to wave to Peter. Then he saw Clancy.

"Hullo!" he said. "Trouble?"

Clancy nodded and led him away out of earshot while the Lone Piners grouped themselves round the sign-post.

"I met Alan just riding out of the farmyard," Peter explained. "He'd had some sleep and was just going on guard again and was jolly surprised to see me ... I say, I think he's very bucked with us. He was awfully nice when I told him about the van. What do we do now?"

"I hate to say it again," Tom replied, "but I'd really like to go to sleep. There's not much left of the night, and before we know where we are Agnes will be banging on the door."

"I do hope the twins haven't woken up and found us not there," Jenny said. "That would be awful ... I think I need my bed, too, but I did enjoy being a sentry with Tom. I kept on thinking how wonderful it would be if something happened or someone came along."

Then Alan and Mr Clancy came over and the latter was all smiles under the moustache.

"You youngsters must get back now," Alan said. "You've done grand work, and we all appreciate it very much. Mr Clancy and I are going to check up with the other farmers, and we shall try and get some sleep, too. We're not telling the police at the moment – not till we've found out something else we want to know. Cut back now and come and see us at Bury Fields whenever you feel like it. You'll always be welcome…"

He stopped and put his hand in his pocket.

"I nearly forgot," he said to David. "You left this behind yesterday," and he handed over the precious map. Then, as he rode away, he called over his shoulder, "Cheerio for the present, and thank you all."

"I'll send on your bicycle, young lady," Mr Clancy said. "And thanks to all. You're welcome over at Three Oaks any time."

Half asleep and bitterly cold, the Lone Piners went back to Clun. The cyclists, with Penny on Jon's crossbar, got there first, of course, but Peter was not very far behind. They waited for her by the front gate and then crept up the steps, across the long hall and up the stairs to their rooms.

Just as David and Jon were crawling thankfully into bed for the third time that night, Tom put his head round the door.

"Just thought you'd like to know that Dickie doesn't seem to have moved. Hope Jenny is as lucky with Mary. Good night, chaps! I don't know how we shall ever get up in the morning. If those kids are really noisy and difficult I'll send 'em to you, David. Good morning!"

Chapter 8

Into Action

The routine at Keep View was badly upset the next morning. Poor Agnes tried again and again to wake the Lone Piners, but only the twins came down for breakfast at the proper time.

"Just you go out there and bang that gong again, Master Richard," she said in despair as she put the plates of porridge in the hatch, "I know there's many a time I've told you not to play with it, but *this* time you can bang it to your heart's content, for I don't know what's come over them all this morning ... Anyone might think they'd all been up all night, except you two precious lambs."

Here Mary smiled a little and then, as she realized the significance of the housekeeper's last words, looked over at her twin very meaningly. But Dickie was only thinking of the gong. He took off his coat and rolled up the sleeves of his pullover, and strode out into the hall. There he met Mr Cantor coming down the stairs in his absurd green plus-fours.

"Good morning, Richard," he beamed. "If you are about to sound the gong again you need not bother, as I heard it the first time and need no further summons to what, I am sure, will prove to be a delicious and satisfying breakfast."

"Acksherly, Mr Cantor," Dickie replied, "I wasn't going to bang it for you. Agnes says I can bang it for the others 'cos they won't get up this morning ... So if you'll kindly excuse me I'm goin' to bang it and crash it as hard as I've always wanted to ... P'raps you'd rather go in and shut the door, 'cos I'm going to make the biggest noise there's ever been in this house."

Mr Cantor looked slightly alarmed and hurried into the dining-room as Mary came out. Dickie picked up the great gong-stick lovingly, but Mary stopped him before he could strike the first blow.

"Just a minute, Dickie. Did you hear what Agnes said?"

"She said I could biff this old gong and I'm jolly well going to biff it off the stand. Watch me!"

"Stop a minute, Dickie. Agnes said that anyone might think the others had been up all night. I believe they have. I just couldn't make Jenny wake up. Penny and Peter *can't* wake up. I went in and tried. You tried the boys, didn't you?"

Dickie lowered the gong-stick.

"Do you really think they've been out somewhere without us all night, Mary?"

His twin nodded. "I bet they have."

Dickie ran for the stairs, flourishing the gong-stick.

"Come on!" he shouted. "I'll *beat* them out of their beds with this. We'll make them confess. We'll make them sorry to leave us out of things. Gosh, Mary! The great hulking beasts. Those boys are the worst. They're bullies. Come on!" and here he fell over the top stair with a crash, picked himself up and dashed along the landing until he reached David's room. Then, with Mary panting only a few steps behind him, he raised the gong-stick with both hands and crashed it against the panels of the door. The stick broke and the padded head fell off. During the brief silence that followed a sleepy voice from inside the room muttered:

"All ri'. Thank you, Agnes. Shan't be a sec."

"Di-di-did you hear that, Mary?" Dickie stuttered with tears of fury in his eyes. "Did you hear him say, 'Thank you, Agnes?'"

Mary nodded happily. She was enjoying the situation, which was certainly of her own making. She had stooped for the head of the gong-stick, and Dickie snatched it from her as she flung open the door.

Jon was still sleeping, but it must have been David who had answered, for he stirred as the twins ran over to his bed.

"Get up, you beast," Dickie yelled as he snatched back the bedclothes. "Get up and tell us the truth ... If you don't tell us everything we'll go straight down and tell Agnes you've been out all night. Have you?"

David sat up in astonishment.

"Hullo, Dickie. What's wrong?"

"What's wrong!" his brother yelled as he danced with fury. "It's past nine o'clock and you've been out all night without us and you've jolly well got to tell us what you've been doing this instant minute."

Mary was watching her twin with astonishment and admiration. She had never seen him quite like this before and was thoroughly enjoying it. Suddenly Dickie wheeled on her.

"Go and do the same to those girls," he shouted. "Yank 'em out of bed. Make them tell you. Chuck water at them. Go on! I'll do Tom next and then I'll come in to them."

Mary ran.

David reached for the bedclothes and began to pull them round him.

"No, you don't," Dickie yelled as he fought to pull them down again. "You beast, David. Have you been out all night without us? Jus' tell me now. That's all we want to know. That's all I ask. Jus' tell me the truth."

David was wide awake now. He put out a strong arm and scooped up his small brother on to the bed beside him. The tears were streaming down Dickie's face although he did not know it as he fought and struggled to escape.

"Steady, old chap!" came David's calm voice. "What's wrong? Just sober down a bit and I'll tell you everything … Don't be a little idiot, Dickie … Stop struggling else you'll get hurt … That's better."

Then Jon sat up in bed.

"What's all the row about? Can't you let a chap sleep?"

Dickie brushed his hand across his eyes and stopped fighting. The truth was that he had a tremendous love and admiration for his big brother and would have stood up to anybody in the world who dared to say anything against him.

"Well, David," he gulped. "It's time to get up and Agnes is mad with you and the porridge is getting cold and we want to know if you've been having adventures without us, 'cos if you have…"

David grinned, and pushed him off the bed.

"Just get off my legs and I'll get up ... Jon! Get up and hurry. We'd better go down in our dressing-gowns."

"Well, have you?" Dickie persisted. "That's all I ask. Have you been out in the night without us?"

Before David could answer Jon reached for his glasses.

"Just trot off downstairs, Dickie, like a good little boy and we'll tell you all about it after breakfast."

"Don't you dare to call me a good little boy," Dickie spluttered. "You're the worst of the lot, Jon. I bet it was your idea to leave us behind. I loathe you. We both loathe you an'..."

David reached for his dressing-gown behind the door, put his hands on Dickie's shoulders and gently pushed him into the passage. At that moment there was a startled yell from the next room and Mary shot out and joined her twin.

"I did it, Dickie. I've *soused* them both with cold water. Jenny wasn't much trouble. She was *terrified* of me. She's getting up."

David shut the door behind him.

"Get on, you two, and no more nonsense. This is serious and you can really help us now. We'll tell you everything as soon as we can but it's up to you both now to do something for the Club ... Go and keep Agnes quiet. Say we're very sorry and will be down in five minutes, and if Mr Cantor is in the dining-room get him out of the way so that we can talk. We shall want your help badly today and I promise we'll tell you everything. Do this for us, chaps, will you?" Mary looked him straight in the eyes, reached for Dickie's hand – something she did now only when it was very important — and led him downstairs.

A few minutes later six woe-begone and bedraggled Lone Piners joined the twins at the breakfast table. Mr Cantor, after a very curious glance, passed them in the hall as they came downstairs. They all muttered a greeting and slipped into the room, hoping that Agnes would not be waiting for them. Dickie and Mary had done their work well, for they were alone and a plate of porridge was ready at each place at the table.

The twins were standing in front of the fire and Mackie was lying at their feet. His tail thumped a welcome as the others came in.

"Now then," Dickie said. "Buck up and tell us. We've let you off this time, but we won't again."

Mary giggled. "You do all look funny! At least, most of you look awful. What's the matter with your hair, Penny? Have you been out swimming?"

Penny's eyes widened. It was a long time since she had been wakened with cold water and she wasn't feeling her best this morning, but before she could reply Peter intervened.

"For goodness' sake let's sit down and have breakfast and do the squabbling afterwards. Is Agnes very mad with us?"

"She was," Dickie said, "but I think we've fixed her. We said we'd go and fetch our breakfast and clear it away and everything. You've just jolly well got to be thankful to us for that ... Come on then – let's start."

"I don't think I want any breakfast," Jenny wailed. "I don't feel too good."

"Just sit down and try," Penny snapped. Then, "Sorry, Jenny, but we none of us feel too bright and we've just got to keep Agnes sweet."

At this Tom, who up to now had said nothing, began to roar with laughter.

"What a lot of fools we all look!" he spluttered. "Have any of you seen yourselves? I'm hungry anyway and I bet Jenny is when she begins … Just tell those kids everything, David, while we eat. I reckon they ought to know. After all it was Dickie and his famous jangling bell who really started us off."

They all – except Dickie and Mary who looked at each other pityingly – began to laugh too and settled down to their porridge. In between mouthfuls David told the twins of the night's adventures. He was often interrupted because they were determined to keep Agnes out of the dining-room if they could and the only way to do this was to keep running to the kitchen and waiting on themselves. But they managed it somehow and Mary once reported that she could hear the housekeeper humming dolefully upstairs.

"… Then Penny had an adventure on her own and she'll tell you that when her mouth is empty. But you do see, kids, don't you, that we couldn't very well drag you in as well?"

"We don't see," Mary said tersely. "You didn't even ask us to the meeting and we're going to make a new rule which says a meeting isn't a meeting at all unless we're all there."

"If we don't get that rule in," Dickie added, "we're through … We'll bust it all up."

David looked helplessly at Peter who had so often saved a situation like this, and she rose to the occasion once again.

"Listen, twins. I know you're mad with us and we all know why. But just think for a minute. It looks as if we're in for just about the biggest adventure we've ever had, and when I saw that van last night I knew we'd got to do something quickly and quietly, but we've hardly done a thing yet. We didn't have a proper Club meeting last night or else you'd have been there, but it *was* you, Dickie, and your cleverness, that got us on to the track of Mr Cantor and there's lots more important things for you and Mary to do, aren't there, David?"

David nodded in silent admiration.

"The truth is," Peter went on before either of the twins could speak, "that we are all tired out this morning, and there wasn't any sense last night in tiring everybody. We've got to have some reserves you know. Every general who fights a battle has to have reserves, doesn't he, Jon?"

"He does," Jon agreed solemnly. "Definitely he does. And in this case the twins are our reserves."

"Jolly lucky we've got them," Penny murmured, crumbling her toast.

"No good without 'em," Tom put in. "We couldn't do a thing."

"So you see, twins," Peter continued hurriedly, "that we can't do without you and that it's lucky for us that you're fresh and strong and cunning this morning ... Now let's clear away these things and make ourselves look a bit respectable ... You boys look absolutely disgusting and you never even apologized to us girls."

David looked a bit sheepish at this attack, but before he or the twins could reply to Peter there was an extraordinary interruption. Macbeth, from the hearth-rug, suddenly growled and Mary pointed dramatically to the window.

"Look!" she squealed. "A policeman. He's coming here."

"Have you been telling us the truth?" Dickie said. "'Cos if you haven't I hope he's come for you," and then there was a tremendous knock on the front door and Mackie started barking furiously. Jon jumped up.

"I'll go," he said quietly, and then from outside in the hall they heard him call up the stairs, "Don't bother, Agnes. I'll go. I saw who it was."

Then they heard the front door open and the rumble of voices. Penny looked excited, Jenny scared, Tom indifferent and David worried. The twins were engaged with Mackie who was struggling and growling, but before any of them could say anything the door opened again and Jon came in followed by a very large, red policeman who removed his helmet and mopped his forehead, although the morning was remarkably cold.

"The constable," Jon began, "is making some enquiries and thinks some of us may be able to help him. I've told him we'll do anything we can of course, but it all sounds very mysterious just when we've come to a quiet place like Clun for a little holiday … Mary! Keep that dog quiet … Come in, constable, and we can close the door."

Penny jumped up with a beaming smile.

"Wouldn't you – er – care to sit down or something? Do come nearer to the fire."

"No thank you, miss, but kindly meant all the same I know … This is just a matter o' routine as you might say, and knowing you youngsters were getting around a bit I am acting from instructions received and am to enquire if any of you have seen a gipsy caravan in these parts," and here he looked at them solemnly and flicked over a page of his notebook with a wetted thumb.

The Lone Piners looked at him in astonishment and Mackie growled again as the door opened quietly and Mr Cantor came in.

Dickie gasped and then said, "Ow!" as David kicked his ankle. Jenny's knees gave way and she collapsed on to the sofa, and then there was a long silence. Eventually Mr Cantor cleared his throat softly and said, "Dear me! How very remarkable. A police constable to be sure, and at breakfast too – how very odd! Can I be of any assistance to you, constable? My name is Cantor and I am staying here on vacation for a short while. I see you are being entertained by my young friends."

The policeman put his helmet down among the breakfast things.

"Thank you, sir, but I was just enquiring whether any of these young ladies and gentlemen happened to have seen a caravan about these parts – and most partickeler a red and yellow caravan looking very bright and colourful," he finished unexpectedly.

"And are the dwellers in the red and yellow caravan wanted by the police?" Mr Cantor asked as he stroked his shining bald head.

"I have been instructed to make general enquiries, sir, regarding any caravans and this one in partickeler."

182

"Then perhaps I can be of assistance to you, constable. It so happens that I did see a red and yellow caravan yesterday on the hills up by the stone circle … It would perhaps be more seemly if, later on, I stepped along and saw you and gave you full details. I shall indeed be very pleased to do so for if there is trouble I am convinced that gipsies will be involved. All gipsies are thieves and should not be at large."

"That's not true!" Peter said angrily. "Not all gipsies are thieves. We know two who live in a red and yellow caravan and they're the very finest people. It's just not fair to say that, Mr Cantor … And anyway the caravan we know is miles away by now, 'cos some of us met it going away the day we came. You don't want to waste your time looking for gipsies, Mr Policeman! You look for furniture vans that drive about here in the middle of the night if you want to find the stolen sheep."

"This is very interesting indeed," Mr Cantor said after another shocked silence. "Perhaps you could explain yourself, Petronella? What is all this about sheep stealing? Perhaps you can enlighten us, constable?"

"Well, sir, I can't say that's rightly in my province as you might say. What I got to do is to make general enquiries about this caravan, and here's this young lady says it was seen going *away* and you now tells me you saw it right handy here, and it don't make sense to me."

"But I do assure you, my dear man," Mr Cantor began testily, and then was interrupted by David:

"Excuse me, sir, but I do think we're wasting a lot of the constable's time and I expect he's very busy." He turned to the policeman. "I think we can tell you about the gipsy caravan we saw two days ago, but I think you should tell us why you want to know. We've got some good gipsy friends and whatever Mr Cantor says – and he can't possibly know them – every single one of us here, and our parents too, will tell you they'd never steal anything."

Then he turned to Mr Cantor, who was still standing just inside the door stroking his chin. "And I think we ought to tell you, sir, in case the policeman won't, that we know there is sheep stealing going on all round the country here and two decent gipsies in a caravan couldn't possibly organize that! You ask the constable, sir. He knows all about the sheep stealing and he can't do anything about it because there's only one of him and he can't be in two places at once. But there's lots of us and we're going to do all we can to help our friends whatever anybody says."

"And we're not going to have our friends accused of being thieves when they're not here to prove they're not," Peter, very pink in the face, said impetuously. "It's just not fair. Anyway, we know how the sheep are being stolen. I tell you I *saw* that furniture van myself last night in the moonlight."

Then, before Jon could stop her – and he tried to interrupt – Peter poured out the story of the van and the two rough men she had met on her journey to Clun, and of the van she had seen last night in the moonlight.

"How do you know it was the same van?" Mr Cantor asked quietly.

"Well, I don't know for certain," Peter admitted, "but it looked the same shape although the one last night had

Manchester on the side and the first one had another name ... At least I think it did."

Mr Cantor glanced significantly at the policeman, who now looked more bewildered than ever but shut up his notebook.

"I'll be glad if you'd step in at my house some time, sir," he said. "At your convenience o' course. I have the young lady's statement about when the caravan was first seen ... I'd like to lay my hands on those two gipsies."

"But aren't you going to do anything about the van?" Peter gasped. "Don't you believe me?"

Mr Cantor opened the door.

"If you will just direct me to your house, constable," he said, "I will make a point of coming along to have a word with you later." Then he turned to the Lone Piners grouped round the fire and spoke specially to Peter. "Of course, my dear young lady, we all believe you met a van and two men on your way here. Of course we do."

"But last night," Peter repeated. "I saw it again last night, I tell you, some time after midnight. It was rushing up the street outside. I saw it clearly in the moonlight."

Mr Cantor smiled gently. "Quite so, my dear. You thought you saw it, but nobody else did. You were tired out after a long day and dreamed it no doubt," and he closed the door behind the policeman, who followed him out into the hall.

"Did you hear what he said?" Peter gasped. "He called me a liar. I'll never, never forgive him. I hate him. I've always hated him. I believe he's absolutely wicked ... David! Why don't you go after him and do something to

185

him? Are you going to just stand there and let him call me a liar?"

Even as she was speaking David strode across to the door, but Jon stopped him before he could open it.

"Just a sec," he said quietly. "Let's be sensible. We'll get our own back on him, Peter, don't you worry. Nobody is allowed to call a Lone Piner a liar and get away with it, are they, Dickie? ... Be quiet just for a minute and see what he's going to do, and then we'd better make our plans."

David went across to Peter and touched her arm.

"Sorry about that, Peter. Jon's right, though. We won't forget. I won't forget, I promise."

She gave him a grateful glance and then turned away so that he could not see the tears in her eyes as Jon, his ear against the closed door, whispered, "He's shut the front door and gone upstairs, and I bet he doesn't want to see us again for a little. Now, David, what's the best thing to do?"

"We'd better get dressed first," David replied, "and while we're doing it will you girls do everything you can to keep Agnes sweet? Go and help her do bedrooms or something and tell her we'll do ours – or better still, you come and do them as soon as we're dressed ... Come on, Jon, and for goodness' sake, Tom, cheer up."

"Just a minute, if you please," Mary said coldly, slipping in front of the door. "I s'pose you think you're all very clever, but we haven't finished about *us* yet."

"Yes, we have, darling," Penny laughed as she gave her a hug. "We can't do without you, but we can't waste time squabbling either. Come and help us," and rather surprisingly Mary gave her a beaming smile and left

Dickie looking slightly sulky on the hearthrug.

Fifteen minutes later the dining-room was clear and the beds made and all the Lone Piners, including Macbeth, were climbing the Castle hill. The morning was bright and cold and a steady, searching wind from the north-east stung their cheeks and seemed to blow their fatigue and short temper away. The twins and Tom were teasing Mackie with a piece of stick and Jenny's gay laughter at their antics echoed back from the ruins above them. Only Peter looked depressed, for try as she would she could not forget the cruel, unfair way in which Mr Cantor had sneered at her in front of them all just when she was trying to help.

"David," she said suddenly, "I've had an awful idea. We've all walked out of the house to make some plans and left Mr Cantor alone and unguarded. He may go off anywhere and do anything, and we won't know where he is—"

"Gosh, Peter, you're right! What fools we are. If I'd thought for a minute I'd have realized that and we'd have met in one of the bedrooms or the dining-room and kept a look-out for him ... We'd better go back at once."

"Let's talk here," Jon said. "Peter may be right, but I've had enough of Keep View this morning, and it's grand out here. Let's chance Mr Cantor for a few minutes just for the sake of some fresh air."

But it was another twenty minutes before they agreed on a plan, and then it was really three separate plans. David, and later Jon and Peter, were insistent about this.

"It's no use us trying to do everything together," he said. "We've got too many things to do and too many

187

people to watch. I'm sure Peter is right and that Mr Cantor should be shadowed every minute. Everything about him is suspicious, and he behaved disgustingly this morning when he tried, first of all, to blame Reuben and Miranda for something he knew nothing about…"

"Or pretended he knew nothing about," Penny put in.

"… Yes, that's true enough. Maybe he knew more than we think. Then there was that business of getting the policeman away from us so that we shouldn't tell him any more."

"P'raps we ought to go back and tell him some more," Jenny suggested.

"Alan told us not to go to the police," Jon said, "and now I've seen the policeman I'm not surprised! David and Peter are right when they say Cantor has got to be watched, and I know who ought to watch him."

"Not me," Penny said promptly. "I'm sick of him."

"Not you," Jon agreed. "We want somebody with more guile than you've got. No, this is a job for the twins and Mackie."

And so it was agreed. Mary and Dickie were prepared to argue at first, but after a little they swore most solemnly that they would never let him out of their sight.

"Shall we go at once?" Mary said. "Suppose he's escaped us already? And what are you others going to do, and how shall we know where you are?"

"Whatever we do we shall have to go back to the house," David said, "because if we go out on the hills again, which I think we should, we must tell Agnes we'll be out all day and get some food … I'm not very keen to be the one to tell Agnes, by the way."

"The only ones she likes are the twins," Peter said. "They're the favourites; they always were. I suggest they and Mackie go back at once. If Mr Cantor has gone out they'll soon know, and it will be up to them to try and follow him. All right, we know you can! Whatever we all do, let's arrange to meet here, at H.Q. Three, at sunset. If Cantor is in, twins, when we get back we shall understand if you don't leave him and we won't come into the room and interfere if we can help it."

Dickie cocked his head and spoke gruffly out of the side of his mouth. "OK, pards. Leave it to us! The ruins at sunset," and set off down the hill. Mary turned and waved as she followed him.

"Try and let us know what you're all going to do," she called.

After a little more discussion it was agreed that the three girls should go over to "Bury Fields" and see if they could do anything to help the Dentons.

"At any rate Mrs Denton will be pleased to see us," Penny said, "and we can tell Alan all about Mr Cantor. Do you think we should do that, David? Shall we tell him how he behaved to the policeman?"

"I don't see why not. Tell him the whole story and that we'll do anything we can to help them."

"That's all very well," Tom said, "but we've got to sleep some time. Don't think I'm not enjoying myself, because I am, but for goodness' sake don't suggest that I sit up on guard again all night."

"What are you boys going to do, then?" Peter asked.

"We'll explore in daylight as much as we can. We'll look for signs of that van of yours, Peter, and if we get a chance I want to go back to that house with the grey walls and see if I can find out who lives there … Anyway, we all meet here, whatever happens, at sunset."

"Now for Agnes," Jon said grimly. "I think we'd better leave her to the girls, don't you, David?"

As they walked up the steps of Keep View they caught sight of Mary through the lounge windows. They couldn't be sure, but it looked as if she was sitting on the arm of Mr Cantor's chair by the fire.

Macbeth barked as they crept into the hall and then Dickie slipped round the door.

"OK," he whispered out of the side of his mouth. "We got him. He's hardly struggling yet. He's telling Mary a story – a FAIRY STORY!" and he almost collapsed with stifled laughter. When he had recovered a little, and after a loud hiccup, he winked broadly and said, "And what are you going to do?"

They beckoned him to the foot of the stairs, whispered their plans and pushed him back to the lounge. As he opened the door they heard Mary's clear little voice saying:

"Oh, Mr Cantor! How absolutely wizard! I mean he was a wizard wizard in that story, wasn't he? Thank you *so* much…"

They met Agnes at the door of the bathroom and she looked at them very suspiciously.

"There's some in this house this morning with guilty consciences," she began, "and I'm the one who'd be liking to know what mischief you're all up to … Don't forget I'm trusting you, Mister David, and that your father and mother are trusting you, too … All the beds

190

made, I see, and a mess of water on the floor and on the sheets in the girls' room ... I'd be liking to know what's going on?"

The boys grinned rather sheepishly, and then the girls took charge of Agnes and led her downstairs to the kitchen. Half an hour later they came out triumphantly laden with parcels of sandwiches and flasks of hot coffee. The twins were still busy with Mr Cantor as they all crept out of the front door, but Mary must have heard them pass, for as David looked back from the steps she appeared with her back to the window and waggled her hand at them.

The sun was high now and the wind stronger and colder as they crossed the bridge and climbed the hill. They had agreed that bicycles would be more trouble than they were worth, so they walked steadily until they reached the signpost at the cross-roads where they had all met in the early hours of the morning.

"Looks different now," David said; "but do you girls think you can find your way? I've found that 'Grey Walls' place on the map, and we're going to get there presently and see if anything happens. But if you don't mind I think I ought to keep the map ... I don't see how you can find us if you want us, unless Alan can tell you how to get to 'Grey Walls' from this place. Come to think of it, though, you might upset something if you appeared on the scene, so you'd better keep away ... We all meet at the Castle about half-past four, anyway. Good luck!"

"Good luck to you," the girls called as they climbed over the gate, and "I hope you know how to read a map, David," Penny added.

When, a few minutes later, they turned round they could just see the three boys leaning over the gate, watching them. They waved and Peter whistled a Peewit call, and then they went on their way.

"Do you think we ought to have our sandwiches before we get there?" Jenny said. "I mean if Mrs Denton asks us to dinner we've either got to say we've had it or else offer to eat ours while she has hers. I think it's jolly difficult."

Eventually they found a little hollow on a hill-top. It was only a few yards from the track, but Peter said it reminded her of one at Hatchholt where she and David had once hidden and watched a woman spy, so they decided to eat their food in its shelter. The cold wind whistled over their heads, but they were protected from it, and as the little hollow was a sun-trap, they lay back on cushions of heather. Penny broke off a sprig and put it in her hair.

"Do you realize how dry this is?" she said. "I bet it's as dry as it is in summer and with this wind it would burn more quickly. Funny that we don't think of fires as much in the winter, isn't it? I wouldn't like to be caught up here in a fire."

They basked and talked for a little, and it was not surprising that they went to sleep. They all slept so soundly that the motor-cycle carrying a man wearing dark goggles which bumped along the track not many yards away did not wake them until he was out of sight. Then Penny looked at her watch and found that it was nearly two o'clock.

"Do you think we've slept at our posts?" she yawned.

"Lots of men have been shot for that. I was dreaming of shooting and thought the bangs were real. Either of you hear anything?"

Peter looked worried. "Funny you should say that. I thought some noise woke me, but I can't think what it would be up here … We'd better go. Come on. The haversacks are much lighter now."

They made no mistake over direction in daylight, and within a quarter of an hour were at the top of the hill overlooking the farmyard of Bury Fields. The place looked deserted.

Peter strained her eyes.

"There's something black against the wall of the barn just inside the gate," she said. "I'm sure it wasn't there yesterday, or else it's something that's been moved."

"There's smoke coming from the chimney," Jenny said. "Let's go down."

When they got a little nearer they saw that the black object was a motor-cycle, and then suddenly they noticed a figure, which was probably the rider, cross the yard. There was something furtive about the way in which he walked that made the girls quicken their pace and then start to run down the hill. The man disappeared round one side of the house and then reappeared by the back door just as they reached the farmyard gate. The door must have been open, for they could hear Mrs Denton's agitated voice say quite distinctly:

"You get out of here, Sam Quickset. You wouldn't dare come into the yard if Mr Alan was at home, and you know you wouldn't … What are you doing in these parts

I'd like to know…? And don't you dare to threaten me either … Just get off these premises."

Even while she was speaking, Penny, followed closely by the other two, dashed into the kitchen. Mrs Denton was standing with her back to the fire facing a man in a dirty cycling suit and leather helmet. A pair of goggles dropped from his fingers as he wheeled round to face the girls as they ran in. Penny's temper was up and she faced the intruder as if she was as big as he was.

"Just you get out!" she stormed. "Get out now before Mr Denton catches you here. Don't you worry, Mrs Denton. Alan is on his way down. We were talking to him just now."

The man stooped for the goggles, turned and brushed past Peter and Jenny and dashed out into the yard. The engine of the motor-cycle started into life with a roar, and then they watched him wobble out of the gate and disappear round the corner of the house.

"He didn't like us much, did he?" Jenny said. "I certainly felt very brave, but maybe I'd be as brave as Penny if my hair was as red."

"Thank you, my dears," Mrs Denton said. "That was well done. Have you really seen my son?"

Penny shook her head. "Sorry, I made that up. I heard you say that he wouldn't dare appear if Alan was here. Who is that man? He looks horrid."

"He is, my dear. He's a real bad lot. Name of Sam Quickset, and used to work for us. We caught him stealing more than once, but we had nobody else to help just then and we gave him another chance, but he was worse next time, so Alan threw him out when he was rude to me. He's a bad lot, and he swore he'd never forget and that he'd get his own back one day. I'm right thankful you came in when you did. And now sit you all down and make yourselves comfortable, and there'll be a cup of tea in a minute … I have clean forgot your name, my dear," she added, turning to Peter, "though I'll never forget the colour of your hair and your eyes. Is there anything I can get you, for you look poorly and very white? Are you all right, my dear?"

Peter sat down thankfully and said she was all right. "Just puffed a bit with running." Penny looked at her suspiciously, but turned back to Mrs Denton as the latter said, "Alan is out to fix a meeting of all the farmers twenty miles around, for we lost more sheep last night. 'Twas as soon as Alan rode over to the road with you, my dear. Somebody must have been watching, but we can't tell how they got 'em away … Let's not worry about that for a bit and enjoy a cup of tea now."

As soon as she turned her back Penny came over to Peter.

"What's wrong, Peter? You look awful."

"Sorry, Penny. I'm all right, really. Just a bit of a shock. That man on the motor-bike was the driver of the van I met on the way to Clun. I'd recognize his squint anywhere."

Chapter 9

Offa's Dyke

When the twins had left the others at the top of the Castle Hill they both realized the importance of the job they had been given. To watch Mr Cantor, to spy on him, and to report on his actions to the Club was something which they both felt they could do better than anybody else. And in this they were right, and for once they did not feel that the others were taking an unfair advantage of them. In their short lives they had had some remarkable adventures together, and although on principle they always made a fuss when they were not included in anything the others did, they were now old enough and sensible enough to know that David would not have asked them to do this if he had thought any of the others could have done it better.

They padded down the hill side by side, with Macbeth gambolling between them, and did not speak until they reached the street. Then:

"Don't let's be out of breath," Mary panted. "It won't be too good if we can't speak to him properly."

"Do you think he'll be there?" Dickie said as he fell into step beside her. "What shall we do if he's escaped?"

"If he has we'll follow him to the end of the world," Mary replied dramatically. "Don't worry, twin. He can't go far … And I'll tell you something else. If his bike's still in the shed we'll take the valve out of a tyre so that he can't escape that way … If we have to go with him anywhere I'd rather walk, wouldn't you?"

Dickie agreed, so that as soon as they reached Keep View they crept round the side of the house to the bicycle shed. Very delicately he unscrewed the valve from the rear tyre of the bicycle with the jangling bell, rolled off the all-important scrap of rubber tubing, and then replaced the metal parts.

"He won't get far on that," Mary observed with considerable satisfaction. "Now let's go and see if he's still in the house. Do you think he's as bad as Peter thinks, Dickie?"

"I'm sure he is. I believe he's the worst villain we've ever had. I feel like seeing him. Come on!"

The telephone at Keep View was in the hall, and when they opened the front door Mr Cantor had just replaced the old-fashioned receiver on the hook. He glanced up quickly as they came in, and just for a moment he didn't look at all like Mr Cantor. It was very odd, and they both remembered it afterwards, but as he turned to see who had opened the door he seemed younger and more alert. It was only a glimpse of something different, but the twins stopped on the threshold and were, for a long moment, silent.

Then the Mr Cantor they knew beamed at them through his heavy spectacles and the strange spell was broken.

"Richard and Mary! Ha! … Perhaps you can tell me whether it is very cold outside? I was just wondering whether I should venture out this morning in the sunshine for a little."

"What for?" Dickie asked rather rudely as his sister nudged him and said:

"Oh, Mr Cantor, I do hope your cold is really better this morning … I was only saying to my brother – this brother, I mean, my twin – when we came along the street that I did hope you would be at home and that your cold was really better."

Before their victim could answer, Dickie took up the tale.

"We really are very pleased indeed that you're here, Mr Cantor. You see, we're rather lonely this morning, and we did hope you would be here when we got back."

Mr Cantor looked a little puzzled, but beamed at them through his spectacles again.

"Lonely? But that is a very extraordinary statement to make, Richard! How could you be lonely? I have rarely met two children who were less lonely. Where are the others?"

"Well, you see, Mr Cantor," Mary explained with eyes modestly downcast, "it's rather difficult and horrid for us to 'splain to you, but I s'pose we must be brave and try and tell you, just because you are so nice to us."

"Oh, yes, sir," Dickie chimed in, "we've always said that, Mary and me have … We keep on telling them how nice and kind you've been to us."

Mary gulped and went on bravely:

"It's just because we're so small that the others are so unkind to us and cast us out sometimes."

"They don't always *mean* to be unkind," Dickie

explained generously. "It's just like Mary says. They're much bigger, you see, and sometimes they do things that we can't do just because we're small."

"An' this morning it was like that, dear Mr Cantor. Shall we go in by that lovely fire and we'll tell you all about it?" and Mary sidled over and took his hand.

"But, my dear child," the victim protested, "it's very good of you to say such nice things of me, but I don't think that just now I can spare the time to listen…"

"I don't s'pose we shall be very long telling you, sir," Dickie said as he opened the door, "but of course you just couldn't understand how wonderful it is for Mary and me to have a friend like you."

Almost without realizing what had happened, Mr Cantor found himself seated in the most comfortable chair in the lounge before a roaring fire. During the next hour it seemed to him that either Dickie or Mary was sitting on the arm of his chair, ready to light a fresh spill for his pipe, to fetch anything he wanted, or indeed, as he realized later, to see that he didn't move out of the room!

As soon as he was comfortably seated Mary went on with the tragic story of their ill-treatment.

"Those big ones don't ezackly *bully* us, Mr Cantor, but they do just jolly well tell us when we're not wanted."

"I think that's the most awful thing of all," Dickie added in a choking voice as he gazed into the leaping flames. "Not to be wanted, I mean. Have you ever been not wanted, Mr Cantor? We're not very old yet, but we do know how awful that is."

"We do hope it's never like that with you," Mary went

on, "but of course it couldn't be. You'll always be wanted, dear Mr Cantor. Nobody could help loving you."

Mr Cantor cleared his throat noisily and polished his glasses, and moved as if he was going to get up. At once Mary leaned across him from her perch on the arm of his chair, and pulled back the cuff of his coat-sleeve so that she could see his wrist-watch.

"What a *lovely* watch, Mr Cantor. How proud you must be to have a watch like that … No. Please don't take it off for me to see … I like to look at it on you," and she laid her little grubby paw on his wrist so that it really was rather difficult for him to move.

"What I was going to say, my dears, was that I am quite sure you are exaggerating this – er – this feeling of being not wanted by your friends. Of course you are. Why, now I come to think of it, I have never seen you parted until today."

"You don't often see us, do you, sir," Dickie said promptly. "I mean, you don't know what they do to us sometimes when we are all out together."

"Only 'bout an hour ago," Mary took up the tale, "we were all just strolling along together makin' our plans."

"And what did you all intend to do today?" Mr Cantor enquired. "From what I hear, and from what you have already told me, it seems that you are getting to know this country very well."

"That's different," Dickie said quickly, with a meaning glance at his twin, who went on with her story.

"Anyway, dear Mr Cantor, we were just strolling along and talkin' a bit when absolutely suddenly, those two big boys – the one with glasses, and I expect you've noticed him, and the other one who's the worst and he's my brother – they suddenly turned round and said … What do you think they said, Mr Cantor?"

Mr Cantor had no idea. He was beginning to look as if he was hypnotized and all he could do was to shake his head feebly.

"We'll tell you," Dickie said. " 'You two get back home at once,' that's what they said, and we were absolutely innocent of everything, sir! Honest, we were. We hadn't done a thing."

" 'Just get back at once,' they said," Mary spoke huskily. " 'You're neither of you wanted here. You're not big enough … You'd better get back to Keep View and stay there quietly and play games with yourselves until we get back.' "

" 'And take that dog with you,' Jon said," Dickie added – and then, triumphantly, "And so here we are and you see, sir, that we just don't know where those bullies have gone or when they'll be back, and we don't even know if we'll get anything to eat today."

It was soon after this that they managed to persuade him to tell them a story. Dickie looked as if he might explode when they realized that it was to be a fairy story, but it was while Mr Cantor was becoming hopelessly mixed up that the other Lone Piners arrived and Dickie made his excuse to slip out of the room while Mary sat on the hearthrug at the feet of the story-teller and gazed at him with wide and innocent eyes. When Mr Cantor paused for a word or because he couldn't make up his mind what his characters were going to do next, Mary helped him. The wizard was entirely her own idea and together they gave him some remarkable adventures. When Dickie came back it was important for him to know what had happened while he had been away, so that took a little more time, and the Lone Piners had at least half an hour's start before Mr Cantor really got out of his chair and walked over to the window. He seemed a trifle warm and mopped his forehead with a spotted handkerchief as he stood looking out into the sunlit street.

"It seems to be a very pleasant, bright day now," he said, "and although I enjoy your most entertaining company I think I will be taking some exercise before the sun goes in."

"Oh, Mr Cantor," Mary wailed, "are you really going to leave us just when you were making us so happy? … I'd quite forgotten how lonely we were feeling, hadn't you, Dickie?"

Dickie agreed fervently, and then added, "Where were you thinking of going, sir? This is just about the time we take Mackie for a walk, so perhaps we could sort of go along together."

"I don't think so, Richard," Mr Cantor said hurriedly, "I would rather take my walk by myself, thank you."

"Oh, Mr Cantor!" Mary said as she sidled up to him. "Is the walk you're going really private? Don't you really *want* us to come with you?"

"I don't think you'd better come with me, my dears. I may be going for quite a long walk and I shouldn't like to get you into trouble by taking you too far."

"Please don't worry about that, sir," Dickie broke in. "We like long walks and you won't tire us out. We're used to long walks and Mackie always comes, too. Although he's quite a small dog and his legs are so short he can go a very long way … Acksherly we have to give him a lot of exercise and he's just got to have some today."

"So if you wouldn't really mind, dear Mr Cantor," Mary went on, "we would like it very much if you'd let us come with you … We were hoping that you could spare a scrap of time to show us some of the exciting places round here that you told us about the other day … O' course if you *really* wanted to do anything very private we'd just disappear quietly, wouldn't we, Dickie?"

"We wouldn't get in the way for anything," her twin agreed, "but we are very lonely today and it would be nice if you could go on being with us."

Mr Cantor moved from the window to the fireplace and stood for a moment looking down at them. Macbeth, on the hearth-rug, got up slowly, stretched, yawned prodigiously, and gently wagged his tail. He seemed to know that a walk was imminent and looked first at his master and mistress and then up at the stranger, whom he seemed to like. There was a long silence while Mr Cantor looked at the three of them; and just for a second or two Mary, who met his eyes steadfastly, had that same odd feeling that he was somebody else – or almost that he was two different people. Then he smiled and said, "Very well – you shall come with me. You shall help me explore and we will look for arrowheads. Let us ask the housekeeper for an early lunch."

Mary thanked him very prettily for this – so prettily that even her brother nearly blushed for her. It was while she was holding Mr Cantor's hand and looking up at him with wide eyes, that Dickie had another idea. Perhaps Mr

Cantor thought that if he promised them his company after lunch this would keep them quiet until then, while he slipped off to his room and planned something else. At all costs Dickie felt that they should go out together now before he changed his mind or escaped from them behind the door of his own room, because it would certainly be difficult for them to follow him there.

"We do think this is wonderful of you, sir," he said, "and we would like you to know how wonderful we think it is." Somehow Dickie felt that this was not as good a start as usual and he went rather red as he felt his sister looking at him in astonishment. He tried again.

"What I mean is that it's very kind of you to take us with you, but we would like you to make the whole adventure just the most wonderful thing that ever happened to us."

"Well, Richard," Mr Cantor beamed indulgently, "what would make the day perfect for you?"

"Let's start *now*, sir. While the sun is out and it's not too cold—"

"You must take care of yourself, Mr Cantor," Mary broke in. "We shall never forgive ourselves if your cold got worse."

"It's better to go out in the fresh air with a cold," Dickie continued hurriedly. "Mother always says that, unless you've got a temperature and we're sure you haven't got that … No, sir, please let's go now and have our lunch at an inn. Do you know that I've had a ginger pop at an inn but never anything to eat in one."

"But that's a marvellous idea, Dickie," Mary said. "*Please*, Mr Cantor, let's do that. There's a funny old inn on the road that leads up to the hills. I'd love to go in that. We could pretend we're weary travellers whose coach has broken down or been robbed by a masked highwayman, and that reaching the inn has saved our lives. P'raps we could sit in the chimney corner and watch the leaping flames while we sipped our wine."

Mr Cantor looked at her in surprise and then smiled again.

"That *is* a good idea, Richard," he said. "Wait here and I will be ready in five minutes. Will one of you tell Agnes that we shall be out to lunch?"

"Can I come up to your room and help you pack or anything?" Dickie asked as he edged towards the door.

"No," Mr Cantor said tersely for once. "You may not. Stay where you are."

Dickie ran his hand through his unruly hair and flopped on the sofa as soon as Mr Cantor had closed the door behind him.

"Gosh!" he gasped. "This is an awful strain, twin … Slip out and see if he's really going into his room. Buck up!"

Mary was back in thirty seconds.

"He's gone in and I heard him lock the door. Oh, Dickie! Do you think we've done the right thing so far? Do you think the others will think we're all right? We are doing all right, aren't we?"

"Well, we can't break down the door of his room," Dickie said reluctantly. "I wish we could. That would be fun … Do you know, twin, I think he quite likes us."

"Do you?" Mary replied. "I shouldn't think he could. I don't think I would if I was him … Do you think he's escaping out of the window? ... Quick, Dickie. You go outside and watch his window and I'll go and play about on the landing just in case he does come out and really means to take us with him."

"I'm feeling worn out before I start," Dickie said. "All right. I'll go. And you'd better tell Agnes what he said. She thinks we're mad anyway so I s'pose she won't try and stop us."

But Mr Cantor did keep his word and came out of his room so quietly that he caught Mary sitting on the top stair gazing pensively down into the hall.

"How you made me jump, Mr Cantor! I was just sitting here waiting for you."

Mr Cantor looked surprised again but said nothing beyond, "Is your brother ready, and have you told Agnes?"

Mary skipped down into the hall before him and opened the front door.

"Mackie went out," she explained. "He's very excited about all this too. He loves exploring ... I'll go and find Dickie."

When the three of them, and Macbeth, went out into the sunshine the clock on the church was striking noon. They crossed the bridge, and as they trudged up the long hill, Mr Cantor told them stories of the border lands of Wales and England which are called the Welsh Marches. He was wearing his plus-fours, a greenish tweed hat to match, and a pair of woollen mittens. He carried a heavy walking-stick and his boots had steel studs on the soles which made a cheerful, clinking sound on the hard road. They soon forgot how funny he looked and forgot too that he was a dangerous and suspicious man and that they had been given the special task of watching him.

He told them again of the forest of Clun and paused at a gate to show them how the bare slopes of some of the hills had been replanted after the Great War with baby fir trees and how, in the sunshine, these looked blue against the green of the larches. In one place their road cut through one of these young forests and when they looked through the wire fence they saw hundreds of rows of thousands of baby trees stretching away in the dark distance and standing up stiffly like soldiers on parade.

Then they went through another gate and he showed them an ordinary field where, he said, hundreds of flint arrowheads had been found in the past. Mary wanted to stay and find one for herself, but Dickie was hungry and wanted the inn.

When they reached *The Plough and Harrow* at last, they realized that Mary's description of it had been very true. From the outside it looked as if it was falling to pieces and the old signboard creaked eerily in the wind as they stood wondering whether anyone had ever ventured over the threshold before.

"I don't like it so much now I'm here," Mary admitted. "I wonder if they'll let us in? I should think a witch lives here."

Mr Cantor then tried the door which, to their surprise, was not locked and led the way into a stone-flagged passage. On the right they saw the flicker of flames through an open door and, with a cry of delight, Mary slipped ahead and sat down on a stool right inside a great fireplace as big as a small room, in which a fire of logs was burning. The floor was also of stone, polished and worn by generations of the men of Clun who trod these hills, and there was a great black table, quite as old, against the window. An old, old woman with beady black eyes who, in another age, would certainly have been thought a witch, stepped into the room behind them and looked at the children as if she did not like them there. Mr Cantor went out into the passage with her and closed the door, and strain their ears as they would, the twins could hear nothing beyond the rumble of voices.

"What shall we do?" Dickie hissed. "D'you think he's in league with her? We must get out somehow and listen to them."

Mary looked worried.

"We can't do that, Dickie. Don't be so silly. If we go out we shall give the game away … I say, Dickie, I'm not enjoying this adventure 'cos I'm beginning to like him."

"Like him?" her twin snorted. "How could you like a beast like that? Have you forgotten what he said about Reuben and Miranda? … Look out. Here he comes … Gosh! I wish I knew what he'd been talking about."

He must have raised his voice for the last sentence for Mr Cantor heard it as he opened the door. He smiled at Dickie, who fidgeted uncomfortably, as he said, "I can tell you that, Richard. I was talking about something to eat. That good woman has promised to find us something cold and a cup of tea."

"She doesn't look good to me," Mary said. "She looks like a witch. I bet she puts a spell on us so we can't move from this place and only a fairy prince can rescue me … P'raps you're a fairy prince in disguise, Mr Cantor?"

Their host looked really startled at this and dropped the pipe he was filling. Dickie dashed over to pick it up, but Mary noticed his strange look at her innocent remark.

They sat, an odd-looking trio, in the fireplace and enjoyed their cold lunch. Mackie had his share too and then lay with his nose on his paws, while Dickie and Mary sipped their hot, strong tea and Mr Cantor puffed his pipe. The flickering firelight glinted on his spectacles as he turned to answer Dickie, who said:

"Can we walk along that Offa's Dyke this afternoon? Will you show us that, please?"

"Why not? If you're not too tired … I apologize, my dears. Of course you wouldn't be too tired but perhaps the strangely-named Macbeth is too weary? He seems to like this fire."

"Oh, no," Mary said. "He'd like to see Offa's Dyke too."

So, a little later, they said "Goodbye" to the witch, who actually smiled at the twins and did a sort of curtsy to Mr Cantor who whispered something to her and then slipped a piece of paper into her hand. Both Dickie and Mary were very quiet as they walked on for they had seen him do this and did not like it. Somehow they both began to feel that they were not finding out very much about their victim, who seemed to be too clever for them. It was puzzling to know what else they could do for, owing to their determination not to let him out of their sight, it was impossible for them to discuss the problem.

Although he kept on talking as they walked – and everything he said was interesting – they did both notice that Mr Cantor was always looking about him very keenly. Once, after they had left the road and were walking on a track crossing a bare hillside, Mary interrupted him to say:

"What do you keep looking for, Mr Cantor? You're looking on the ground all the time you're talking."

"Arrowheads, my dear. You look too. You wanted one for yourself, didn't you?"

"You don't mind if I don't, do you, sir?" Dickie said. "We can't all be looking on the ground all the time, else we shan't get anywhere."

Soon after this they reached the top of a little hill and paused under two tall fir trees.

"Now," said Mr Cantor, "if I have brought you the right way by the map we should see the dyke from here."

"I see it," Mary said quietly. "It's grand. Look, Dickie!"

North and south of them for as far as they could see stretched the shape of the earthen wall with a deep ditch on the Welsh side that was built by an army of slaves over a thousand years ago.

"See how it goes up and down the hills but keeps straight," Dickie said. "Let's go and walk on it. You promised that we could, Mr Cantor," and he dashed off down the hill with Mary and Macbeth at his heels. Not until they had scrambled through the dead, brown bracken and scratched their knees on the heather in the great ditch did they realize that Mr Cantor was no longer with them.

"P'raps we'll see him when we get to the top," Mary gasped as she pulled herself up the steep sides of the bank, but when they reached the top and looked back at the two fir trees there was no sign of their guide.

"He's vanished, Mary. Or do you think he's tricked us? But where could he go?"

Mary was still struggling to get her breath and before she could answer Macbeth yelped excitedly from somewhere below them.

"Come here, Mackie," Dickie called. "You know you can never catch rabbits. Come here!"

But Mackie, who was in the big ditch, barked again and again, and Mary said, "I don't think it's a rabbit, Dickie. He generally dashes after rabbits and then comes back with his tail down looking rather silly. He sounds as if he's found something. Let's go down and see."

"It's more fun up here," Dickie complained. "Don't worry about him, Mary. He'll find us when he's ready … I wish I knew where old Cantor has gone. He's much more important."

"And why is old Cantor so important, may I enquire?" said a voice behind them, and they both reddened with shame as they turned and saw that their companion must have climbed the other side of the bank while they were calling Macbeth. He stood still, looking at them very seriously, and they both agreed later that he had really been very decent about Dickie's rudeness. Mary started to make some sort of lame excuse and then the dog started barking again and Mr Cantor said quietly, "Never mind that, Mary. What has your dog found? He sounds excited."

His voice sounded different. Firmer, more definite and not so much the voice of the elderly gentleman they thought they knew.

Dickie started to apologize. "I'm really very sorry, sir, for being so rude—"

"All right, Dickie" – and for the first time he said, Dickie and not Richard – "never mind that. Just run down there and see what's the matter with your dog."

The twins glanced at each other and obeyed him without another word.

This side of the bank was very steep and pitted with rabbit holes and in the ditch itself the dead bracken stood nearly as high as their heads. Mackie was still barking and as they turned in his direction Mary said suddenly, "Look, Dickie. This is funny. There's a little path here ... I mean it looks as if it's been used a lot. It's quite smooth."

"I wonder why there's a path here?" Dickie said. "P'raps Mackie has found something after all ... I say, Mary, is Mr Cantor" – and he said Mister Cantor this time – "is Mr Cantor still there? Don't let's both look. You look."

Mary glanced back. "Yes, he is. He's standing still watching us. I'll wave."

"Find the dog!" came his voice from above. Macbeth barked again in answer to Mary's call, so they hurried along the little track which twisted and turned between the bracken and heather. Suddenly Macbeth hurled himself at them, jumped up, licked their knees and urged them to follow him. A few more yards and they shared his unpleasant discovery, which was a dead sheep lying beside the track.

Mary stepped back and wrinkled her nose in disgust while Macbeth sat down and looked at them both for the admiration which he thought was due to him.

"It looks very dead, twin," Mary said at last.

"Not very long, I should think," Dickie replied doubtfully. "Somehow it looks sort of newly dead. I don't like it much."

"It's got a big A.D. painted on its side," Mary added. "I'm sorry for the poor thing. I wonder what killed it? Or p'raps it was just ill? … Mackie, darling! You made a lot of fuss about one dead sheep, didn't you? … Come on, Dickie. Let's get back. I don't like this."

"All right," her brother said slowly. "I don't like it either … Mary, just a sec! I think Mackie is interested in something else. He keeps on fidgetin' around … You know, Mary, I think it looks as if somebody else has been here. Everything is a bit squashed down and trodden on. Shall we explore a bit further down this path?"

Mary shivered. "No. Let's go back and find Mr Cantor. I don't like this place and I hate the wind and it's getting so cold that my teeth are chatterin'."

Before Dickie could answer Mr Cantor hailed them.

"What have you found, children? What about the dog?"

Dickie turned and called, "All right sir. We're coming back. Only a dead sheep."

His clear little voice carried far, for Mr Cantor heard his reply and shouted back.

"Stay where you are. I'm coming down."

But Dickie was still looking uneasy and puzzled. Macbeth too was very restless, and although he came back when he was called, he kept ranging round and sniffing along the track as if there was something else that he had to discover. And just at that very moment, while they stood in the great ditch of Offa's Dyke by a

213

dead sheep, with a bitter east wind whistling round them, waiting for Mr Cantor, the discovery was made.

Either the wind changed direction a trifle, or perhaps blew a little more strongly, for suddenly Macbeth, who had just returned from one of his short foraging expeditions and was panting with lolling tongue at Mary's feet, cocked his head, whined softly and barked just once.

Dickie looked down at him with interest.

"He can hear something we can't, Mary! What is it? Listen!"

They stood still. Above them the bitter wind stirred the dead bracken fronds and rustled through the dry heather. Once, twice came the distant sound of Mr Cantor's descent into the ditch and two large, black and evil-looking birds flapped slowly over their heads. Mary's teeth chattered, Macbeth whined again, and then they heard what he heard. Faint, from very far away it seemed, there came to them on the wind the sound of sheep bleating. They looked at each other without words as Macbeth barked again and dashed away down the track. Then Mr Cantor called to them, Mary answered in rather a shaky voice and Dickie said, out of the side of his mouth, "What shall we do, Mary? Shall we tell him? We must follow Mackie and get him back."

Mr Cantor was puffing rather heavily when he joined them. His green tweed hat had slipped to the back of his head and his spindly legs looked thinner than ever under his old-fashioned plus-fours. When he saw the sheep he took off his glasses and looked at it very carefully.

"So that is what your dog found? Where is he now?"

"He's run off down the path there," Mary said. "He's

excited … P'raps he's found something else."

"Let's go and see," Mr Cantor said in a voice which suddenly seemed quite different from his Keep View voice and they both turned obediently as he put a hand on their shoulders.

They walked a pace or two ahead of him down the unknown track but stopped when he said suddenly, "That man … That sheep farmer you know and went to warn last night. What's his name?"

"Alan Denton," Dickie said.

"Yes. Of course. A.D."

And just when they both realized that the dead sheep was probably one of those stolen from Alan, several things happened at once. First Mackie came bounding along the track and, as soon as he saw that they were following, turned to run back before Mary could catch him. As she grabbed for him she stumbled and fell forward into the heather at the side of the path. She was not hurt, but as Dickie put out a hand to help her he stopped half way and stooped to pick up something from the ground – a clean, white cigarette end.

"Someone else has been here…" he began, but before he could say more they all heard again, quite clearly, the bleating of sheep, followed by Macbeth's excited bark.

Mr Cantor cocked his head, smiled grimly, took off his glasses again and crammed them into his pocket.

"Buck up, kids," he said briskly. "Find that wonder dog of yours and the sheep he's found. I was sure he'd found something … Go on! Don't stand there gaping at me … Or let me get in front. I think maybe I'd better."

They were both staring at him in astonishment, for

suddenly the Mr Cantor they had known had disappeared and a stranger had taken his place in some miraculous way. They had no time to decide whether they liked this stranger or not, but he seemed to have a mind of his own and the way in which he said, "Buck up, kids," convinced them that he meant it. So they turned from studying him and dashed up the track so that they should be the first to share Macbeth's new discovery.

The ditch just here had very steep sides and narrowed as if they were running down a tunnel. Dickie sniffed as he ran and smelled sheep, and then they turned a sharp corner and realized that once again they had done something worth while for the Lone Piners.

They stopped short at the edge of a flat circle of grass which had been trodden and soiled by sheep. At the far side of the little clearing Macbeth was standing before a hurdle intertwined with bracken and heather and barking furiously.

He had always disliked sheep and chased them when he could and now the world, on the other side of the hurdle, consisted of nothing but the smell and noise of sheep and it made him very angry.

Mr Cantor joined the twins and stood still looking keenly about him while Mary dashed forward and picked up the protesting little dog.

"Look!" she called over her shoulder. "There's millions of sheep parked in here. Somebody has made a roof of these hurdle things and covered it all over with heather. It's all disguised and secret. Isn't Mackie a clever little darling to find it?"

"He is," Mr Cantor said quite grimly. "He certainly is.

I shouldn't be surprised if he doesn't get a medal – and both of you, too!"

"I think we've found the stolen sheep, haven't we, Mr Cantor?" Dickie asked. "It's jolly lucky we came to Offa's Dyke, isn't it? I s'pose we ought to go back and tell that policeman."

"I think so, Dickie," Mr Cantor said solemnly, with a twinkle in his eyes which was now more easily seen without his glasses. "I think perhaps it's time the police knew all about this. Come on. We're going and quickly."

The next half-hour was a nightmare to the twins. Within five minutes they were too tired to protest and could only follow Mr Cantor as he trotted back the way they had come. They climbed up to the hill with the two fir trees and here Mary said she had a bad stitch and could go no further.

"What are we dashing about like this for?" she panted with her hand against her side.

"Listen, kids," the surprising new Mr Cantor replied. "We've tumbled on something important and I'm in a hurry. It's getting dark and I don't want to leave you alone here. I've got to find a telephone quickly. Can you stick it a bit longer? You've been grand kids and I'm proud of you, but I'm in a hurry ... You wouldn't like me to leave you here, would you?"

"You couldn't," Dickie said between clenched teeth, "we'd follow you. What are we waitin' for?"

As they trotted along behind Mr Cantor, Mary whispered, "This is awful, Dickie. I'm all muddled up and don't know what side I'm on. What do you think he is and do you think we've done right?"

"We haven't left him, anyway," Dickie replied, "and we've kept our word there. Shan't we have something to tell them presently. It's nearly sunset and we ought to be home."

Mr Cantor really got along very quickly and it was soon obvious that he wasn't nearly as old as he had pretended to be at Keep View. Indeed it was soon obvious that he wasn't what he had pretended to be at all! They reached the road at last and turned in the direction of Clun, and after only a few minutes they heard a car coming along behind them.

"Stand each side of the road and put your hands out," Mr Cantor ordered. "We've got to stop him."

The car, an ordinary black saloon, pulled up at their signal and Mr Cantor stepped forward.

"Sorry," he said, "but thanks for stopping. Take me and these children into Clun as quickly as you can, please."

The man in the driving seat looked surprised at the tone of voice and was about to protest when Mr Cantor put a hand in his waistcoat pocket and produced something which the children could not see. But they did hear him say "Police" and "Hurry" before they were bundled into the back seat and Mr Cantor got in next to the driver.

"Gosh," Dickie whispered. "Did you hear that? He's a detective. A real one. I've never met one before! ... Mary, what do you think he'll do to us for fooling about with him like we did this morning?"

"P'raps we're completely in his power," Mary murmured as her head slipped back against the cushion at the back of the seat. "I'm so tired now I don't care much what he does to us, but I think after all he's turned out to be nice … I like dashing along like this, Dickie. It's fun! Here's the bridge already … Listen! He's stopping outside that policeman's house, so it must be true I suppose."

Then they found themselves on the pavement and Mr Cantor, who now had his glasses on again, spoke in his old voice.

"I am deeply indebted to you, Richard and Mary, for a most interesting and instructive afternoon. Thank you very much for your company. I shall see you all soon doubtless, but now I must fulfil the promise I made to the policeman this morning. And good day and thanks to you, my good sir, for your courtesy," he added to the mystified driver of the car, who drove off hurriedly before something else unexpected happened to him.

The twins watched the door of the policeman's house close behind Mr Cantor and then looked at each other in triumph.

"It was all worth it," Dickie said. "Just think of their faces when we tell 'em … Think of Jon's face when he knows that Mr Cantor was a detective all the time."

"Think how they'll look when we tell them how we found out!"

"Think how mad they'll be when they know it was Mackie and us who found the place where they hide the sheep … Oh, Mary! What a wonderful day it's been."

" 'Tisn't over yet, Dickie … Let's go up to the ruins … It's getting jolly dark so it must be time to meet the others. Come on … You'll have to walk now, Mackie. I can't carry you any farther."

They trudged up the hill in the dusk while the cruel, cold wind sang through the ruins of the Keep. Twice Dickie tried to whistle the Peewit's call but his signal was blown back to him and there came no answer from the bulky black shapes of broken stone above them.

Macbeth bounded ahead with a joyful bark and they heard a welcoming call which sounded like Jenny's. Two minutes later they found the three girls, crouched down behind a great buttress, but warm and out of the wind.

"Well?" both parties said simultaneously when they were near enough, and then Dickie grinned and said, "Where are the others hiding, anyway? Don't fool about, chaps, 'cos we're jolly weary and we've got the most terrific story to tell you ... But we must wait for the others."

They waited behind their buttress while an angry sun sank into the west. The cold increased and they lit a little fire of twigs to keep them warm. The girls were soon aware that the twins had a secret, but they could not persuade them to tell it until the boys came.

"No," Dickie gloated. "We're not going to tell you yet. This isn't a proper meeting unless all the members are here anyway, so we gotta wait."

"But you will be surprised," Mary added, but all Peter said as she looked at her watch by the flickering light of the flames was, "I'm worried. They're over an hour late and now it's dark and getting colder. What shall we do? ... I do wish they'd come."

Chapter 10

The Boys' Adventure

As soon as they had left the girls, David, Jon and Tom set out for the mysterious house with the grey walls. David had his map with him this time, and although he had to put up with some sarcastic remarks from his companions on the subject of map reading, he led them over the moor and hilltops without any mistakes. They strode along with their hands in their pockets, for the wind was bitterly cold, and when Tom wasn't whistling he was yawning.

"It's no use, chaps," he said when they were rude to him, "I just can't help it. I could go to sleep right here ... And I may as well tell you that I think all this business is very rum ... Young Mary would call it funny peculiar, I s'pose. Either we're asking for plenty of trouble or else we shall be made to look very silly. That's what I think."

David laughed. "I know your trouble, Tom – you just don't like walking, and that's why you're grousing now. You don't enjoy exercise, do you?"

Tom grinned. "I get all the exercise I need on the farm. D'you know that before I came to Ingles and lived in London I never walked anywhere much – not even to school."

"Did your mother push you in a pram?" Jon asked solemnly.

"Bus or tram," Tom answered as Jon dodged out of reach of his avenging hand. "No sense in tiring yourself out ... Of course, this Mr Cantor business and the sheep stealing is very important for the Club, but we don't seem to do anything else but be yanked out of bed and walk or bike madly about in the cold ... I'm fed up with it."

And having expressed his opinion with his usual bluntness he began to whistle in the peculiarly sweet and melodious way which he made his own.

"We ought not to be far from that little wood now," David said after a few more minutes. "Have a look at the map, Jon. I think this is the track we're on."

"Not on your life!" Jon replied. "You're doing the map. If we're lost I'm not going to have anything to do with it, are you, Tom? ... Besides, three people reading a map is always a hopeless mess ... A glance round the countryside just now made me feel that we might be in the middle of the Sahara desert in winter-time – if it has a winter. This is the rummest country I've ever been in. I don't like it much."

"Neither do I," Tom said. "I keep on telling you I couldn't care less about it ... I wonder how the twins are getting on with old man Cantor? I bet they're giving him a marvellous time ... What's happened to David? He's disappeared now."

They turned and found that while they were talking David had stopped to wrestle with the map and been left behind. They watched him trying to fold it in the stiff breeze, and laughed when he heard their guffaws and shook his fist at them. They laughed still louder when the map blew away and fluttered over the heather.

Then Tom suddenly stopped laughing and said seriously: "Jon, look at the ground here carefully. I'd swear that these marks are the tracks left by the wheels of a big lorry."

When David, rather out of breath and red in the face, caught them up they were on their knees at the edge of the track.

"So you've gone mad now," he said with considerable satisfaction. "I felt like it just now with that map, but now I can see that I'm the only sane one. Shall we all three lie down and roll in the dust?"

Then they showed him what they had found.

"You're right," David said. "I don't know which of you found it, but, of course, it would have been me if I hadn't been busy with the map. Now I know we're on the right road! Bet you that these tracks lead us to the house."

Five minutes later they reached the little clump of fir trees which were swaying and moaning in the wind, and soon they were looking down on the mysterious house. As before, there was no sign of life, but the walls were too high for them to see over into the garden or grounds. The windows in the upper floors seemed to be uncurtained and stared at them with blank eyes. The chimney stacks might have been made for show. The great double gates with the little sliding wicket were closed as grimly against an intruder as they had been on their first visit, and the track on which they were standing ran down the hill and stopped abruptly before them.

"Let's go down," Tom said. "We shan't find out much from here, shall we? Let's make a row outside until they have to open the gates."

"Someone must live there," David replied; "and, anyway, we know that they do, and I've got the feeling now that something is spying on us."

"Bet it's old Cantor," Jon said.

"If it is, then the twins are spying on him," was David's comment. "Look here, chaps! The tracks here are clearer than ever, and I'm sure there are marks of car tyres as well. We didn't see those tracks further back, did we?"

Down they all went on their knees again and were still grovelling when a smooth, silky voice behind them said:

"Of course, there's no reason why you shouldn't spend your time like that, but it would interest me very much to know what it is that you have lost."

Jon and David jumped up, but Tom seemed to be transfixed with either surprise or fright and remained on all fours until the others hauled him to his feet. When they turned round they saw a large, powerful-looking car, which must have glided down the hill with the engine cut off, standing a few yards behind them. In front of the car and smiling at them under a small black moustache was a tall, handsome and very well-dressed middle-aged man. He was holding a pipe between his teeth and wearing a light-coloured overcoat with a belt. By the door of the car stood a very different type of man who was scowling at them under a battered felt hat. He looked rough and tough, and as the car seemed to be a very expensive model David began to wonder what the two of them could be doing together, even before he had puzzled out how they could have managed to have come up behind them so quickly and quietly. Before he answered the smart stranger's ironic remark David looked again at his companion. Surely there was something about one of his eyes which was rather peculiar? While he was still puzzling over this the man moved forward and said rudely, "Come on, now. All lost your tongues? What are you doing here, messing about on the ground?" and as he spoke David saw that one eye squinted horribly, and suddenly he was sure that this was the eye which had watched them through the wicket *from inside the gate* on their first visit.

Before he could answer either question the first man turned and very softly said, "Thank you, Quickset. I do not think that our young friends here will appreciate such direct speech ... Get back into the car and turn it."

"*Turn it*, guv'nor?" the man with the squint protested. "*Turn it*? ... OK! OK! I'd as soon be sitting in the warm as standing out here in this perishing wind."

When he was back in the driving-seat the other man turned again to the boys.

"And have you lost anything? I fear I disturbed you and perhaps should apologize. When the car came over the top of the hill and I saw you all on your hands and knees, I felt that I would like to share your surprise, so I crept upon you, hoping for some fun, but, as the uncouth Quickset remarked, you do seem to have lost the gift of speech ... Is there not one of you who is not afflicted?"

Jon was the first to recover his wits. He said afterwards that he had no shame for the lies he told, but that in any case he knew at the time that the man did not believe him.

"Well, sir," he said at last, "you certainly startled us.

Only a few minutes ago we were saying that this country was like a desert in winter, and then suddenly you were behind us. Were you dropped by helicopter?"

"Nothing like that." The man was still smiling. "Nothing like that. But tell me what you have lost or what you hope to find on the ground up here in this remote part of the world?"

Jon went on: "We were told down in Clun, where we are staying, that there are lots of flint arrowheads round here, and we're very keen to find some … The three of us have got a sort of competition on to see who can find the first."

The stranger still smiled. "Really? But how odd that you should all look in the same place at the same time?"

"Not odd really, sir—" Jon began, but was then interrupted by David, who was beginning to lose his patience.

"I wonder, sir, if you'd mind telling us who lives in this big house and why the gates are always closed?"

"Are they? Have you been here before, then?"

"Yes, we have. We were lost round here the other day and went down and rang a bell at the side of the doors because we wanted to know the best way to get home to Clun … But nobody answered the bell."

"But you found your way back to Clun, nevertheless, and have come back specially to look for arrowheads?"

Jon nodded. He could not trust himself to speak!

"Do you live here, sir?" asked David in a very meek and mild voice.

"I do," the stranger admitted. "Why are you three so interested in it?"

"We're always interested in houses, sir. Jon and I are

going to be architects one day, we hope ... I wonder if we could ask you a favour? We're sure you've got a marvellous house and grounds inside these walls. Has the house got a history?"

"It has," the man said rather grimly as he relit his pipe. "Go on! Don't think you're being impertinent, will you?"

David faltered a little at this attack.

"We don't mean to be. We're just interested, as anyone else would be. After all, this does look a jolly mysterious place, and it would be fun if we could have a look at it from inside the walls."

By this time the other man had turned the car until it was facing up the hill towards the fir trees. He leaned from the window and called, "Buck up, guv'nor! Time's getting on ... What shall we do with these kids?"

The first man silenced him with a look and turned again to the boys.

"That house down there happens to belong to me, and that answers your first impertinent question. But there is something much more important for you to remember than that – I do not like, and will not have, curious and inquisitive strangers spying on me. Please remember that ... Now jump into the back of the car, and I will take you back to the road."

"But look here," Tom began impetuously, "we don't want to go back to the road, thanks all the same. You can't stop us from stopping here or make us go either. We can do what we like here because we're not on your property."

The man took his pipe from his mouth, opened the

door of the car and laughed.

"Jump in, young cock sparrow," he said.

Tom hesitated, but David nudged him, and under his breath whispered.

"Hop in, Tom. It's all we can do. I've got a plan."

Then he turned to the handsome stranger.

"It's good of you to give us a lift, sir. Thank you very much ... But we *can* walk, you know. We walked here."

By now the car was moving off slowly up the rough track and passing through the gloomy shadows of the pine trees. David tried to follow the twists and turns the driver made, but it was impossible to pick out landmarks or to memorize the route. Once or twice it seemed that they left the track entirely and just bumped along over the heather, but it was not very long before they reached a road. The boys remained silent throughout the drive, except that Tom muttered mutinously once or twice; but he had nothing to say when the stranger turned in his seat and opened the door of the car.

"Goodbye," he said cheerfully. "I'm glad to have been able to put you on your way. There are two other things I forgot to mention. First is that there never have been and never will be any flint arrowheads found round my house ... There's a big field up here somewhere where they were found once, but you'll not find any my way, and you'll be wasting your time looking for them ... The other point I've mentioned already. I'm an ordinary enough sort of chap, except for one thing. I hate strangers and won't put up with them ... Good afternoon!"

The boys got out rather sheepishly and the man put in a parting shot.

"I nearly forgot to tell you. Because of that feeling I have about strangers I keep a big Alsatian dog up there inside those walls. He's nearly wild and he doesn't care for strangers any more than I do," and the car moved off, leaving them standing on the edge of the road.

There was a long pause.

"Dear me!" said Jon at last – and he often used old-fashioned phrases like that – "Dear me! We have been clever, haven't we? Caught out properly and with nothing much to say for ourselves either! What have we found out, David? Anything we didn't know?"

"Only that the guy with the squint is the man who glared at us through the little wicket in the gate and refused to let us in the other day ... The other thing is that the smart-looking gentleman doesn't care for strangers; but perhaps you both noticed that? What shall we do next? I *know* what I'm going to do, but maybe one of you has got a suggestion."

"All right, David," Tom said. "I know what you're going to do, and I'm with you. I don't like those men – particularly the beautiful one – and if they think they're going to scare me off with a yarn of a wild Alsatian they've made a big mistake ... I think we're on to something ... What are we waiting for?"

So for the second time that afternoon they followed the track to Grey Walls, but this time, at Jon's suggestion, they went very carefully just in case the car returned the same way. As they walked they discussed plans.

"It's obvious enough," Jon said, "that if we are to fasten anything on to the people who live in that place we've got to have some proof of what they're up to ... I

229

mean it's no use going back to Alan Denton or to the police and saying that we think the people who live here drive about in expensive cars and look suspicious."

"I'm sure the only way to do that," was David's comment, "is to get inside the place and see what's happening there."

Tom laughed sarcastically. "You *are* bright, aren't you? How did you think of that? And have you thought how we're going to get past those locked doors or climb those high walls with broken glass on the top?"

"Of course I have. I've just had a brainwave. There's only one way to get in, and that is when the gates are opened."

The others looked at him as if he was mad.

"I know! You needn't look like that. The way to get in is on the back of, or behind, a lorry when it comes down the track. I'm sure they do come down this way some time, and I'd bet that's just about the only time they open the gates. I think our best plan is to hide in the little wood, or, better still, much nearer the gates if we can get down there without being seen, and then when the lorry stops or slows down, try to hop on the back or slip in behind it. Are you game, and can you think of anything better?"

Jon shook his head. "I can't, and although it's a crazy plan I'm game enough. I agree that it's the only way to get a chance of seeing inside. But I think it would be silly for all three to try and get in at the same time. That seems stupid to me. Two's one too many really, but then perhaps we ought to hunt in pairs, so maybe we'd better toss for it."

"I reckon I ought to be one of those who try it," Tom said. "It's my turn to have some fun, and I don't like those men. Let me go, anyway, David."

But before either of the others could answer Tom gave a whoop of joy and pounced on three empty milk bottles lying in the heather at the edge of the path just as they had been tossed by some careless picnicker in the past.

"I've got the idea," he shouted triumphantly. "Listen! Let's bust up those bottles and spread the broken glass in the track fairly near the gates, so that when the lorry comes the tyres are punctured and they just have to stop."

"Suppose it's a lorry with solid tyres?" Jon asked.

"It won't be," Tom answered triumphantly. "Look at the tracks. You can see the pattern of the tyres in the sand."

By now they had reached the shelter of the little wood again.

"Wait here a sec," David said, "and let's make sure that the coast is clear. It would spoil everything if they saw us now, and it's going to be difficult for us to get down close to the gates without being seen."

It was nearly dusk now and the wind was stronger and colder than ever. They crouched down in the heather at the edge of the trees and watched to see if any sign of life came from the house. But there was no sight nor sound of any living thing – not even a wild Alsatian dog. Only the bitter wind moaned through the branches above them and stirred the heather which crackled between Tom's fingers as he pulled himself forward on his stomach.

"Gosh!" he said over his shoulder. "This heather is dry and wouldn't it burn in this wind? ... There's only one way to do this job, I reckon, and that's to crawl, one by one, through the heather on the right of the path and get down into that big ditch that runs by the walls ... If we can crawl along the ditch to where the track sort of stops it going any further – as if it was a bridge, you know – then maybe we could hide there and hear what old Squinty says when his tyres go pop!"

"How shall we spread the glass without being seen through that little spyhole?" David asked. "And do you think one of us ought to wait in the wood?"

"We'll take the bottles down with us and smash 'em up in the ditch and then throw the bits up out of the ditch on to the track and hope for the best ... Maybe one of you two ought to wait in the wood. Better decide among yourselves. I'm going to start crawling down now, and we must be jolly careful not to be seen ... Cheerio!" And with that Tom left them looking blankly at each other.

"Well," Jon said as he polished his glasses with a very grubby handkerchief, "that's that! I didn't know Tom decided things for himself in this club."

"Neither did I," David agreed. "He's never been quite like that before. He didn't seem very keen on the adventure when we started, but now he's quite excited."

"He doesn't like those men," Jon grinned. "He's told us that several times! ... Look, David. I still think it's a good idea for one of us to stay up here. Whoever stays may have the chance to come down on the back of the lorry as it comes under the trees; and, anyway, suppose you two manage to get inside those gates and don't appear again – there ought to be someone outside to go for help and tell all we know."

David looked serious. "I hadn't quite thought of it that way. This is a crazy idea, you know, Jon, and it must be nearly time for us to be getting back to meet the girls. I'd forgotten all about them."

"So had I," Jon agreed, "but we've got to go through with this now. It's too good a scheme to miss. Now let's toss for who goes with Tom."

David won.

"If a lorry or car hasn't come in half an hour," he said, "we'll come back here and make for Clun and try the same trick another day. Do you agree?"

Jon nodded. "I suppose so, but I wish we could stay here all night and see what really is going on round here. Anyway, good luck, David, and just restrain Tom a bit if you can! He's an amazing chap when he gets excited. If I can't get on the back of the lorry I'll watch from here and see what you do, and then if you don't come out soon I'll go back and tell the others and warn Denton as well. I'd better do that, hadn't I?"

"I suppose so. Nobody can say what will happen if we do get in but let's have a shot, Jon. If you're on the back of the lorry as it comes down drop off just where the big ditch ends by the track. That's where we'll be hiding and we'll throw the broken glass as far up the track as we can … Cheerio, Jon. Hope we don't have to wait too long," and he dodged through the trees and then crawled through the heather after Tom.

It took him longer to reach the ditch than he had expected and the journey was very unpleasant for he dared not raise his head too often to see where he was going. The hill sloped down steeply to the house and if a watcher was hidden behind the peephole in the closed doors he could easily have seen anyone approaching in the normal way. David had to stop several times to rest and take his bearings, but he rolled over the edge of the ditch without knowing that he had reached it. He got to his feet cautiously and looked round. The light was going fast now and with a shock he realized that he did not know which way to turn to find Tom. He was just making up his mind to climb the side of the ditch and look round him when he heard the peewit's whistle from his left. Thankfully he answered, and in two minutes found Tom, who was crouching under a hawthorn bush which was growing within a few feet of the top of the bank.

"So it's you, is it?" he grinned. "Don't talk loud because we're at the end of the ditch here and the gates are only a few yards away ... Can't you see them? And the wall? Where's Jon?"

David answered the last question first.

"In the wood. If a lorry or anything comes through he's going to try and hop on the back ... If nothing comes in half an hour I told him we'd go back to him and try again tomorrow."

"Glad it's you, David," Tom whispered unexpectedly. "Jon's a good chap but us two have had a lot of fun together and maybe this will turn into something. I didn't think it could be so cold as this, did you? ... I wish those gangsters would come for I'm in just the very mood for them!"

"Have you heard anything?" David asked.

"Not a sound. It's the rummest place I've ever struck and yet we know that those men must live here and that something suspicious is brewing."

"Have you done the broken glass, Tom?"

"I've busted it up very quietly and cut my hand, but now you're here and it's nearly dark I'll crawl up through the heather and spread it about by hand. It would be grim if we didn't throw it in the right places ... I don't think we could be seen now, do you?"

David shook his head.

"All right, Tom. It's worth risking I think but I'm worried about those girls. We ought to be in Clun now you know and they'll waiting for us."

"It's hard luck for them, David, but they'll understand, I'm sure. Have you thought what we're going to do when we do get into this place?"

"Have a look round and then ask them to open the doors so that we can walk out," David laughed. "Go and do your stuff with the broken glass if you're going and if you lose your way back whistle the call. Buck up!" but even before he had finished speaking Tom had disappeared over the top of the bank.

Left alone David began to think, and the more he thought the more convinced he became that they were all crazy. Even if the mysterious van did come down the track and the gates of the house were opened and they got inside, they were certain to be discovered sooner or later. And somehow David did not like the idea of being found by the smoothly-spoken stranger who had warned them off this afternoon. He might have been romancing about the Alsatian dog; on the other hand it might have been the truth. He shivered, and not altogether because of the cold, for he was at least sheltered from the bitter wind where he was hiding. Twice, while he was waiting, he thought he heard an unusual sound. The first was undoubtedly the clink of glass on stone, and the second was a rustling which might have been made by someone moving about in the ditch. He wondered if it was Tom and whistled softly but the answering call, when it did come, was from above his head and to the right. Before he could signal again Tom rolled over the edge and clutched at the heather to check his fall.

"I've chucked the broken glass up the track all right. I bet that will do the trick … I say, David, as I was crawling back I could have sworn I saw something or somebody moving about along there just below the top of the bank … I'm going to have a scout round … You stay here, David, in case the van comes…" and he slid down the bank and slipped off into the shadows of the ditch.

David began to think that this adventure belonged entirely to Tom, for he had never known his friend to be so enterprising and excited. It was nearly dark now, so he pulled himself up to the top of the bank and looked up to the little spinney where Jon would still be watching. The half hour he had promised to wait must be nearly up and he felt rather unhappy about the girls and the twins, who would now almost certainly be at the meeting-place in the castle ruins.

Then he heard the throbbing of a heavy car or lorry in the distance; and at the same time Jon whistled the peewit call which he answered as loudly as he could. Next he saw twin headlights between the trees and the shadowy shape of a large van lurching down the track towards him.

Wishing that Tom had not dashed off like that and hoping that he would have the sense to come back, David crawled forward a little nearer to the track and remained hidden behind a stunted hawthorn tree. As the lorry came nearer the headlights were switched off, and a spotlight low down by the left-hand front wheel suddenly sent a long clear beam along the rough track. David almost cried out with exasperation for, even from where he was hiding, he could see the pieces of broken glass glinting in the strong light. Then he heard a shout and the headlights went on again.

The lorry swerved violently but too late for there was a loud report as one of the tyres burst. Again the van slewed across the track, righted itself a few yards from David, and stopped with the engine still running. A man got out on the far side and walked round into the glare of the headlights. He was a very unpleasant-looking man, and it was at once obvious that he was in an ugly mood; David winced as he heard his language when he bent down to examine the wheel and found the broken glass.

"Glass all over the road," he bellowed. "Spread everywhere and the tyre is flat. Come and see for yourself if you don't believe me."

More growling and swearing followed, and the driver got out as well, and the two of them began to kick the broken glass out of the way. This was David's chance for he knew that while they were in the glare of the lights looking at the ground the two men would not be likely to see him if he moved. He wondered where Tom was and if Jon was behind the lorry.

It could not have taken him more than five seconds to dart, doubled low, across the heather to the back of the van, but it seemed like five minutes. At the edge of the track he stumbled and would have fallen flat on his face but for a strong hand that reached out from the dark shadow and helped him up.

"Nice work, David," Jon breathed in his ear. "Where's Tom? He certainly worked the glass trick all right."

"Don't know where he is. He dashed off like an idiot because he thought he saw someone moving about in the ditch ... Shall we chance going in on the back of this, Jon?"

"Listen," Jon whispered. "Gosh! But aren't they mad?"

The rumble of voices was still coming from the front of the van.

"Gipsies, I reckon. Just let me get my hands on the next lot I meet. I'll make 'em eat broken bottles."

"The other tyre's gone too. What about the rear ones?"

Jon and David held their breath in suspense, then, "One each side of the track in the heather if they move," the latter breathed, "and if they see us run for it up the hill." Then the driver growled, "Cut down and get the gates open. We can't change the wheels here and I'm not going to try either. Let the others take a turn at some of the dirty work. I'm going to drive in as we are."

The boys felt the van shift as the man climbed again into the driving seat and they both sighed with relief.

Under cover of the engine's roar Jon said, "There's a tailboard thing down here. I think it's safe enough because I came down the hill on it. Hop on, David. You'll have to hang on to that steel bar that locks the double doors. I tried to get into the van but couldn't move that bar ... Look out! We're moving!"

David jumped up beside Jon as the van lurched forward again.

"I can smell sheep," David whispered as they tried to flatten themselves against the closed doors.

"None in there now, I'm sure," Jon gasped as they were nearly flung off the tailboard. "We should hear them. I reckon the van's empty ... We've stopped again. Are we through the gates? Be ready to hop off."

"We're not in yet ... Hold me on and I'll look round the corner ... The gates are still shut but I can see that chap tugging the bell we tried. I s'pose they've got a code signal ... I say, Jon! We've got to get inside this van somehow else we're sure to be caught. Let's try this bar again ... Ready? When I say 'three' let's give it all we've got together. One. Two. Three...!"

As they pushed together with all their strength the van moved forward again and the extra jolt moved the bar a little so that as Jon pushed upwards he was able to free it in the socket. David struggled to pull one side of the great door open and as the van bumped slowly through the now open gates the two boys scrambled in and pulled the doors closed behind them.

"Hang on to it, Jon," David grunted. "Don't let it swing open."

"We've done it, David! We're in! Bit of luck for us that

the bar shifted, else they'd have got us by now. It's dark as the inside of a cow in here. Are we alone, d'you think?"

Then the lorry stopped and the engine was cut off. In the sudden silence they heard the rumble of men's voices from outside and one of them seemed to be apologizing.

"Sorry, guv'nor, if we're a bit behind, but two tyres went on the hill outside. Gipsies been chucking glass about. Someone will have to change those wheels."

Then the voices moved away and David, in relief, moved his hand from Jon's arm, which he had been gripping fiercely.

"Phew!" he gasped. "What do we do now? I'd like some light and fresh air. Smells a bit strongly of sheep, doesn't it?"

"Wait a minute or two," Jon said as he rubbed his arm, but even as he spoke there came a new sound – the deep, resonant and angry bark of a great dog. They heard a man shout and then the barking came nearer and almost before they had time to press the door into place the dog, in a frenzy of rage and excitement, first dashed round and round the van and then began to jump up at the back and hurl himself at the doors, on the other side of which both boys felt themselves go cold with terror.

Chapter 11

Tom on His Own

When Tom left David so suddenly and ran off down the great ditch after a shadow in the dusk, he acted for once without thinking first. This was not like Tom for although he was quick-witted he was, by instinct, cautious and liked to make up his mind before taking action.

But somehow this adventure at Clun had changed Tom, and this may have been because it was a real holiday for him. He rarely thought about it, but this was only the second time that he had ever had more than a day or two off from his uncle's farm since he came to Shropshire. He was very fond of his uncle, but Mr Ingles was rather loud and overpowering and never seemed to think that anybody else could have an idea or a mind of his own. And Tom had plenty of ideas and a very strong character and never minded saying outright what he thought, and during these last few days he had begun to realize this.

For instance, he had suddenly made up his mind half an hour ago that he wanted to get inside Grey Walls, so he had said so and left David dumbfounded. For almost the first time since he had joined the Lone Piners he was acting entirely on his own, and he enjoyed that too as he trotted along the narrow track at the foot of the great bank which towered above him.

He was certain as he rolled over the top of the dyke after scattering the broken glass that he had seen the outline of a shadowy form moving away from them into the ditch, and he knew that whether the mysterious lorry came back to Grey Walls or not, this chance of following a mysterious stranger might never happen again. But there were other reasons for Tom's enthusiasm. He was beginning at last to realize what work on the farm and with animals really meant. He knew now from his own experience how the wrong weather at the wrong time could ruin a farmer and that it was the long, patient work put in by those who worked on the land that made it possible for the townsmen to live. Tom was beginning to have a way with animals, too, and had recently learned to milk. Only just before Christmas his uncle had told him that he was thinking of starting with a few sheep this year and, one evening round the fire, he had talked loud and long to Mrs Ingles and Tom about what he hoped to do. They had looked at the farming papers together and Uncle Alfred had told him a little of the different breeds of sheep and how some were light and some heavy, and how some throve on the plains and others on the mountains and hillsides. Tom had realized then how interesting sheep farming could be, and it was not so difficult for him as for some of the others to understand what sheep-stealing, and the constant threat of it, must mean to the farmers of Clun Forest.

There were two other reasons for his quick decision. First, he had taken a tremendous liking to Penny's friend

Alan Denton and an even greater dislike to the men in the car who had surprised them earlier in the afternoon. Tom had always had a quick temper, but the smooth-spoken, well-dressed man with the little moustache who had threatened them with a dog had made him so angry that he hoped, now most fervently, that his quarry some forty or fifty yards ahead might be this man.

The light was failing fast now and Tom, as he trotted along cautiously, suddenly remembered that the girls and the twins would be waiting for them at H.Q. Three by the ruins of the castle. There was no sound but the sighing of the wind in the brown bracken fronds and in the branches of the few stunted hawthorns at the top of the bank, but down here he was sheltered from its sting.

Suddenly he stopped and hoped that nobody else could hear the beating of his heart. Ahead of him, in the dusky shadows, he saw a point of light which was not the beam of a torch but a little orange star, that flickered for a second or two and then disappeared. He waited, and then the light came again and he guessed that the man in front of him had stopped to light his pipe. Tom crept forward and sniffed like a bloodhound on the trail. After a few more steps he was rewarded with the unmistakable smell of tobacco. He was so excited now that he quite forgot David and Jon waiting for a lorry to open the gates of Grey Walls for them, and hurried forward until he was able to distinguish the figure of the man in front of him. He waited a few seconds while his quarry lit another match, and then hurried forward again when he saw a much bigger flame flicker into life unexpectedly at ground level.

Tom could not see much beyond the flames, which were small; and although the new Tom wanted to dash forward and see what was burning, the old Tom had enough sense to realize that a false move now into the unknown might mean the end of the adventure for him. Underlying all his keenness was the wish to prove to his old friends, and to Jon and Penny in particular, that he could be trusted to do something important on his own. So he waited for a long half minute watching the flames and wondering whether the man he was following would see them also and turn back.

The flames flickered, and died down. Then, as a gust of wind came down the gully, there was a red glow and the fire started into wicked life again. Tom ran forward and as he got nearer saw that the heather was on fire at the side of the narrow track. Here then was where a lighted match had been dropped, and such carelessness was enough to start a big heath fire.

He stamped on the burning clump, noticing as he did so how dry it was and how a burning twig ignited some more dry stalks nearby. When he was sure there was no more danger he went forward again and, after a little, heard the unmistakable sound of bleating sheep. For a moment he thought he must be dreaming, but as he stood stock-still and listened the sound came again and he knew that whatever the others were doing at this minute he would not change places with any of them.

As he stood waiting and listening the moon came up over the top of the dyke, the dusky shadows fled and the cold world looked colder still as it became patterned in black and silver.

Tom never forgot this moment and the way in which the silent, silvery light slid down the side of the great bank on his left and picked out for him a strange scene, the sight of which sent him flat on his face in the heather.

He was hiding at a turn in the track and when he raised his head cautiously he saw that round the bend the ditch itself appeared narrower, with steeper sides. About forty yards ahead of him was a patch of ground bare of heather, and beyond that it seemed as if the ditch was either filled or else turned so sharply that it was not possible to see beyond this particular point. The moonlight had already reached this miniature arena and Tom saw quite clearly a man with a pipe in his mouth, a stick in his hand and a cap on his head. But what he liked much less than the man was the dog at his heels – a restless dog which barked sharply once or twice as the bleating of invisible sheep increased.

Tom, of course, had no idea that the twins had already discovered this secret hiding-place from the other side, so he was astonished when he saw the man lean forward and then throw to one side a hurdle which he afterwards knew to be camouflaged with dead bracken and gorse. The dog barked again as the man spoke to it, and suddenly the ditch seemed full of sheep as they came tumbling, in a panic, out of their shelter.

Tom had to think quickly, for he realized at once that the only direction in which the sheep could be driven was along the ditch towards him. It would perhaps be possible for him to scramble up to the top of the bank and hide until he could see which way the flock would be driven and then follow it. But the sheep were now coming towards him so fast, and the dog was barking and the man cursing, so that the only course open to him seemed to be retreat. He wriggled backwards out of the heather in which he had been lying until he was round the bend and then got to his feet and ran as fast as he could back the way he had come.

As he ran he guessed the secret of the cunning sheep-thieves, for although he did not know how the sheep reached the hiding-place he realized now that large flocks could be driven right along the bottom of the ditch out of sight of any inquisitive strangers or even of the farmers themselves, right up to the gates of Grey Walls. What happened then Tom had no idea, but he was quite determined that he was now going to find out.

Tired, footsore and breathless, he dashed on along the narrow track which he now realized had been made by the hooves of sheep, praying that neither the man nor the dog would see him in the moonlight. He tried to keep in the shadows, but stumbled and fell twice. Actually it was only a very few minutes before he looked up to his right and saw the grim walls of the house above him. He stopped and looked ahead for David, but could not see him. He whistled the peewit call, but there was no answer.

Suddenly he felt unreasonably angry. At the very moment when he wanted the help of the others David had apparently wandered off somewhere and would not even answer his signal. Then he grinned ruefully to himself as he remembered that he had run off on his own without giving his friend a chance to argue, and that it was possible that the agreed half hour was up and that

David had gone back up the hill to the spinney to meet Jon. But this did not seem much like David, who would certainly never desert a friend if he could help it. Tom's anger disappeared as quickly as it had come, and for a moment he felt uncommonly foolish as he realized that he might have upset all their plans. Then he heard the sheep behind him and began to climb frantically up the bank to the hawthorn tree where David and he had hidden half an hour ago.

Once up he could see at once that the great gates were still closed and that there was no sign either of a furniture van or of David or Jon. For a moment he wondered if David had been forced to change his hiding-place and had moved to the ditch on the other side of the gates. He raised his head and whistled the peewit's call three times. The third time he thought he heard an answering call, but it was very faint and far away and certainly did not come from the other side of the ditch.

Tom was puzzled now and rather worried. It was possible that Jon, if he was still at his post in the spinney, had heard him and answered; but the signal he had caught – if it was not imagination – had not seemed to come from that direction. Then he had no more time for wondering what had happened to the others, for he looked down and saw sheep below him. He crouched lower in the heather and saw that the man was now in front of the flock, which was pushing and scrambling and bleating frenziedly in the narrow track.

Tom knew that he was in a most dangerous position, for if the sheep were to go in through the gates they would have to be driven up the side of the bank. There

247

was no chance for him to move, for if he attempted to do so surely either the man or the dog would see him? In despair he tried to wriggle still lower into the heather and wondered, if his luck held, how he would be able to follow the flock into Grey Walls when the gates were opened.

But now came the greatest surprise of all. He could hear the man below him cursing the sheep and his dog, and the sound of his stick as he struck some of the frightened and bewildered animals. Then, when he plucked up his courage to raise his head again, he saw the man bending down over something at ground level on the far side of the ditch. Although this side of the dyke was in shadow, it seemed to him that the man lifted something which might have been a board, or perhaps another hurdle, and then stood to one side. Tom strained his eyes, but could see nothing more than a darker patch of shadow which might perhaps be a rectangular hole in the bank.

It *was* a hole in the bank! He almost yelled in excitement as the dog barked again from further down the track, the man shouted and used his stick and the sheep began to vanish, one by one, into the cavity.

This, then, was the secret of Grey Walls! A secret passage right under the walls through which stolen sheep could be driven without even bringing them out of the shelter of the ditch.

"Jiminy Cricket!" he whispered to himself. "This is a go! Somebody once told me that a good way to send yourself to sleep was to count sheep going through a hole in a hedge. I reckon this is better than any hole in any hedge! Won't the others be mad when they know what I've found? ... Gosh! What a stroke of luck! ... There they go ... forty-three ... forty-four ... forty-five ... That seems to be the lot, and I'm not asleep yet ... The dog's disappeared now, and where's the man?"

He peered down into the shadows and was just able to distinguish the form of the stranger as he bent to pick up the hurdle. Then it seemed as if he got into the hole backwards and pulled the cover across the entrance again from the inside.

Tom lay still and listened. From the other side of the wall came the slightly muffled sound of the bleating sheep and the sharp, excited bark of the dog. There was just a chance, Tom thought, that the shepherd had not followed his flock and might still be in the ditch, so he waited for a few minutes before sliding down the bank. He was too excited now to remember David or Jon or any of the others! This was a thousand times better than any film which he had ever seen, and he was determined to make the most of it and this wonderful chance to get inside Grey Walls.

The bottom of the ditch was still in deep shadow, but his eyes soon became accustomed to the dark and after a little searching he found the heavy hurdle leaning against the side of the bank. He crouched down and put his ear against the rough bracken with which it was disguised, but could only hear the plaintive, monotonous call of the sheep. Very, very gently he pulled the hurdle across until there was a gap large enough for him to squeeze through. The floor of the tunnel was smooth and dirtied by the sheep, but before he went forward he pulled the hurdle back in front of the entrance and then slowly stretched upright. His head hit the roof, so he went down on his hands and knees and crawled forward.

The sound of the sheep was much clearer now, and suddenly he heard a man's voice only a few yards away calling directions to the dog, and guessed that the sheep were now being driven into pens. After what seemed a very long time he heard the man whistle the dog, and then footsteps which died away in the distance.

He crawled forward cautiously. The tunnel sloped down for a few yards, turned a little and then ran uphill. As he crawled up he sniffed the fresh, cold air again very thankfully, and noticed with surprise that some windows on the ground floor of the big house were lit up. This was the first sign of life in the house behind the grey walls seen by any of the Lone Piners.

Tom put his head out into the open and looked round cautiously. Although the house itself was in shadow, the ground in front of it was bathed in moonlight. He glanced first to his right and saw at once that his guess had been correct: the stolen sheep were crowded together in a pen made of hurdles. When he had given a quick look in the other direction he shot back into his tunnel like a startled rabbit, for, not more than fifty yards away, standing on a rough drive, was a large furniture van. Two men were wrestling with the wheels, and when he turned again and there was a lull in the bleating of the sheep, Tom could hear the mutter of their grumbling voices.

Unless the van had been there all the time, which did not seem very likely, it must have arrived while he was following the shepherd down the ditch! It was just then that Tom began to wonder what had happened to the other two and whether he had really been a little too clever. Perhaps it would be better to creep back down the tunnel and find David and Jon? After all, he *was* the first to get inside the grey walls – at least he thought he was – and he had seen the stolen sheep, the furniture van, the driver and his mate and the lights in the windows. Surely he had enough evidence now for a policeman?

And yet Tom hesitated. He hated going back without getting nearer to the house. It would only take a few minutes, and he might be able to dodge across the patch of moonlight when the driver and his mate went to the other side of the van. It was true that he ran a big risk of being seen from one of the windows, but his luck had held so far and was hardly likely to break now.

Then his mind was made up for him.

Somewhere at the side of the house a door opened. Tom could see the sudden glow of orange light and hear a burst of radio music as a man stepped out, put his hands to his mouth and shouted, "Come on in, you two … Boss wants you right away … Buck up!"

The two men dropped what they were doing and strolled over towards the open back door, and Tom, on sudden impulse, left the shelter of the tunnel and started to crawl over towards the van. Somehow he felt an impulse to examine this first, and with the guards called off this was his big chance.

He grunted with pain as suddenly a sharp flint cut his knee. After that every wriggle forward hurt him badly, so he jumped to his feet and dashed as fast as he could for the van.

As he ran his scalp tickled with terror as the silence was broken by the deep baying of a great dog. He looked back over his shoulder and saw an enormous animal like a wolf bounding across the moonlit patch towards him.

So the smart man had been right about the Alsatian!

"What a fool I've been!" poor Tom panted as he tried to spurt. The only thing he could possibly do now was to jump for the van and hope that the back would be open.

"But it *must* be open," he prayed.

The dog was gaining on him fast, and he thought he heard men's voices shouting as well as he made a last great effort and scrambled up the tailboard of the van. At first glance it looked as if the big double doors were closed, but suddenly one of them pushed outwards a little and a strong hand grabbed him and pulled him in. Before he could cry out he was flung on the floor of the van and another hand was put over his mouth. The door closed with a bang as the great dog, snapping and snarling, hurled himself against it.

Tom began to struggle instinctively. A man shouted outside, and then another voice that he knew breathed in his ear:

"Gosh, Jon – it's Tom! ... But we're for it now, for they've heard the dog. Here they all come ... Lie flat on the floor and let's hope for the best!"

Chapter 12

The Girls to the Rescue

High on the hill above Clun, while the bitter wind howled through the ruins of the ancient castle and the light of the moon threw black, fantastic shadows over the frosty turf, Penny, Peter, Jenny and the twins crouched in the sheltered corner of H.Q. Three.

Peter, in her jodhpurs, her scarlet sweater and a short but warm coat, was leaning against the wall looking down at the others who were crouched round a little fire of twigs. She was bareheaded as usual and her face was very grave as she listened to Jenny.

"It's no use staying here, I tell you. We'll all die of the cold if we're here much longer, and there's no sense in it. Let's go home now and get something to eat and tell Agnes not to worry ... Of course, something dreadful may have happened to them, but I don't think it could really, 'cos Tom's with them."

Penny opened her mouth at this last remark and Peter's chin went up indignantly, but before either could say what they were thinking Jenny went on as breathlessly as usual.

"... And another thing ... Why won't you twins tell us what you know? You say you've found out everything, so why don't you tell us? It's just silly staying here like this."

"I think so, too," Penny said. "I think maybe the boys are playing a trick on us. Or else they've forgotten all about us ... I'll have something to say to them when they do turn up. Maybe they're at Keep View now eating their heads off round the fire."

Peter flushed with anger.

"I don't know how you *dare* to say such a thing, Penny. It's the meanest thing I've ever heard you say, and it just shows you're the newest member of this Club ... Of course they'd be here if they possibly could. Something's gone wrong, and I think they're in great trouble, but David will get them out of it..."

Before anyone could answer this outburst she reached across and pulled Dickie to his feet by his collar.

"No more nonsense now, twins," she went on. "This is serious. Tell us what you know."

For a moment Dickie looked mutinous, but then Mary got up and slid her hand into the pocket of Peter's coat.

"All right, Peter," she said quietly, "we'll tell. We think it's good news."

Between them they told their story in less time than usual, for they realized that Peter was very serious.

"...And so, you see," Mary finished triumphantly, "that Mackie and us found where they hide the sheep, and if we hadn't stuck close to darling Mr Cantor we would never have discovered that he's not an enemy but the most wonderful, brilliant detective that ever lived ... Now I think we'd better do as Jenny says and go home and look for him ... He'll find the boys for us."

Peter swung round and put her hands on the little girl's shoulders.

"You're not playing a game now, are you, twins? What you've told us is really true? Every word? ... All right, Mary darling ... I can see it is ... I'm sorry I found it so difficult to believe ... And you really think Mr Cantor is a detective?"

"Oh, yes," Dickie nodded. "He's got a badge, and I reckon he's got a Sheriff's star, and I bet he packs a gun."

Penny was grinning wickedly.

"I always knew he was all right," she said.

Peter smiled, too, and said, "Sorry I snapped just now, Penny, but I was worried. Honestly, you can be sure that David and Tom would be here if they possibly could ... And I'm sure Jon would, too ... I think something has gone wrong and that we'd better get back now. When we find Mr Cantor, I s'pose we ought to tell him that the boys were going over to Grey Walls to see what they could find. What d'you think?"

"Maybe we should," Penny agreed. "I don't know Agnes very well, but somehow I don't think it would be a good idea to let her know what we're up to – she might telephone your people in London and my aunt, too, and that would spoil everything."

Peter nodded and put an arm each round the twins' shoulders.

"Right, let's go! It's agreed that we tell Mr Cantor privately but try to keep it from Agnes. But how on earth we're going to come in late in the dark and pretend the boys are just round the corner I don't know."

"Let's have one worry at a time," Penny said. "That's my motto ... Maybe I'll think of something to say to her, and if I don't one of the twins will ... And I wish you'd cheer up, Jenny. You've got your way now and you're going home."

"I'm awfully sorry," Jenny said. "But you know what I am! I keep imagining the most awful things. It's never so bad *doing* things, but I hate thinking them and I can't stop thinking them just now … Let's run down and get warm."

They ran and slid down the slippery slope and waited a few anxious minutes by the bridge in the hope of seeing the three boys coming down the hill.

"How I hate waiting for people," Penny said as she blew on her hands. "Some of the most awful moments of my life have been spent waiting for people to come. Stations are like that. I hate seeing anyone off 'cos it means goodbye, and I hate going to meet them 'cos they may have missed the train and not turn up."

"I don't often go to stations," Jenny said. "But that's just the sort of thing I think."

"You both sound crazy to me," Peter said briskly. "Come on! We've got to go and face Agnes sooner or later, so we'd better go now and get it over. Anyway, I'm so cold I can hardly move."

The twins were unusually quiet as they trudged along the street to Keep View, and Peter felt very unhappy. She had the feeling that something must have gone very wrong with the boys' plans, but did not know what to do about it. She was sure that the twins were telling the truth about Mr Cantor, so supposed that the only thing to do was to tell him what had happened. But she wished they could tell Alan Denton first. He would be so much easier to talk to, she was sure.

She and Jenny were walking in front. They waited on the steps of the house for the others when they came up.

"Look here, twins," she said, "you go right away and see if you can find your friend Mr Cantor. If he's downstairs just get him in a corner and ask him if we can all come and talk to him privately. If he's not about, go and knock at the door of his room. We'll try and deal with Agnes."

"All right, Peter," Dickie said quietly. "We'll try."

"You're Captain of the Club while David's not here," was Mary's comment as they tip-toed into the hall.

The twins went into the lounge at once, but Penny walked briskly up the hall and knocked loudly on the kitchen door.

"Here we are, Agnes dear," she called cheerfully. "Back at last and safe and sound!"

The door opened and Agnes stood before them. Her face was pale and anxious but her mouth was set in a hard line as she looked them up and down.

"There's but three of you," she said quietly. "Where are those little ones?"

Peter stepped forward and put her hand on the housekeeper's arm. She shook it off angrily and raised her voice:

"Where are they, girl? Answer me!"

Peter gulped. "They're all right, Agnes; they're here. They've just gone upstairs to wash."

Agnes relaxed a little. "Come in here," she said and led them into the lounge. The three girls stood before her feeling uncommonly small and foolish, and there were tears in Peter's eyes long before Agnes had finished speaking.

"So you come back when it suits you," she began, "and me responsible for you all and worrying myself sick just because I'm not to know where you are. You girls should know better. Here's your supper been in the oven this hour or more…" She pushed her spectacles up her nose and said suddenly, "And where are those boys? Are they back?"

Peter tried this time.

"We're very, very sorry, Agnes dear. I know we're wrong and it's all my fault. I'm responsible and I really know it was rude and thoughtless of us to be so late. We've been out exploring and having some adventures, and just didn't know exactly what the time was … Please forgive us?"

"Where are those boys?" the housekeeper repeated grimly.

"I don't think they'll be long," Penny said, a little too brightly. "We haven't been with them for some time but we know they'll soon turn up … Don't worry about our supper, please Agnes … I mean, we'll get it and clear it away and wash it up, and do the same for the boys when they come in."

Before Agnes could reply the door opened and the twins entered. They were quick to sense the atmosphere, and while Mary rushed over to Agnes and flung her arms round her, Dickie looked soberly at Peter, put his finger to his lips and shook his head.

"It's so lovely to be back, Agnes darling," Mary said. "Please don't be too cross with us. We've had the loveliest adventures and now we're cold and hungry – only just now I said to Dickie that the loveliest thing about going out and having fun is coming back home and being looked after by Agnes. Didn't I, twin?"

"Yes, you did! ... Did you happen to notice when Mr Cantor went out, Agnes? We want him very extra specially."

The housekeeper's mouth relaxed, for she never could resist the twins.

"Ah well," she said, "maybe I was a bit hasty in what I said. I know there's not one of you means any harm but you mustn't worry me like this. Now be sitting down as quick as you can and enjoy some nice hot soup ... Mr Cantor, did you say, Dickie? ... He dashed out in a great hurry about an hour gone, and I must say he seemed very strange and his voice was that different too ... But there, I suppose I was imagining things because I was anxious and worried ... When will he be back? ... Now it's odd that you should ask that for he shouted to me from the front door-step that he didn't know when he would be back, and I must say I've been having a very upsetting evening ... I can't think what's come over you all."

When the door closed behind her they all looked at each other and sighed with relief.

Jenny collapsed on the sofa.

"I just don't know how you do it," she gasped. "I think Agnes is a pet but when she looked like that at us I was just terrified ... Oh, dear! I do wish Tom would come ... I hate this adventure now."

"Talk like that doesn't help us or the boys," Peter said. "If you want something to do why don't you go and help Agnes in with the soup, and don't let her talk about the boys."

The hot supper was very welcome but Peter nearly choked once when she looked at the three empty places and then noticed Penny doing the same. It was so utterly unlike David not to turn up when he had promised that she was now really frightened. She tried to persuade herself that nothing really serious could have happened to them but was not helped in this when Penny, who was opposite to her, put down her knife and said, "Peter. Suppose they managed somehow to get into the Grey Walls place, and s'pose they were caught when they were spying around. What do you think would happen to them? Nothing really bad could happen, could it? I mean nobody would ever dare to kidnap them or keep them prisoner, would they?"

Jenny's eyes were wide in her white face.

"They wouldn't *torture* them or anything, would they?"

"Don't be so silly," Peter snapped and then, as the twins looked concerned said, under her breath, "Do have some sense Jenny, and remember these kids."

"Don't call us kids, please," Mary said. "Dickie and me are going out now to find Mr Cantor. He's the one to help us."

But before they could move Agnes came in again and shut the door firmly behind her.

"Now I'm having no more nonsense," she began, "but unless those boys are in this house by nine o'clock news time – and that's just under the hour – I'm going to the police station and you're all coming with me. This is beyond a joke for me, I can tell you, and I should, by rights, be ringing up Mr and Mrs Morton and Mrs Warrender and Mr Ingles too this very minute."

"They'll be here any minute now, I'm sure," Peter pleaded. "I'm sure they will, Agnes," but she said it as much to convince herself as the housekeeper.

When the door closed again Penny said, "She's crying, Peter. Did you notice? Gosh! This is grim, isn't it? Let's try and think what the boys would do if they were here and we were about three hours late ... Let's be sensible but don't ever let them know what I said!"

Before she answered her Peter spoke to the twins.

"Why don't you two go outside for a bit – just on the steps – and keep a look out for them and listen for the signal? Will you?"

Mary looked at her suspiciously.

"You just want to get us out of the way, don't you? We're not going. We're staying here until nine o'clock and then we'll just see what's what. When Agnes comes back – if the boys haven't come – we'll tell her 'bout Mr Cantor."

The others didn't even try to argue. They were too tired and too frightened to say much now and sat quietly and miserably round the fire waiting. For a long time the only sounds that broke the silence were the ticking of the clock and the tumbling embers in the grate. The twins sat side by side on the floor looking into the flames with Mary leaning against Jenny's knees. Once or twice the little girl's head nodded and Peter, watching her, felt that lovely feeling of warmth and sleep creeping over her as well. Only Penny, her chin on her hands and her elbows on her knees, seemed really wide awake. It was only because she really did want to be loyal to her new friends and to Peter in particular that she sat so still. It was always so difficult for red-headed Penny to sit still. She hated waiting, but just because she was beginning to know Peter better she rather grudgingly admired her steadiness and was prepared to accept her leadership for the present. But she had a rather horrid feeling, that she hardly recognized as fear, when she thought of Jon and wondered where he was and what had happened to him. She thought of his slow speech and his slow smile as he made fun of her, and remembered too the way in which he would polish his spectacles when they were already clean. Suddenly she made up her mind and wondered why she had been sitting for so long doing nothing, but as she jumped to her feet the door opened and Agnes came in again. She had a scarf over her head and an old tweed coat round her shoulders.

"Now," she began, "if you know where these boys are you'd better hurry and say for I'm off right this minute to the police."

Peter got up and stood beside Penny.

"We think we know where they might be, Agnes, but we've got something to tell you ... The twins have been out with Mr Cantor, as you know, and they've found out he's a detective.

Agnes raised her hands in horror. A detective was apparently as bad as a murderer to her.

"I never heard the like..." she began, but Dickie interrupted her.

"It's true, Agnes. Honest it is. We'll come with you to the police station. I promise you that Mr Cantor is the chief policeman. We expect he'll be down there ordering all the other policemen about. He'll find the boys for us. Don't you worry! Mary and me will take care of you."

The housekeeper had already turned to the door when she realized that Peter had admitted that they knew where the boys might be, but before she could speak again Penny interrupted:

"You go on with the twins, Agnes, and see if Mr Cantor is there. We'll come along in a few minutes ... Yes, of course we will, but we've got to get our coats and things ... The twins will look after you and I do hope that you find Mr Cantor."

The twins sensed that the others wanted·to get rid of Agnes and led her out, looking very bewildered and unhappy, into the hall. As soon as the front door closed Penny whirled on the others.

"Listen, Peter," she said as she tossed back her curls. "I know what we must do and it's the only thing we can do. I'm not going down to the police station for anybody and I don't care if Mr Cantor is the Lord-High-Detective of all England! ... Here we have been sitting mugging round the fire waiting for the boys, and then for Agnes to do something. Why don't *we* do something? Let's jolly well go out now on our own. Let's go to Grey Walls and explore that and see if we can see any sign of them. Maybe they're wanting us..."

"But, Penny," Jenny began.

"There aren't any buts," Penny stormed. "Can't you see that's what we ought to have done just as soon as we found that Mr Cantor wasn't here...? I don't care about the police. Let's do this on our own. Are you game, Peter? Are you, Jenny?"

"Yes, I am," Peter said shortly. "Of course you're right, Penny ... Coming, Jenny?"

"You're both so quick," Jenny wailed. "But of course I'll come. I'd rather do anything than stay here thinking."

"Let's put on everything we've got," Peter said. "We'll be no good if we're cold, and let's hurry … I'll leave a note on the hall table just to say that we've gone to Grey Walls. That's only fair and sensible, isn't it? Anyway, the twins knew the boys meant to go there and they'll tell Cantor or the police, I s'pose … Come on!"

Penny led the way upstairs three at a time and they were all out of the house in four minutes, tying scarves and fastening buttons as they ran down the steps. The street was empty now and as they trotted over the narrow bridge the wind whistled round them and stung their cheeks and finger-tips. They looked back from the top of the hill and saw the ruins of the great Keep glistening in the moonlight, and once an owl drifted silently over their heads and sounded his mournful cry so that Peter was reminded again of Witchend. When they reached the signpost at the crossroads they paused for breath.

Jenny spoke first. She was the youngest of the three and as she leaned now against the gate through which they would have to go in a minute she looked small and rather bewildered.

"While we were coming along I was thinking again," she began. "I do hope you won't reckon I'm silly, but don't you believe it would be more sensible to go to Bury Fields and tell the Dentons what's happened?"

"No, I don't," Penny almost snapped. "Why, Jenny? Are you scared?"

"I don't think I am any more," Jenny said very quietly

as Peter looked at her in surprise. "I was at first and I generally am to begin with, but I'm sure I'm not now."

Penny had the decency to look ashamed. "Sorry, Jen," she said, "that was beastly of me … I can't see any sense in going to the Dentons, though, 'cos I'm sure the boys won't be there."

"I don't suppose they will," Jenny agreed, "but what I mean is that if Alan is there he could come with us and help us to find the boys, or maybe he could get together some of the other farmers to help or make a search party or something. Do you see what I mean?"

Penny shook her head, but Peter looked doubtful.

"I mean that if we all go to Grey Walls now and find out something there's not much us three girls can do about it, is there?"

"Why not? If the boys can do it we can, can't we?" Penny said.

"I don't know about that … I know there's lots of things that Tom does that I couldn't, but don't you see that if something extra special has to be done in a hurry, Alan, or some of his friends, are sure to be able to do more than we can do anyway."

"You can do what you like, of course," Penny said, "but I'm going to Grey Walls right now … Back in the summer Jon and David rescued me and the twins and if they can do it for me I don't see why three girls – or two girls, anyway – can't do the same for them … You do what you like, Jenny, but I'm going after the boys. They never deserted me and I'm not going to leave them in the lurch now. Are you coming with me, Peter, or are you going with Jenny?"

Even while Penny had been speaking Peter had been confident that Jenny's suggestion had been very wise. And although she didn't hesitate to answer Penny now she still believed Jenny was right. But if Penny thought she had a duty to rescue Jon, surely the vice-captain of the Club had a greater duty to rescue the captain?

"Of course I'm coming with you, Penny, and you'll come with us too, won't you, Jen? Your idea isn't bad, but we can't desert the boys – surely you see that?"

In the moonlight Jenny's chin went up in a way which Peter had never noticed before.

"I'm not going to desert the boys," she said stubbornly, "but if you're right and they've been caught by whoever lives in Grey Walls, then they've got to be rescued and I don't think we can rescue them as quickly as Alan Denton and his friends can … Besides, there's another thing. I'm sure that Alan ought to be told about Mr Cantor and that the boys haven't come back … I don't care what either of you say but I'm absolutely sure I'm right. You two can go down to the house if you like and I bet you won't see anything or anybody. I'm going to Bury Fields … You needn't look at me like that, Peter. I'm not a bit afraid of going on my own … It's funny, but I'm not … I'll find Alan and we'll come over to that little wood above the house and look for you there … Cheerio!" and to the astonishment of the other two she set off by herself down the moonlit road.

Peter felt a lump rise in her throat at the sight of the little figure trudging along so bravely by herself. This self-reliant, confident and courageous Jenny was someone Peter had never met before.

"Jenny!" she called suddenly. "Wait a sec. I've got something for you," and over her shoulder she said to Penny, "Wait for me. I'm coming with you."

Jenny stood still in the middle of the road and did not turn until Peter touched her shoulder.

"It's no use, Peter," she said. "I'm going to Bury Fields. I've made up my mind that one of us ought to go and if you and Penny want to go to Grey Walls I don't blame you ... Honest, I don't, Peter! ... But don't make me change my mind, Peter, please."

When Jenny looked up Peter saw that tears were glistening on her friend's cheeks although her voice was steady enough – steadier than her own when she said, "That's all right, Jenny. I understand. And you know why I feel I've got to go with Penny, don't you?"

Jenny nodded. "Oh yes, I do. You won't let her rescue Jon if you don't rescue David, will you? I feel like that about Tom, but I'm going to do it a different way ... What are you doing, Peter?"

Peter was fumbling under a scarf, a coat and her red sweater.

"Take this, Jenny, will you? It's a whistle the gipsies, Reuben and Miranda, gave me once. They told me that if ever I was in trouble and blew it and the Romanies were near enough to hear that they would come to my help. I'll lend it you now, Jenny, 'cos there's only one of you and two of us! ... Maybe there aren't any gipsies about here now but if you'd like to carry it I'd like you to have it ... Quick! Penny's calling. Here you are. Put the cord round your neck ... Good luck, Jenny! Up the Lone Piners!"

As she ran back to the gate Peter smiled at the thought

of the look on Jenny's face and at the way in which she had stepped off briskly down the road whistling cheerfully.

Penny looked at her curiously as they climbed over the gate.

"That was brave of Jenny, wasn't it? I like her, Peter ... I like you all ... I think you're grand and I think this is fun ... Do you know the way?"

"I believe I can remember ... The place we've got to make for is that little spinney where we hid when the boys went down to explore ... Lucky the moon is up but I hate this wind. It's colder than ever."

Although the moon was high in the sky big clouds were now piling up from the north and it was darker than it had been when they were waiting at H.Q. Three some hours ago. Twice they missed the track and once went half-a-mile out of their way after two trees on the skyline that were nothing to do with the spinney for which they were searching.

"I wonder what Agnes is doing," Penny said suddenly, "and whether they've found old Cantor? I shall always think of him as old Cantor, won't you?"

"By what Dickie said," Peter answered, "you'd think that he'd changed into a different man altogether ... It's funny, Penny, but I never liked him, did I? Maybe I shan't like him any more now that he's on the same side as us ... Ow! Let go. You're hurting my arm, Penny."

Penny relaxed her grip slowly and pointed ahead.

"Look, Peter. Surely that's the spinney just down in that dip? And can you see something else? Two little squares of yellow. Do you know what those are?"

"Yes, I think I do, Penny. They're lighted windows in the house, but it's funny we can see them from here and never seemed able to see the house in daylight."

Penny started to move off again towards the pine trees and, for a moment, did not realize that her friend was not with her.

Meanwhile Peter stood still looking down on the two lighted windows and feeling vaguely uneasy. She was aware that Penny, twenty paces ahead, had turned and was waiting for her but for a moment she felt that she could not move. She brushed a hand across her eyes and then, with a great effort, broke the strange spell and hurried on down the path.

"What were you doing, Peter? Dreaming?"

"Think I must have been," Peter said. "I wonder if we shall be able to watch those windows all the time ... That's rum, Penny. They've disappeared now. You know you can only see down on to the house from certain places ... There they are again. They must be windows of rooms right at the top of the house ... Let's wait a sec under the trees and shelter from this wind. I can't feel my feet ... And keep your eyes on those windows."

They leant against the trunk of a great fir tree while above them the branches tossed and threshed and moaned.

"I *loathe* wind," Penny said suddenly. "I think I can stand any weather but wind ... It gives me the shivers when it makes a noise like this at night ... Peter! One of those lights has gone out ... No, it hasn't. It's on again ... Peter, look! They've gone mad ... It keeps going on and off. Can you see it, too?"

Peter suddenly yelled out in excitement.

"Penny! Watch! Somebody is signalling … That's Morse. Do you know it?"

Penny shook her head gloomily. "Never could learn it. I know I'm a fool at that sort of thing but I just couldn't be bothered with Morse … What is it, Peter? Have you got it?"

Peter was murmuring to herself, "Dash. Dot? That's N … Now what? Nothing else. Just an N. Maybe he'll start again … Here he comes again, Penny! Now I can do it. Just remember the letters as I spell them out. Dot, dash, dash, dash – that's J … Now three dashes, and that's O, and then dash dot again. Doesn't make sense to me. Suppose that's part of a word."

"Of course it is, you chump!" Penny shouted. "Can't you see we've found them? That message is J-O-N, which is short for Jonathan … We've found them, Peter. Do you realize what we've done? We've found them, and they're shut up in that place. All we've got to do is to get into the house somehow and rescue them … Peter! PETER! What's wrong, Peter? Are you ill? Answer me, Peter. I hate you like this. What is it?"

Peter was still leaning back against the trunk of a tree at the edge of the little wood with her hands over her eyes and did not answer.

"Peter! What's wrong? Are you coming down with me or are you scared?"

This time Peter answered, but her voice was low and muffled behind her hands and the wind was making such a noise in the branches overhead that Penny could not hear her. She came back to her friend's side and put her hands on her shoulders.

"Look at me, Peter! PLEASE, PETER! What's wrong? I can't hear you."

Slowly Peter lowered her hands and Penny hated the dazed look on her face. She looked straight ahead, as if she was hypnotized, at the two rectangles of light below them and said in a strained voice:

"Don't go, Penny. Stay here with me a sec. I *am* scared, Penny ... I've been here before."

"Don't be an ass, Peter," Penny said uneasily. "Of course you have. You know you have."

"I mean this has all happened to me before ... Penny! I know it has. I remember the trees and the wind and the cold, and I remember you, though I don't remember the lighted windows ... Penny, I've been here before at this very time ... I remember now, Penny! ... There ought to be a fire! *Look behind you, Penny! Look behind you!* Is the heather on fire?"

Penny turned at the note of urgency in her voice and then felt her scalp tingle with fear as she saw a belt of red and orange flames and billowing smoke sweeping down towards them from the top of the hill. Even as she stared the acrid smoke swirled round them and the evil crackle of the fire as it was fanned to fresh fury by the wind sounded louder every second.

Peter was still too bewildered by her strange experience to move, and Penny tugged at her sleeve to make her realize what was happening.

"Peter! We can't stay here ... The flames are coming straight at us ... Come on, Peter ... Buck up. We must get down to the house, and they'll have to let us in ... They can't keep us out ... They dare not."

Peter flicked back her plaits.

"I remember it all," she said quietly. "I remember running down the hill with you and how the heather scratched my legs. I didn't know who you were, Penny – not then, I didn't."

"What do you mean, Peter – *not then*?"

"Oh, I don't know, really, except that this has happened to me before ... Sorry, Penny. I sound crazy, I know."

The wind strengthened and a clump of flaming heather dropped between the trees behind them, and as the smoke stung their eyes Peter forgot everything except that David, Jon and Tom were in the house below them and that somehow they must be rescued. This was all that mattered now, and she turned and smiled naturally at Penny and grabbed her hand.

"All right, Penny. Don't look so worried. There's nothing the matter with me, really ... Let's show those boys what we can do," and side by side they began to run down the rough track towards the great double gates. But as they ran down the hill together the feeling that all this had happened before came back to Peter more strongly than ever. She remembered the clear, cold night in which the moon rode high, and the wild, desolate country around them. She was not surprised when she turned and saw the vivid red reflection of the flames in the sky, and she knew that Penny would suddenly turn her head and smile at her in friendship. They did not have to speak to each other, for they each knew that in spite of the danger behind them they had a job to do and were determined somehow to do it.

Penny loved danger. She was impulsive, moody, quick

to love and quick to hate, but she liked excitement and an adventure. Peter's courage was of a different sort and not quite as spectacular perhaps, but she never lost her head once she had made up her mind.

They were half-way down the hill when Penny stopped with her hand to her side.

"Stitch!" she gasped. "Just a sec … Gosh! This is grand fun! … Look, Peter. Come back a bit … I thought I noticed them signalling from the window again."

They turned and went back a few steps, but were now too far down the hill to see the house above the high walls. The fire was spreading rapidly and roaring down towards them. Even as they watched, the first flames reached the cluster of pine trees and one of the latter flared up like a great torch. Sparks and glowing twigs were whirled towards them down the wind and even Penny stood in awe for a moment at the majesty of the fire.

"It's bad," Peter said quickly. "It's coming so quickly because of the wind … We must dash for it, Penny … Let's get down into the ditch just by the gate. Can you run again?"

"D'you think they're watching us from inside?" Penny panted as she fell into step beside Peter again. "Surely they'll open the gate for us."

Peter was too worried to answer. She had no idea how they were going to get into the house, and even if the gates were open for them they had no plans made for getting to the boys. Almost as if she had read her thoughts Penny went on:

"All we've got to do, Peter, is to get in. Once we're in one of us will think of something to say or do. We'll get to the boys somehow, I'm sure ... Here we are, anyway. What shall we do? Ring or knock or shout or all three? Or hide in the ditch?"

They had reached the flat space in front of the gates as she was speaking, and they both turned at the same time to see whether the fire was gaining. From that moment everything happened so quickly that it was not until long after that they pieced the order of events together. But neither of them ever forgot that astonishing scene as they stood alone with the closed gates of the house at their backs and the great fire roaring down towards them.

The skyline was alight for as far as they could see to the left, and right up to the spinney above them. Even as they watched another tree flared up and the sky was blotted out by the billowing clouds of smoke. And all the while the wind that Penny hated blew harder. It roared down at them steadily and relentlessly; it fanned the flames crackling through the dry and brittle undergrowth and urged them on and on and never let them rest and die. It was a cold, hard wind that the girls never forgot.

"It will burn itself out when it gets down here," Peter whispered almost to herself. "It can't spread over this patch of grass. But we'd better get down in the ditch, Penny."

"Sparks are blowing down the ditch now, Peter. There's plenty of gorse and stuff to catch fire down there, isn't there? ... LOOK, Peter! LOOK! I can see HORSES!"

And then, as if to complete the fantastic picture of a moorland fire in the middle of a cold winter's night they saw some six or eight horsemen come galloping through the flames and smoke straight towards them down the hill. The leading horse was carrying two people – a small, wiry horse with flying mane and tail that was coming, sure-footed, as fast almost as the wind itself. The man in front, who was riding as easily and comfortably as if he was part of the horse, suddenly yelled and pointed to the two girls. The figure behind him shouted, too, and the voice was vaguely familiar.

Peter wondered if she was dreaming again, and then suddenly she recognized the riders.

"It's Reuben, the gipsy," she shouted as she grabbed Penny's arm. "I don't see how it could be, but it is ... and that's our Jenny behind him! Hi, Reuben! It's us! Hi!"

Then they found themselves scrambling down the sides of the ditch as the horsemen shouted at them. Reuben smiled as he soothed his horse and Jenny, with shining eyes, flung herself between them.

"The whistle worked, Peter. See how it worked! And Alan is about somewhere, 'cos we found him almost at once ... I told him about Cantor and the boys and he said he'd help. Have you found anything?"

The ditch seemed full of plunging horses and shouting, swearing men who had no time for anything but care of the terrified animals. Peter saw Alan in the distance struggling with his hunter and decided that she would not be welcome at the moment. The sky seemed full of flying sparks and burning twigs, and although some of them fell nearby no fresh fires were started, probably because in the dyke they were sheltered from the wind, but there was so much noise that the girls had to shout to each other to be heard.

"Have you found anything else?" Jenny shrieked. "Do

you know that they're here? I told Reuben and Alan that they were. I hope I was right!"

"You are," Penny shouted in her ear. "Jon has been signalling to us from inside and we got the message ... I wish the horses weren't so scared, and then we could talk to these men you've brought, Jenny. You said you were going to get help, and you've certainly done it. Thanks for going!"

When they turned round Peter was shouting at Reuben, who was still holding his horse. Penny, in exasperation that they weren't doing something more spectacular, skipped back out of the way of the horses' restless feet and felt something move against her back.

"But *do* something, Reuben," Peter was yelling. "I'll hold your pony ... Go over and get hold of Mr Denton ... Tell him we know the boys are inside there and that we're sure they're prisoners."

"In just a little minute..." the gipsy began, and then Penny pulled at Peter's sleeve and dragged her away.

"Look what I've found. It's a way in under the walls. Come on, Peter and Jenny! Crawl in behind me and we'll be the first in after all ... Never mind the others, Peter. They'll be busy for a bit with their horses. Let's do this on our own and see what happens ... I'd give anything to get to the boys first. Coming?"

"Of course," Peter said. "And let me go in front. I'm the vice-captain, anyway."

"I'm coming," Jenny laughed. "You couldn't keep me out of anything after what I've done tonight ... Go on, Peter ... Buck up ... Someone'll notice us soon."

And this was the way in which they found the tunnel

and got into Grey Walls. Peter shouted something to Reuben, and when the sparks were flying more thickly than ever, crawled into the tunnel which Tom had found earlier that same night.

As they came out the other side two men were running across from the house towards the gates. The girls shrank back into the shadows and looked up to see if they could find the lighted window from which Jon had signalled.

"I don't know where we are," Penny cried. "It looks different from inside. Which window was it, Peter?"

While she was speaking there came the sound of breaking glass from their right and the tinkle of the fragments as they broke on the ground beneath.

"Over there," Peter called. "Come on. This way. Don't worry about those men, anyway. They're busy with the gates, I think ... There are the boys! Look! We're here, David."

She stopped and pointed to a window that had been just out of sight when they came up from the tunnel. In the moonlight and the red glow of the fire they recognized Tom leaning out of the broken window beside David. Tom had his hand to his mouth and was shouting something.

"Can't hear you!" Jenny called. "How do we get in to rescue you?"

"LOOK OUT FOR THE DOG!" David yelled. "Get back somewhere out of the way ... LOOK OUT! ... RUN!"

They heard that shout above the clamour outside and the bleating of the sheep nearby, and as they turned they heard above everything the furious bark of the huge

Alsatian that came bounding towards them. Instinctively they began to run, for even Penny was frightened when she saw the great dog's eyes shining in the dark, and the white gleam of his teeth. And while Penny and Jenny ran back towards the tunnel Peter stood her ground and then walked forward confidently to meet the dog.

"It's all right, old boy," she said quietly as she put out her hand towards him. "Here, boy! Come here. Good boy!"

The dog, with lolling tongue, stopped short at the sound of her voice. She spoke to it again gently and held out her hand. The dog sniffed at it, licked it and wagged his tail. Peter put a hand on its head and made a fuss of it, and then slipped her other hand underneath his collar and led him towards her two friends, who were watching wide-eyed.

"He's all right now," Peter said quietly. "He won't touch us, I promise ... Oh, I don't know, Penny. Animals seem to like me, and something like that happened once before, so I thought I'd try it again!"

"Lucky you did," Penny said. "I was terrified."

"What about the boys?" Jenny asked; then, "ALL RIGHT, TOM! We're all right!" she yelled up to the broken window. "Peter did something magic. What do you mean? Go over there where you're pointing? All right."

They turned again to see a big furniture van drive in through the open gates. As they started to run towards it the back opened and six or seven policemen jumped out, followed by a well-known figure in a plus-four suit.

"It's Mr Cantor," Peter shouted as she began to run

towards him. "The twins were right and we're all saved now ... Look, Penny. They've grabbed those men who ran across to open the gates. One of them is that man with the squint who tried to frighten Mrs Denton that day ... Hullo, Mr Cantor! I bet you're surprised to see us."

Mr Cantor certainly was! He was so surprised that his mouth fell open before he was able to say anything.

"I s'pose you know that the boys are prisoners in this house?" she went on. "How can we get them out? They're in a room right up under the roof, and they've just broken the window. Will you help us with a policeman, please?"

Before he could answer – and he was leaning against the tailboard of the van – a familiar voice said plaintively, "I haven't heard any shooting, so I reckon we can come out now, Mr Cantor," and Dickie and Mary popped their heads over the back of the van. "I think we must have been asleep for a bit."

Then a look of absolute disgust crossed Dickie's face as he recognized the girls.

"How did you get in here first?" he demanded.

Penny giggled, but it was Mary who spoke next as she clambered to the ground.

"Hadn't we better do something about those boys? They're makin' a lot of noise up at that window."

Chapter 13

Explanations

Just before four o'clock the following afternoon Alan Denton came down from the hills with Lady at his heels and strode cheerfully into the big kitchen of "Bury Fields".

"It's warmer," he said as he paused on the threshold. "Snow on the way, and I'm glad we'll see the back of that wind … My word, Mother, but that table's a grand sight. Can I start before those kids arrive – although I'm so tired I don't know how to keep my eyes open?"

Mrs Denton looked up from the great glowing kitchen range with a smile of welcome. Her cheeks were rosy with the warmth of the fire and her eyes had lost the worried look they had been carrying for the last week.

"I've done the best I can in the time, son, but I've forgotten how many you said would be coming. If there's not enough room for all, some must sit on the floor, but every plate and cup we've got in the place is out on that table."

She straightened her back.

"And you'll leave those boots *outside*, please. Sometimes, my boy, I wonder if you'll ever grow up … But tell me … is all cleared up now and safe and sound, and those rascals under lock and key? … And our flock! Is there a chance of finding the sheep, do they think?"

"It's all cleared up, I believe, Mother, but we'll hear more presently, for that detective chap Cantor is coming. I saw him for a minute in the town this morning, and he did say that there might be a chance of getting the sheep back, so I asked him to come along with the children ... And that reminds me ... They wanted to bring their housekeeper who is looking after them at Keep View, and I said that was all right. Hope you don't mind?"

Mrs Denton laughed.

"If she's anything like her poor sister now in hospital, I'll be glad to welcome her, and we shall want some help, too ... Now, Alan, tell me about these children again, for I get them a bit muddled in my mind."

"We all owe them a lot, you know, Mother. It's odd that I should have met two of them in the train on the way home the other day and that they should have all turned up here ... They're grand kids, you know – every one of them. It's a long time since I had anything to do with youngsters like these. I like 'em. Even those saucy young twins."

"Saucy is the word," Mrs Denton said grimly, "but there was something about them, I'll admit ... Then there's the red-headed little spitfire that scared Quickset out o' here the other day and the smaller redhead with the big eyes that comes from over Stiperstones way."

"Penny and Jenny!" Alan laughed. "But you can't mistake the quieter one of the three, can you, Mother? You couldn't forget the girl they call Peter, could you?"

Mrs Denton looked out of the window into the dusk. Snow-laden clouds were banking up above the line of the hills as she struck a match for the lamp. Her kind, wrinkled face stood out sharply as the flame flared up.

"If there could have been a sister for you, my boy, I would have wished her like that child Petronella … There's something about her eyes and the way she holds up her head that I like … And I'm old-fashioned enough to like a girl who wears her hair in plaits."

Alan was at the window.

"Yes," he said quietly, "a nice kid … And here she comes over the hill now on that little nag of hers … Now, Mother, do you remember the boys, and will you be sure to call them by their right names? … Listen, and I'll tell you again … First, there's David, and he seems to be the leader of the gang. He's the twins' brother and special pal of your friend Peter. The tall, lanky chap in the spectacles who looks as if he ought to be in college is young Penny's cousin, and I met him on the train, too. His name is Jon. Last is young Tom – small and tough and quick. Think you can remember 'em?"

His mother laughed. "I'll do my best … Go out now and look after that girl's pony and tell her to come right in."

Three minutes later Peter came in, her eyes bright and her cheeks flushed with the cold.

"I do hope I'm not too early," she said. "If I am perhaps I could help a bit … The others are only about ten minutes behind, but I felt I wanted to come on Sally. And did Alan tell you Agnes is coming, too? Mr Cantor is bringing her in a car, but the others all said they'd rather walk … And what do you think? The twins and Jenny are carrying hurricane lanterns like carol singers."

Rather shyly she slipped off her sheepskin coat.

"Can I help, please, Mrs Denton? Isn't it wonderful that they've caught those awful men, and now you won't be worried again about losing your sheep?"

"Seems from what I hear that you youngsters had something to do with the catching of 'em. I reckon we're proud of you round here, but maybe we'll get the full story when this special policeman and the others arrive ... Why, girl! You're yawning your head off! You must be tired out."

"It's not so bad now," Peter laughed. "But we've not caught up yet! You see, when we got home last night it was very early morning and we all went straight to bed. Then when we woke up it was dinner instead of break-fast, and then we all went to sleep again until about an hour ago ... It was when we'd had our dinner-breakfast, as Dickie calls it, that Agnes told us that you'd asked us all here ... We think it's marvellous of you, Mrs Denton, and we're all thrilled about it, but do please excuse us if we yawn a bit ... Look! Here they are. They've lit their lamps and I can see them coming over the top of the hill. I'll run out into the yard and meet them."

Alan, who had by now put Sally safely in the stable, strolled across to the gate with her.

"Just like a circus, Peter," he grinned as the Lone Piners came straggling down the track. "They're making such a noise they'll have lost their voices by the time everyone has to tell their story."

Peter laughed.

"I s'pose other people think we're a bit noisy, but sometimes we can be quiet, you know ... After all, we know each other very well now, and we've had lots of adventures together ... Listen, Alan! I can hear one of the twins – I think it's Mary."

Voices carried well in the quiet of this evening for the great wind of yesterday had dropped.

"I'm like the page in Wenceslas," came Mary's clear treble. "Jus' you all mark my footsteps well and remember you wouldn't know where you were or where you're going if we hadn't brought these lanterns ... Are you all right behind, twin?"

"Just about!" came Dickie's faint answer. "I keep watching for stragglers, but they're sticking it jolly well – even Tom."

Alan laughed. "Call them, Peter! Let them know we're waiting for them."

Peter put her fingers in her mouth, and in a most unlady-like manner whistled the peewit's lament loud and clear. Alan looked at her in surprise.

"That's an odd way of calling them," he said. "Why a peewit?"

"I could do an owl as easily," Peter said. "Listen now, and you'll hear Tom answer. He's the best whistler of us all."

They heard Penny's clear laugh next, and then the reply to the signal as the party came hurrying down the last few yards of the hill to the gate.

"Good evening," Mary said politely as Alan opened the gate for her. "It's lovely to be back again but the others wouldn't be here now if it wasn't for me and Dickie and our lanterns."

As the others crowded round the sky was lit up by the

headlights of a car which came scrunching down the track. Dickie stood in front of the open gate waving his lantern until the car stopped a few inches from him. A stifled scream came from inside the car.

"Richard!" the shocked voice went on, "I've a good mind to wash my hands of you for good and all, for when you're in bed I'm worrying to know whether you're really there, and when you're up you're nothing but a worry to me and ought to be in bed … And now, after all I've been through these days, and last night in particular, you go standing right in the way of this great motor-car, and if it wasn't for Mr Cantor here beside me you might well be squashed flat to death."

But before she could say more Agnes was pulled out of the car by the twins and hugged until her now famous Sunday hat, from which dangled a large bunch of artificial cherries, was cocked over one eye. She was introduced to Alan, who then shook hands with Mr Cantor, and the whole party moved over to the house.

Mrs Denton was waiting for them at the open door and the great kitchen glowed so warm a welcome that most of them – even the twins – were silent with wonder. Nobody ever knew where she had got so much food in so short a time, and this was indeed, as Dickie remarked when he had found his tongue again, the "highest high tea" he had ever seen.

Not until they were all together in the lighted room and the red curtains had been pulled across the window, and Mrs Denton and Agnes had retired together into the scullery, did the Lone Piners have a real opportunity of looking at Mr Cantor, who was standing on the hearthrug chatting to Alan just as if he were an ordinary person and not a detective.

He certainly looked different, and although he was still as bald and still wore glasses, he looked younger. He had got rid of that peculiar greenish plus-four suit that had looked as if it was twenty years old and was wearing a checked sports jacket and grey flannels. He looked up suddenly from lighting his pipe and caught Peter's eyes on him.

He twinkled at her and said, "Well, Peter. Forgiven me?"

Peter flushed scarlet. She hated being caught at a disadvantage like that and knew that she had been staring at him.

"I don't know quite what you mean," she whispered. "I think you ought to forgive me, for I did think the most awful things about you, and sometimes I was very rude, too."

"No, you weren't, Peter – not really ... But I didn't like you hating me, you know ... I'd like to sit next to you in a minute. I seem to know the others better than you, and I'd like us to be friends ... I've enjoyed meeting you children, and I'd like to say now—"

"Silence, all!" Dickie yelled suddenly. "I've just heard our famous Mr Cantor say he's got something to tell us."

Mr Cantor looked a little embarrassed.

"Speech!" said Penny very loudly and distinctly. "Go on, Mr Cantor. You can't get out of it ... I say! I s'pose you know I was the only one who stuck up for you ... I'm jolly glad you'll never know the awful things some of the others said about you."

"I was only going to remark," the detective said as a sudden hush fell on the crowded room, "that you're a grand lot of kids and I've enjoyed working with you ... Maybe your names will be mentioned in my report."

"Will we get medals?" Dickie said. "Mary and me'll take them if you ask us. I don't mind telling you, Mr Cantor, that I'd like a police medal to take back to school."

When the roar of laughter following this remark had subsided, Jenny spoke up.

"Of course, we're all half asleep, but we do want you to tell us *everything*, Mr Cantor. We want all the truth, and we don't want you to hide anything. We can *stand* the truth, Mr Cantor."

Jenny's shadowed eyes were wide in her pale little face, and she did not even smile when the others laughed again. Jenny was always mixing the many dramatic stories which she loved with life itself, and sometimes, as David told her once, she forgot which was real! But before Mr Cantor could answer the door opened again and Mrs Denton, Agnes and a strange man came in.

Then Penny remembered him and came forward.

"Why! it's Mr Clancy, who rescued me that night your sheep were stolen."

Alan slipped over to his mother's side. "I found him in Clun this morning and asked him if he'd like to come this evening. He said he would, but I never believed it. I'm so sorry, Mother, that I forgot to tell you."

Meanwhile, Mr Clancy was shaking hands with Penny and looking very nice and human.

"I'd remember that head of hair anywhere," he said,

"though I couldn't see it properly the other night ... I mind seeing a crowd of your young friends then, but it looks bigger than ever now..." Then he stopped suddenly and fumbled in his pocket for a pair of gilt-rimmed spectacles. He had seen the twins for the first time. "But those are new to me," he murmured.

"We're twins," Mary began brightly, but for once the two of them were howled down as their hostess led them all over to the loaded table. Mrs Denton sat at one end and Alan at the other. Next to Alan and on his right was Mr Clancy, then Jenny, Tom, Mary, Dickie and Agnes. Opposite Agnes and next to Mrs Denton was Mr Cantor, with Peter next to him as arranged, and then David, Penny and Jon.

In one of the few lulls in the buzz of conversation Dickie was heard to say, "It's funny, but it's nice, but we always seem to finish an adventure with a jolly good feed ... Do you remember that mighty feast in H.Q. Two at 'Seven Gates', twin?"

Mary nodded happily, gulped and whispered back, "Don't let the others know or let Agnes see, but I can't acksherly stop yawning ... This being sleepy is awful when you're so hungry."

At last nobody could eat or drink any more, and even Mrs Denton and Agnes, who had been so busy looking after everybody else, had had something themselves. Agnes, with her flock safe and home again and with the twins by her side, was at peace. Her kind face was rosy and shining in the heat and lamplight, and the cherries in the wonderful hat nodded happily over one ear. Mrs Denton looked down the table at her son, now lighting his pipe, and was content. The Lone Piners had each other and had made some new friends as well, but it was Penny who spoke up and spoke for them all when she said:

"Mr Cantor! Please, we're all waiting to hear what you've got to tell us about this adventure and about the men in 'Grey Walls', and whether you've really caught them all and how long they've been in that house and—

"Stop!" Mr Cantor shouted. "Go easy, girl! One thing at a time, but I promise I'll tell you all everything I can presently ... You've got to remember that you've all been asleep since early morning and that there's plenty I don't know ... It seems that you all split up last night, which was sensible enough, and it seems that you all got into 'Grey Walls' somehow, but who was first?"

"I think we were," David said. "Jon came down the hill on the back of Sam Quickset's van and I joined him when the tyres burst ... Of course, Tom was in this, too, but he'd gone off on his own."

"Right," Mr Cantor said. "We'll deal with Tom presently ... Will you tell us everything that happened to you two, then, David? And I'd like to know, too, what started you off on this hunt for sheep thieves."

"You know that really, Mr Cantor," Peter interrupted. "Don't you remember that I told you about meeting the furniture van on the road to Clun and how I was sure it had sheep in it? And don't you remember how I heard the van again in the middle of the night and saw it dash through Clun from my window?"

Mr Cantor nodded. "Yes, I remember, Peter. When it's my turn to talk I promise I'll tell you why I was rather rude to you that day. Thanks for reminding me, anyway ... Now, David, will you go on?"

Between them Jon and David told the full story. Sometimes David stopped for a word which Jon would give and sometimes, much more slowly and methodically, until Penny nearly collapsed with suspense, Jon would take up the tale. He told them how he had waited shivering in the little wood while David and Tom watched down by the big gates, and how, when he had almost given up hope, he heard the lorry coming, and when he had seen the tail-board down jumped on it and hauled David up when it stopped at the gates.

Then David took over, and Tom smiled to himself until Jenny nudged him as he remembered how he had dashed off on impulse and quite unexpectedly found his friends again.

David caught his eye and winked, and then went on with his story.

"It was rather grim lying on the filthy floor of that van in the dark and wondering when we were going to be caught, but the worst moment of all was when we'd actually bumped into the place on two flat tyres. It was then that I began to get really scared. I don't know how Jon felt, but—"

"Awful!" Jon said. "I don't think I've ever felt so terrified as when we realized we were really inside and the dog started to bark."

"I was coming to that," David went on. "The dog came nearer and nearer, and I'm jolly sure that if he'd got to us we'd have had a bad time. I know I thought my last moment had come..." He looked across at Jenny, grinned at her and said, "That's what great explorers and heroes sometimes think, isn't it, Jen?"

Jenny gulped and nodded. She had no words while she was living this adventure with the boys.

"Well, anyway, there we were. So far as we could tell we were just inside the gates, and even before the dog started that horrible racket we'd heard Quickset and his nasty mate grumbling to the man who had come across from the house to open the gates. Our luck held because the men were so mad about the burst tyres and the gipsies they thought had done it, that they just didn't or wouldn't believe that the dog meant business and that we – or anyone else – could possibly be inside the van. Anyhow, while we were shaking – I was, anyway—"

"And me," Jon added gloomily.

"...on the floor of that van," David went on, "the chap who had come from the house wanted a chat with the others, and our two could hardly speak for rage, so all three of them were mad with the dog for doing his job, and before long they dragged him away, and I suppose they went back indoors." Here David took a deep breath and looked round at his listeners. "I'm afraid I'm not telling this very well," he said. "You see, everything happened so quickly, but I shall never forget how I felt while that dog was barking and snapping outside the van … You go on now, Jon … It's your turn."

Jon polished his spectacles and then returned Penny's flashing and encouraging smile rather sheepishly.

"I shan't tell this better than David," he began, "but there is one thing we ought to say now. While the men were muttering and cursing outside we did hear the one who came from the house say that the van would be wanted later to take more sheep out so that the wheels would have to be changed. Anyway, after they had dragged the dog away they started up the engine again and the van limped across to what we knew later was a big garage. We could see a crack of light through the van doors and there was a rather uncanny throbbing noise which puzzled us until we realized that it must have been an engine generating current for electric light."

Here he paused and took a long drink of tea.

"Go on!" Penny hissed. "Don't be so greedy. Do your eating and drinking when you've finished telling us."

Jon smiled at her, but spoke to Mr Cantor.

"Are we telling you what you want to know, sir? Stop us if we're not ... All right. Good! ... I s'pose it took them about half an hour to get those wheels off and mend two punctures. Obviously they had to mend two because they had only one spare wheel, and I can tell you that we heard a few things while they were at work."

And here Jenny, who had long given up eating and was listening entranced with her chin on her folded hands and her elbows on the table, said what all the others were thinking.

"Tell us! Tell us, Jon! *Do go on!* What did the men say?"

"They said lots of things we can't repeat here," David said modestly as he nudged Peter beside him, "but it was clear, although they did nothing but grumble, that they were scared stiff of someone they called the boss, and, as you'll hear presently if you don't keep interrupting us, this boss was the man who brought us back to the road in his car and threatened us with the dog earlier in the afternoon … Shall I go on now, Jon? Right! … You'll see that we were in a real mess and there wasn't much we could do, because all this time the van was never left alone. We did manage to prise open the big doors a bit so that the crack between them was wider and we could see more outside. As soon as the wheels were changed the driver said he'd move the van over on to the drive again, and we guessed he did this because it was nearer the sheep pens – of course, we didn't know about the sheep pens until we saw them from the back of the van. When the driver made his way back to the house his mate came running across and pointed to the walls about forty yards away from us … The moon was very bright, you'll remember, and we could see all this clearly, but you can guess how excited we were when we saw sheep coming up out of a hole in the ground. There was a sheep dog, too, and the sheep were driven into the pens by the men, and we heard one of them say they wouldn't be able to get away for another two hours.

"Then we were sure our chance was coming, but a lot of things all happened at once that spoiled that. When the men went in to the back door they must have let the dog out, for he started barking again, and at the same time we saw somebody coming out of the hole under the wall. We didn't recognize Tom until we had him in the van because he was out of our line of vision as he ran across, but we were jolly glad it was him."

"So was I!" Tom said. "Never been so scared in my life as when that dog was after me."

"Now I think the really interesting part of the story

begins," Mr Cantor said, "but tell us as quickly as you can and then I'll ask you any questions after ... Will you go on, David, please?"

Everybody, even the twins, was quiet. The three men lit their pipes, Mrs Denton had picked up some knitting, while Agnes was so astonished at the revelations of what these boys had done while in her care that she could not take her eyes off them.

David went on. "The next part wasn't so pleasant, but I'll tell you as quickly as I can. This time the dog was so furious that the men began to realize that something was wrong, but they were still arguing about it when the man they called the boss came sauntering across the yard. I was watching through the crack in the doors and saw him. He was smoking a cigar and wearing a light-coloured overcoat with a belt round it. He spoke to the dog and put his hand on its collar, and then he told the men to open the van!"

It was at this stage of the story that Jenny screamed and that Peter gripped David's tweed sports jacket without the latter noticing.

"Well?" Mr Cantor prompted.

"We weren't very clever then," David went on apologetically, "but of course there wasn't much we could do."

"What exactly did you do?" Alan asked.

"Well," Jon said after a long silence, "we had a bit of a scrap ... You see, none of us liked that smart chap with his little moustache."

"And we'd been shut up in that van a long time," David added as if in excuse.

"I see," Mr Cantor said as he filled his pipe. "I think Jon's reason is the sounder of the two. What happened?"

"When we got sorted out they hauled us off indoors," Jon continued. "Trouble was that they were just too big for us, but I bet there's one of 'em will remember Tom for quite a long time. Tom's much quicker than I am, you know ... Anyway we were taken into a marvellous big room with a carpet about six inches thick – did you notice it had peacocks on it, David?"

David shook his head. "I thought they were lobsters."

"But you can't have purple and green lobsters," Jon replied.

"I don't see why not—" David began, but was interrupted by a crash as Mr Cantor banged his fist on the table.

"Go on with your story, boy! What happened in that room? Who was there and what questions were you asked?"

David sighed. "You don't give us a chance with your interruptions. Where were we? Oh, yes. The lobster carpet."

"Peacocks," Jon said quietly.

When the pandemonium had subsided David tried again.

"The smart guy was there by himself. He sat on the arm of an enormous sofa and smoked his cigar and drank his drink and looked at us and asked us questions ... If the other two felt like me they were scared of him. I was."

The other two nodded and Tom added, "But I always hated that chap."

"What did he ask you?" Mr Cantor said quietly.

"He asked us why we had come back asking for trouble and how we had got in. Tom said that we'd jumped over the walls, and Jon said we'd swum in and that annoyed him because I think he must have suddenly remembered that we'd been found *inside* the van, and that made him madder than ever for a minute and he swore at us."

"I didn't mind him doing that as much," Tom put in. "I hated him most when he was quiet. I think I'd have made a set at him again but we knew those two toughs were waiting just outside the door."

"He asked us if anybody had sent us down to spy on him and of course we said, no, it was just that we were interested in the country, and he didn't like that either ... Then, quite suddenly, he flung his cigar away and told us that we were going to be locked in an upstairs room until we came to our senses, and before we could argue he called in the toughs and we were marched off. When we got to the door he said, 'If you break the window I'll break your necks, and anyway you'll be too far from the ground ... And if you did jump the dog'll be waiting for you ... Don't argue. Off you go and maybe I'll have a word with you in the morning ...' You go on now, Tom."

Tom ran his fingers round the inside of his shirt collar.

"It wasn't much of a room. No carpet or lino and only one small iron bed, a chair, and a bare sort of chest. The chap with a squint they called Sam and his mate had to fetch another fellow before they could get us up the stairs, but in the end they shoved us in and locked the door and then we heard them push something in front of it as well. It was Jon's idea to signal and he did it by moving his coat up and down in front of the light."

"What did you signal, Jon?" Penny asked suddenly. "We saw you and Peter spelled it all out. Bit of luck for you that she was there 'cos I could never be troubled with morse."

"Sometimes I did S O S and then our names. It was too difficult to do long words or sentences. It was something to do anyway, although we didn't see how you girls could reach us."

"Oh, didn't you?" Penny stormed. "And who *did* reach you, we'd like to know? You just wait till you hear what we did after waiting for hours and freezing to death up at those ghastly ruins."

They smoothed her down and at last Tom was able to continue his story.

"There's not much more to say, I don't reckon. After Jon had been signalling for a bit we saw the fire come over the top of the hill and then Alan and the rest of them dashing down on the horses. Gosh! It was better than the pictures ... When all the excitement started outside and everybody was dashing about we tried to get the door open but couldn't manage it. Then we saw you girls prancing about down there and remembered the dog, so I bashed the window and I reckon that's all."

"Oh you do, do you?" said Dickie, breaking the hush that followed this story. "You reckon that's all, do you? You've quite forgotten who came and rescued you, I s'pose? You don't know who found a policeman while the flames of that prairie fire were lickin' the very gates and led him right through the enemy's camp till we found

you there and busted open the door and rescued you ...
You reckon that's all, do you?"

Poor Tom was so taken aback by this attack that he
could only gasp, and was thankful to Jon who said, "You
go too fast, Dickie. I was just going to thank you and
Mary publicly, now, in the name of the three of us ...
Thank you, Richard. Thank you, Mary."

The twins inclined their heads in recognition of this
tribute, but the wink that Mary gave Jon made him feel
a little uncomfortable. It was obvious that Mary was
growing up.

Now they begged Mr Cantor to tell his story but he
said again that he wanted to hear all that they had to say
first.

"Let me tie up the threads at the end," he said.

David yawned behind his hand.

"I want to know how the girls popped up out of that
tunnel, and I seem to remember hearing that Jenny had
an adventure we know nothing about ... Let's have that
next."

So Penny began the girls' story. She told it impulsively
and with all the generosity of her warm heart praised
Peter until the latter protested and hid her burning face
in her hands.

"So, you see," Penny finished, "we didn't do much
really and it was luck that we found the tunnel under the
walls ... What I want to know is what happened to Jenny
and how she came riding down through the fire on
Reuben's piebald..." Here she leaned forward to speak
to Mr Cantor. "And if there's anyone here who ought to
have a medal I think it's Jenny 'cos she's the bravest of

any of us. I know I wouldn't have liked to have gone off by myself in the dark like she did."

It seemed that Jenny was much better at reading stories than telling them, but in the end she was persuaded to try.

"I do wish you wouldn't keep on at me so," she began, and then Tom whispered something to her and she took a deep breath and tried again. "I hated it after Peter had left me to go back to Penny. I hated it. It was so cold that I felt a bit sick, and although I'd pretended to be brave I knew I wasn't and all the time I walked along – and sometimes I ran a bit to keep warm and to get there quicker – my teeth chattered like anything. They chattered so much that I made up tunes on them ... I was jolly lonely and after a bit I got lost. I knew I ought to have known how to get here but the moonlight seemed to make everything different ... Do you know I've never noticed that before? ... I mean things that are still sometimes seem to move or not to be in the same place, and yet everything is so still and quiet ... I got rather scared about some hawthorn trees –" she turned to Peter – "The sort that grow up the Black Dingle at home, Peter. Do you remember?"

Peter nodded sympathetically. She remembered, and she knew too just exactly how Jenny felt about the black shadows of a weirdly-shaped tree cast by a full moon on the frosty ground.

Jenny went on. "Well, anyway, I kept on walking over the hills in the heather looking for this place and after a bit I saw what looked like a little flame. When I got nearer I saw it was a camp fire still burning near a caravan. Then I remembered what Peter had given me and as I was lost and scared and cold and jolly miserable, I took out the little whistle the gipsies gave her and blew it hard. I blew it once or twice as I walked nearer and then the caravan door opened and there was Reuben ... I was quite sure it was magic – him being there I mean – but I didn't care and I called out to him and he called me, and I was never so pleased to see anybody any time as dear Reuben ... I told him how I got the whistle and that Peter had lent it to me, and then I told him that I wanted to find Alan 'cos you boys were probably prisoners and p'raps being tortured ... Then he said it was quite all right for me to have blown the whistle and I must come up on the piebald horse with him and we'd be at 'Bury Fields' in about five minutes, and so we were. On the way he told me that because of what David had said he'd come back to Clun just because he wasn't afraid of being accused when he was really innocent.

"I was jolly uncomfortable on that horse. It was just *awful* but it was fun ... Reuben knew all the farms and the farmers seemed to know him. I don't know where we went but soon there were four men, and when we got here there were five 'cos Alan was just going out to find someone to ride and keep watch with him. I told him more about us than I did the others and then he spoke to them, and I could see they were all just crazy to help us and rescue you if you were really there, if you know what I mean?"

Her charmed but bewildered audience tried to pretend that it did know, but had hardly taken a deep breath again before Jenny resumed – "I ought to tell you, and specially you, Peter, that twice Alan spoke jolly nicely to Reuben ... Mind you I think Alan was a beast about Reuben and Miranda once upon a time, but he was awfully friendly this time ... That's about all that happened to me except that all the time we were coming down that hill with the fire behind I never stopped screaming."

At last it was Mr Cantor's turn, and when he had thanked them all for their stories he asked Mrs Denton if she would excuse him standing up by the fire to talk. So some turned their chairs to face him, and the lamp-light glowed warmly on their faces as they listened. First he explained that sheep stealing had been going on in all parts of the country during the long winter nights. It had started very cleverly in a small way and in so many different districts that it was some time before the police realized that the thefts were organized. Always it seemed that the sheep were moved to another part of the country as soon as possible where they would be sold for slaughter in the black market.

"We've got most of 'em now," he said, "and you'll all be glad to know that this beauty here – the one that Tom likes so much – and who seemed to have been a sort of ringleader, is now behind lock and key. We haven't found out yet how they got 'Grey Walls', but it was the ideal place for a headquarters. I think most of you realized that for some odd reason the very lie of the country round it makes it invisible from the side we know except from the spinney ... By the way, none of you have asked me if the fire is out? Yes – it is. It burned itself out last night when it reached the level ground down by the house, but I'll tell you more about that in a minute.

"The dyke of course was an ideal hiding-place for sheep. It seems the farmers round here do know it, but never seem to take much interest in it, and I don't believe one of them would have thought of searching it. This morning my chaps found four more hidden pens for stolen sheep in two miles of ditch. I'm not sure why it was considered necessary to make that tunnel under the walls, but maybe it existed before this chap got hold of the house and he had the sense to use it. We think sheep stolen in the day were generally hidden in the dyke till dusk and then driven into the pens at 'Grey Walls' in the dark. Sometimes the farmers' brand marks would be changed or obliterated before they were driven out again in the van … By the way, Peter, they seem to have had only one van operating from here, but we've discovered that they changed its colour and the name of its supposed owner by fitting false sides.

"From here the stolen sheep would go sometimes into Wales but more often into Shrewsbury or Birmingham … Just before you youngsters arrived we'd been suspicious that the thieves were working from some-where round here, but it's wild and lonely country, and I spent some days in the district on my horrible old bicycle, but I never found 'Grey Walls' until the same day that you did … I don't know whether you realize it but you've all been very helpful indeed. I'm sorry I had to mislead you all at first, but I was suspicious and afraid you might be a nuisance. Then if I'd given you a glimmering of the truth there was a risk – though I know now it wouldn't have been a risk – that you would let something out, and it would get back to 'Grey Walls' that the elderly gent roaming the hills for flint arrowheads was not so elderly, and certainly not a gent...

"I'm afraid I blamed the gipsies for the same sort of reason. I didn't want to talk about stolen sheep to anyone for a few days, but to find out more in my own way. It was more natural for elderly Mr Cantor to blame gipsies and I didn't want Denton and Clancy to start such a fuss that the thieves would close up activities here and move. I'd been told that I'd got to get hold of the ringleader at all costs, so I didn't want him to slip out of the noose – as Jenny would say, I think – before I was ready for the lot of them.

"After the twins had found the hiding place in the dyke yesterday I got busy. The furniture van which arrived full of policemen was borrowed, but can be returned tomorrow! I didn't know that Jenny and Reuben had been round collecting the farmers and I wasn't sure how I could most easily get inside the gates..."

"I gave him the idea," Dickie said. "We were inside that van with some marvellous policemen and when we stopped for a council of war up beyond the pine trees I had the idea ... Mary or me did anyway ... It was one of us ... Or maybe we both had it at the same time..."

"What idea?" Tom bawled. "Do get on with it, Dickie."

"It was a good idea," Mary said quietly. "We thought of it ... We told Mr Cantor to go out with a box of matches and burn everything up till they all came scuttlin' out like rats in a trap." And after making this simple statement Mary's head slumped forward and, with her curls in her plate, she slept. Agnes started up in alarm, but Mr Cantor waved his pipe at her and said, "Please don't wake her now. She's all right, I'm sure. Only tired ... What she says is right enough, so we tried the fire idea and it worked far more quickly than I thought. The men I had with me went out and started about six fires and the wind did the rest. Not until they were well alight did we see the horsemen who were really racing the flames and not coming through them. That's so, isn't it, Denton?"

Alan nodded. "Yes. We were coming up a track below the level of the hill parallel with the dyke. Of course we couldn't see you or any of your policemen because they were the other side of the hill, but the flames frightened the horses and as we'd made up our minds to get into the house somehow we all turned and came down the hill as fast as we could, and tried to calm the horses down in the dyke. How did you get the gates open, by the way? Did you knock or ring?"

Mr Cantor smiled specially at Dickie.

"Dickie doesn't realize it, but I shot the lock out. I couldn't wait ... And now is there anything anybody else wants to know before I say thank you to Mrs Denton for us all for her hospitality, and thank you to my new friends for helping me to do my job?"

Mrs Denton looked up from her knitting.

"Sam Quickset? You've got him? ... He was always a bad one and he hated us for discharging him for stealing ... He tried to threaten me t'other day, but the bigger of those two redheads – Jenny, isn't it, Alan? – Penny, then!

Penny! and it seems a strange name to me – frightened him off the place."

"What did he threaten and why?" Mr Cantor asked.

"Said that if I didn't pay something to keep 'em safe our sheep would be stolen. He's a poor specimen, is Sam Quickset. I never liked him."

Then Agnes began to show signs of unrest. The cherries nodded as she leaned across and whispered to Mrs Denton and looked meaningly at the twins. Mary was now asleep against Tom, and Dickie, although yawning continuously, refused to be drawn into any conversation with Agnes. He knew only too well that, very much sooner than he wanted, any such conversation would turn to the subject of bed. But all the Lone Piners were yawning now and were too weary to realize the full significance of what they had heard. It was just as Agnes pushed back her chair and rose to give battle that there came a thunder of knocks on the outside door. When David glanced up in surprise he saw Mr Cantor look hurriedly at the watch on his wrist. Then he caught David's eye and winked as the door opened to admit the large policeman from Clun, who looked solemnly round the crowded room until Mrs Denton poured him out a cup of tea.

"I'm obliged to you, Mrs Denton, and right sorry I am to break up this handsome party, but I'm to ask if there are in this house twins of the name of Morton?"

"And what would you be wanting with those poor innocents?" demanded Agnes as she rose protectingly in her wrath.

"Innocents?" said the policeman as he put his helmet

on the mantelpiece and swallowed the tea at a gulp. "Innocents? That's as may be. I've come to take 'em away."

Dickie gave a whoop of joy and leaned over to shake his twin.

"Wake up, Mary. We're going to prison … Honest. Mary! This policeman has come to arrest us."

Mary shook back her curls and opened her grey eyes wide.

"Say that again, twin. It sounded stupid to me … It sounded as if you said someone had come to arrest us."

"So I did. So he has. There he is."

"Don't be silly, twin. There's only one policeman in the world I'd let arrest me and that's my lovely Mr Cantor." She smiled at him sleepily. "He's the king of all policemen."

Here the Clun policeman guffawed loudly and then pretended to have a bad cough as his superior officer looked at him coldly.

"What shall I be doing about the car, then, sir?" he said.

"No need to do anything. We'll be out in a few minutes, thank you." He turned to the twins. "He has come to fetch you though. You've helped the police, so they've sent a big car to fetch you … I'll do my best to arrest you another time, Dickie."

At this the party began to break up and there was great confusion while everybody began to thank everybody else again.

Penny found herself next to Alan on the hearthrug.

"Lucky I met you on the train that day, wasn't it?" he said.

"It was at Charing Cross waiting in the taxi queue. Fancy you forgetting! Things happen to me at Charing Cross as a matter of fact, Mr Denton."

Jon forced his way through the crowd to them.

"Come on, Newpenny. Time to go. I hate breaking up this party, though. It's been grand."

"Come again," Alan said. "Always welcome here. Come and learn something about sheep ... When are you going south again?"

"School next week," Penny said, "so we shan't be here much longer, but we'll try and come one day."

Then they said goodbye to Mrs Denton and Mr Clancy, who seemed to find so many children in one room too much for him, and trooped out into the dark where the two cars were waiting in the yard.

"Don't worry about Sally, Peter," Alan said as he walked over with her. "I'll take care of her tonight and bring her over tomorrow. Or if you'd rather, come and fetch her when you're ready. It will snow tonight, so I should keep her where she is if I were you."

"I'll come and fetch her, thanks, Alan. I'd rather do that."

"And thanks again for all you've done, Peter. You've helped us no end and we shan't forget. We can't put you all up, you know, but you're always welcome here."

Then the twins managed to separate themselves from Agnes and when, at the top of the hill into Clun, they passed a caravan swaying carelessly down the road in the dark, Mary asked the friendly policeman who was driving to stop.

"We'll walk the rest, thank you very much," she said,

and then turned and shook Jenny in the corner. "Wake up! We've just passed Reuben's caravan."

Meanwhile Dickie had jumped out into the road and stopped the other car which was carrying Agnes and the rest of the Lone Piners. The housekeeper's protests were in vain for the twins refused to go in until they had spoken to the gipsies.

Peter was the first to greet them and Jenny the next, and there was then such a chattering that Miranda asked them to be quieter and not to wake Fenella.

Then Reuben beckoned the twins and lifted them up beside him on the driving seat.

"Take the reins," he smiled, "one each, and drive in to Clun."

The Lone Piners walked down the hill beside the caravan like a guard of honour. The oil lamps on the front gleamed like the golden eyes of a sleepy animal and the little chimney sent out a plume of smoke.

"Snow soon," Reuben said as he stopped the other side of the bridge and helped the twins down. "Farewell, my lucky ones. We shall meet again!"

"Come to Witchend," Mary pleaded. "Come again, please."

"Come to Hatchholt," Peter said as she looked up into Miranda's dark eyes.

"Come to Ingles for a good cup of tea," Tom laughed.

"Come to Barton Beach again, please," Jenny said.

Miranda rested her hand on Peter's, but looked down at Penny's red head.

"And you?" she asked. "Have you a welcome for the Romany?"

Penny laughed. "I'm a bit of a one myself, I think, so I'll always be glad to see you … We live a long way away in the South!"

"Then come this way again, my beauty," Miranda said, "and I'll tell your pretty fortune for you."

Then Reuben flicked the piebald gently with his whip and clucked with his tongue, and the caravan rumbled on its way.

There was a long silence until Dickie said, "Do you know what Agnes told us? There's an old saying in this place that says, 'Those who go over Clun bridge come back sharper than they went,' and I should think that's true about us."

"Mackie is going to sleep on my bed tonight," Mary said. "I was so tired this afternoon when we went that Agnes tricked me and made me leave him behind. The poor darling must be pining."

Back at Keep View they found Mr Cantor waiting to say goodbye to them. Then the twins were hustled off to bed, and Penny said, "Let's go up to the Castle just for a few minutes and finish the adventure where it began."

"Moon should be up in a few minutes," Jon said as they toiled up the slope, "and here comes the snow."

They leaned against the rough walls and watched the moon break between the heavy clouds. Clun, but for a few lighted windows, seemed already asleep. Round the hill below them the little river curled, and up and beyond them and round them the mysterious hills the ancient Britons knew still held their secrets.

"It's all been far more wonderful than I thought it could," Penny said at last, "and that's thanks to you all."

"I didn't think a holiday could be such fun," Peter said quietly. "It's the best I've ever had," and turned to smile at her new friend.

Jenny shivered and held her hands out to the falling snowflakes. "Nothing like this has ever happened to me before. I wish you'd all come to see me at Barton next holidays and see what happens there. I'm cold now. Let's go."

"Yes, let's," David said. "I'm cold and sleepy and sore, but I'd like that scrap on the stairs again, wouldn't you, Tom?"

Tom laughed. "You know I really hated that chap. I think it was his moustache. P'raps we'll be snowed up here for weeks now. Look, chaps! Doesn't he remind you of Witchend?"

He pointed upwards and they saw a big owl drift soundlessly by, above the ruined castle.

"Too-whit! Tooo-whit," Tom called in perfect mimicry, and the dusky shadow answered him as they all ran down the hill.

THE END

Written at Westend Farmhouse,
Wheathampstead, St. Alban's.
September, 1946–*January*, 1947.

THE MALCOLM SAVILLE SOCIETY

The Malcolm Saville Society was formed in 1994 to bring together fans of Malcolm Saville's work. Through newsletters and meetings, the society allows enthusiasts to exchange news, information and speculation about the books and the real locations which inspired them.

For further details please send an SAE to:

The Malcolm Saville Society
10 Bilford Road
Worcester
WR3 8QA